ROUGH
MUSIC

also by Alison Harding

ORNAMENTAL ALPHABETS
AND INITIALS
(Thames and Hudson)

ALSO GEORGIANA

Alison Harding

ROUGH MUSIC

MICHAEL JOSEPH
London

MICHAEL JOSEPH LTD

Published by the Penguin Group
27 Wrights Lane, London W8 5TZ, England
Viking Penguin Inc., 40 West 23rd Street, New York, New York 10010, USA
Penguin Books Australia Ltd, Ringwood, Victoria, Australia
Penguin Books Canada Ltd, 2801 John Street, Markham, Ontario, Canada L3R 1B4
Penguin Books (NZ) Ltd, 182–190 Wairau Road, Auckland 10, New Zealand

Penguin Books Ltd, Registered Offices, Harmondsworth, Middlesex, England

First published in Great Britain 1990

Made and printed in Great Britain by
Richard Clay Ltd, Bungay, Suffolk
Filmset in Monophoto Baskerville

A CIP catalogue record for this book is available from the British Library

ISBN 0 7181 2928 8

The epigraph quote on page vii is from Charles Causley's *Collected Poems*, Macmillan,
reproduced by kind permission of David Higham Associates Ltd.

for Lawrence

Why do you travel so far for what is most near?
The smallest coin in your purse buys what is most dear.

Charles Causley, *Collected Poems 1951–75*

A stranger, crossing the river at the crooked bridge, pauses before the turning of the road. Here, where patches of garlic lie white beneath rough leaves of alder and the sapling birch, it seems the track must end. There is a gate, grey with lichen and scarcely supported by its iron hinge, a mass of flies gathered on dried mud beneath; beyond – more like river-bed than road – the stony surface has been scarred and pitted by the downward rush of winter rain. Even at summer's height it looks uninviting to the traveller, who has walked some miles already from the station to the village, from the village to the bridge.

There will be little shade, at this time of day, from the grass bank which rises steeply to one side as he climbs, leaving the shelter of the woods; and little respite from the flies that whirl and buzz about his head and hands, drawn by the fine sweat on his pale smooth skin. He does not appear to be a country man, as he halts to take off his dark-blue jacket, folds it neatly and puts it between the handles of his heavy foreign-looking bag. He is breathing hard, unaccustomed maybe to such steepness and exertion. Yet he is young still, thirty-five or so perhaps; and he continues walking with suddenly increasing speed – as if he knows that when he rounds the shoulder he will sight a group of trees, set with unexpected grace in a fold of ground below the summit of the hill. High chimneys, without the hoped-for haze of smoke; a roof of ragged shining slates; and, rising from the green of uncut grass, a massive wall – marked with a widening crack, from the angle of the gable-end down past a small square window to the buttressed corner of the house.

From the gateway at the bottom of the yard the crack is more clearly visible. In the mid-day brightness it gives the house an uneasy air, as if the stillness of its grey stone is threatened by some unknown element within. For some minutes the traveller stands at a little distance, one hand gripping his bag, the other resting on the gatepost as though seeking reassurance from the strength of its roughened wood; he stares at the house but seems in no hurry to go to the door. Then he straightens up decisively, crosses the yard, glancing quickly at the heaps of straw and rubbish, the swinging stable-doors and the empty hen-hut in the corner by the mounting-block. At the stone step his bag is at last flung down, the jacket falling with it by the open kitchen door; with his foot – the polished leather of his shoe whitened by dust from the track – he pushes, almost kicks both jacket and bag inside, with a violence matched by the strength with which he hammers at the door.

If he expects an answer, he does not wait. Brushing at his forehead with his hand he turns, and now is half smiling to himself. The weariness with which he climbed the road is gone as he crosses the yard again – this time towards a door set in the high cob wall. When he opens it there is a glimpse of hillside grass, its green warmth seductive as he gazes, hesitates, then passes through and takes the path which lies beyond.

PART ONE

1

Each year it was the same. Each year, when the bracken had changed from summer green to gold and at length to a dusty deepening bronze, the gipsies came down from the High Moor.

No one knew for certain where they had been. Sometimes they were seen at Bampton, recognized by farmers as they bargained among the pony dealers at the Fair; or perhaps at Simonsbath a wary keeper noticed wagons in the shelter of a combe, where deer lie warm among the heather and the shining river Barle runs fast and clear, southward to join the Exe. This year they had travelled inland from the coast. Challacombe lay behind them; and the western evening light, striking across the sea, illumined all the indentations of the shores from Lynton down to Barnstaple, beyond the sweep of Westward Ho! to the cliffs at Hartland Point.

They came by the high ridge road, past ancient barrows and strange upstanding rocks, remnants of Exmoor's long-forgotten tribes. Edged with tall fern, the track lay white and narrow, the dust of summer lingering between the autumn brown, the dry sweet scent of heather mingled with acrid drift from a stubble fire on a distant valley farm. The curving shapes of the gipsy wagons – three in all – moved slow and dark against the pallor of the upland sky, soon to be touched with red by the lengthening fingers of the setting sun. Though the hour was late the wagons' pace remained unhurried, silent –

save when a sudden rut or rock caused the ill-sprung vehicles to lurch and creak protestingly, or the ponies' harness jingled as they shook their heads against the searching flies, persistent even in the cool September air.

The road kept to the line of the ridge precisely, with almost Roman straightness, and no turn to left or right for several miles. Suddenly the leading wagon stopped, where a granite post marked the entrance to a lane – scarcely the width of a cart and dangerously steep, winding down across open moor to a lower ridge, to disappear into the depths of a wooded valley below. Without apparent haste – yet not pausing for any consultation – a young man left his seat on the front board of his wagon and carefully led his pony round the sharply-angled bank down into the lane. The second vehicle, its wood and canvas even more worn and fragile-looking than the first, followed at a cautious distance; it was guided by an old man and a boy, one each side of an unwilling mare with the long dark mane and tail of the Exmoor breed. Another barefoot boy walked behind, careless of the dust thrown up as the wagons took the bend. Two lurchers leapt at his heels while a third, a pup, ran between the iron-clad wheels and snapped at the yellow hens that swung in their wicker basket below the van. The boy glanced back, shouted something unintelligible, then without waiting for an answer and picking up the puppy as he went, vanished into the lane.

The last of the wagons, lagging some thirty or forty yards behind, halted just short of the turn. Less shabby, more substantial than the other two, its wooden curves were brightly painted in Romany fashion; lace curtains at the small square windows, shining pots and pans by the narrow door. It was also distinguished by the fact that its driver was a woman. She was tall, well-built and fair – yet her skin, burned brown by wind and sun, contrasted strangely with the substantial braids of light-coloured hair looped close to her head. Her features were strong – no hint of civilized delicacy about them. As she moved down from the front of the wagon, her hand firm on the pony's bridle when he stopped, it was clear she was older than a first glance might suggest.

Grace Penfold heard the boy shout, acknowledged him with an inclination of her head. Now, standing beside her pony, she continued to gaze at the expanse of countryside that stretched below the ridges of the moor. Only the quick compression of her lips, the tightening of lines about her deep-set eyes, showed the depth of her emotion – which, from pride and for her children's sake, she must constantly suppress. A year ago Grace had not seen the beauty of the land: a year ago, almost to the day so far as she could calculate, she was too absorbed in grief to notice such external things. But, with the distancing that comes even in so short a time, the pain – if not the grief itself – was less. She had come to terms with the death of Will and her responsibility for them all.

This year she felt a sense of peace – of homecoming, almost – when she saw again the folded misty valleys, small fields between high dark hedges, smoke rising from villages she had known since childhood. Grace could hear the sound of the other wagons' wheels, their steady rumbling magnified as they descended the lane; then, from beyond the ridge, the sound of water flowing fast over stones from the moorland height to the shelter of the woods, down to the spinneys of willow and birch and the spreading commons where, so many times, the travellers had halted in the past. This land through which they had moved so slowly and so frequently was hers – as much as if she had owned each acre. Only those who come to know a landscape well – its quiet places, hidden paths, and secret life – can understand the sense of possession which grows, with each year that passes, in such wanderers as Grace: transients, yet closer to the earth than those whose lives are limited by ownership,

7

whose daily contact with the land fills their pockets rather than their hearts.

Even as she looked Grace was conscious of the evening chill, of the darkening moor behind, shadows lengthening across the fields, the line of distant Dartmoor hills growing fainter as the sky became a deeper fiery gold. It was as if the coming night were draining life and colour from the land. Grace drew her shawl more closely about her patched and faded jacket, and turned away.

A girl stood beside the wagon. She held a basket filled with heather, gathered as she walked along the road. Almost as tall and with the same straight carriage as Grace, her body was more slender beneath the coarse skirt and heavy shawl; her hair, a rich red-brown, worn long and loose. The likeness was unmistakable. But Grace gave the impression of inner strength; the girl of light and movement – her hair bright, features expressive, gentle rather than angular and hard. As the woman reached to take the basket she glanced questioningly at her daughter – who at once shook her head with a fiercely passionate gesture. A gesture of defiance in which Grace, with a sudden sharp renewal of her pain, saw so much that reminded her of Will . . . The anger, quickly flaring, quickly spent; the recklessness, so eager yet so dangerously blind; the limitless capacity for love. His strengths and faults that she had known so well were living in his child – who mourned him still, could not accept his death . . . The closeness of the two women was clear from the way they looked at one another. Yet there seemed to be some tacit disagreement that made the girl walk rapidly away along the track, towards the granite post.

She was standing there when the wagon reached the lane. She watched while Grace led the pony down, watched while the painted wheels ground through the dust. Then she turned and gazed along the ridge at the straight road that stretched away across the moor. The girl stood there for so long that when at last she moved the van was almost out of sight. Slowly Alice Penfold followed her mother's wagon down, towards the lights of the village which lay below.

That night the gipsies camped at Heasley, in the shadow of a disused mine. Some of the buildings were ruinous, stones and timbers filched for the repair of cottages further along the lane; others were roofless, but even so sheltered the wagons from the cold wind blowing off the moor. Furze and brambles and small trees had grown up there, and there was plenty for the gipsies' fires. When they slept, their horses grazed among the broken props and spoil that still littered the ground near the long-abandoned shaft; they slept to the sound of the river Mole, which had once powered the workings of the mine. Near by, in the fold of the hill, the village rose to its usual tasks – only the night poachers knew that the gipsies had returned. The young man too found pheasant and rabbits easily enough by the early morning light, then vanished to walk the four miles to the nearest public house, to stumble back in darkness and sleep until the women wakened him again. While he was away the boys re-tethered the ponies and polished some tinware for their mother to sell; two smaller children, free at last from the confinement of the wagon, ran in the sunlight among the ruins until dusk. The old man sat all day in the shade making baskets from strips of birch, for Alice to fill with heather. But Grace knew there was no hope of selling such things here: the village was too poor, and too much under the domination of its chapel minister to tolerate the tinkers – as all itinerants, Romany or not, were called.

Next day they took the Molland road, between high tree-topped banks and stone walls covered with heavy moss and tufts of hart's-tongue fern. By the road ran a small stream, broadening as they followed it, until it escaped through a ragged gap in the bank to fall noisily down the hillside to the river flowing fast below. Even in dry weather there was mud, and the wagons' progress was very slow; small birds flew up from the stones of the wet track, while overhead the branches tangled close together, shutting out the sun. When they came to the village the women sold their tinware and some heather. They went to a farm for milk, were greeted warily but not refused. The people were taciturn and observant, neutral rather than unwelcoming: they seldom saw strangers here – only workers from the estate, the hunt coming down from the Moor, sportsmen at the Black Cock after a shoot.

At Molland too there was a chapel, set at the crossing of the ways. The wagons reached it at midday, taking the downward turn. And here, at last, the gipsies left the Moor behind.

First came a twisting steep descent to the valley floor, with its shining threads of river, railway line and road. The smoking chimneys of a market town – South Molton – set on a rise above the mills and weirs, meadows and wooded margins of the Yeo and Mole, their moorland waters joining at the western limit of the facing ridge. Then, as the wagons laboured upwards, Alice Penfold looked across at the receding hills – the Exmoor hills whose roughnesses of heather, peat and fern were softened by the haze of early afternoon, the clefts of many shadowed combes enclosed by the massive smoothness of their curving tops.

How she had longed to take that high road on through Somerset; or, as they crossed the railway, to follow it to Bampton, Taunton, and beyond. Beyond to Bridgwater, to find out for herself the truth about her father's death. For Grace had told them nothing on that other autumn day a year ago – when the streets of Bridgwater were wet with rain, deserted almost after the nights of laughter, the torches and dancing, singing and drunken fighting of the Fair.

10

Grace did not look back. Yet even as they walked in silence at the pony's side she sensed the girl's rebellion. She understood the pride that prompted it, shared her bewilderment and grief. But she knew that Alice must not go.

'Charlie would go with me, my mother,' the girl had said at Heasley, when they sat in the shadow of the van beside the embers of the fire, waiting for the young man to return. 'He said that he would take me –'

Alice had repeated it, certain that she would be checked yet determined she would try just one more time. She cared too much for Grace to disobey outright – to go back to Somerset alone. Yet she had thought of it in those moments on the Moor. And here in this oppressive place, shut in by heaps of spoil and the scattered debris of the mine, she had felt no comfort in the warmth of sunlight or the steady flowing of the stream – no pleasure in the carefree play of the children whom she loved. Her father's voice, his steady gaze restraining or protecting her, the rough affection of his touch: she needed these! The wildness of his singing and the passion of the fiddle's music when he played still haunted all her dreams, came every day between herself and all the petty tasks which for her mother's sake she undertook. But Will was dead – and Alice was forbidden to know how or why.

'Charlie's a fool!' The word was out before Grace could prevent it – yet she knew it was untrue. Charlie was like his father. The Penfold men were cunning and resourceful, skilled in the gipsy arts of persuasion and deceit. Takers of risks, gamblers and heavy drinkers too – but never fools.

'*Dinnelo si!* And you would be another!' Grace had emphasized the Romany words, conscious of her harshness yet compelled by her concern for Alice to be forceful with her. She was angered that her daughter should persist, angered at herself for hiding what she truly felt –

11

a longing to defy necessity. If ever there had been a moment since her husband died when she had longed to speak more openly to Alice – to tell her what she knew and all she feared – it was then, as they sat together in the dusk at Heasley . . .

But Grace had kept her counsel, even then. She had always known that truth and pride were luxuries, belonging to a life within four walls. Acceptance – she had learned that the hardest way, learned it afresh each day of her married life with Will. Acceptance, survival for herself and for her family, were more important now than any obligation to the dead.

There could be no looking back.

Ahead of them the road ran straight across a level tract of unfenced common land – high enough to be impassable in winter, blocked by curling drifts of snow or frozen hard by the winds which swept unchecked from every side. Now, from wide verges, clouds of butterflies rose among the heather and coarse grass. Larks sang; buzzards turned, their wingbeats imperceptible, in warm air far above the steady movement of the horses and the gipsy vans.

A pheasant with her chicks, half grown, fled from the approaching wheels. The laughing shouting boys pursued them, urging the dogs and throwing stones, running behind the wagons with the dead bird swinging and feathers scattered on the road.

There was sunlight on Dartmoor, casting shadows of moving clouds across the lower slopes, still summer-green; glinting on the weather-vanes and corner pinnacles of square-towered churches – seven of them, Grace remembered – on the hills which flank the valley of the Taw. And, much closer, sunlight and shadow on the small rough fields, the woods of willow, ash and oak; the isolated farms on Saxon hill-top sites; the roadside cottages where ragged children watched the wagons pass.

Midway between the two great Moors lies a half-forgotten land. No railway crosses it, and the lanes that wind through its narrow valleys are scarcely more than tracks. The finger-posts at crossroads point to hidden villages with ancient names: Rose Ash, James Week, Maryweek; Westcombe and Narracombe; Penniford and Garland, Easter Ash and Beere. Here and there the landlord – Earl of Portsmouth, cousin of the Poltimores – has planted coverts neatly hedged with beech or made a stretch of broader metalled road. He owns a many-windowed mansion set upon a southern-facing slope; his family's memorials are crowded in King's Nymet parish church, with its shining copper spire which rises, curiously frail, above the clustered cottages of stone and cob and thatch. Though his agent is well-known, the landlord rarely comes. For many he is just a name – a faded coat-of-arms painted upon the signboard of an inn or carved above the lintel of a farmhouse door. His absence, and his tenants' quiet lives, are part of an age-old pattern which, within a generation, will have fragmented, irrevocably changed.

In such countryside as this, land that has lain untouched, small dramas are intensified. Even the quiet slow turning of a leaf, its fall from the tree, takes on dimension and significance beyond its shrivelled entity, its grains of dust. There is a sense of forces tending to tragic consequence: the cry of a buzzard high above the hill, the gathering murmur of water flowing from the dark wood; rustle of badger in the deep goyle, leap of trout among rocks, haunting of dragonflies across the marsh – pieces of blue light between the rushes. A pair of half-fledged kingfishers waiting wide-beaked on a branch above the stream; a family of weasels playing on sandy earth, worn down by the tread of cows; the conflict of stags in rut, a rattle and clash of horn on horn throughout the autumn night.

It was dusk when the gipsies came.

2

The rabbit trapper saw them first, when he set his evening gins a couple of hedges away.

He had heard the rattle of the wagons' wheels when they left the metalled road at an unmarked cross-way by the corner of the wood. He watched from the lee of a high bank as they halted in the rutted sunken lane; he listened to the gipsies' voices while the ponies were unhitched and tethered where the grass grew lush beneath the overhanging birch.

Silently, a man accustomed to the darkness and the rough descent, he was gone, down through the thickets of the covert to the cottage by the bridge.

By morning, a cold wind blew. It spun the fine-veined curling leaves from the highest birches at the top of Jason's Wood, bearing a scent of smoke across the hill towards the village of Ash Ford. It blew across the pools and shallows of the river Aish, drifting a random freight of twigs and straw against the northern-facing bank and scattering bubbles gathered where the current turned. Thin rain, driven along the valley by the wind, began to darken stones at the water's edge, clinging to strands of cobweb thick against the reeds. Between the river and the wood, the marsh lay chill.

The shot, when it came, reverberated through the trees. The second shot, caught up in the echo of the first, seemed to lengthen and intensify the heavy penetrating

14

sound which moved almost tangibly across the water and the whiteness of the marsh. As the echo died, there was a rush of wings above the reeds; then, only the gusting drops of rain and the distant barking of a dog.

To Martin Ford, climbing the hill with his face against the wind, the sudden noise was like a violation of the early day, denying him the peace he hoped to find. For an instant only, he hesitated, tempted to look back. Then he continued climbing, leaving a swathe of shining flattened grass and frail webs broken by the rapid pressure of his boots. He was determined to ignore the challenge – or were the shots intended as a summons even? Francis, he knew, was capable of anything.

The rain, now falling more insistently, enclosed him with a fine cold curtain drawn against the world. It blotted out the valley, isolating Martin as he climbed, almost erasing from his mind the thought of Francis, almost – but not quite – cancelling the anger and the pain that drove him on, anger and pain which since last night's quarrel must always come between the two of them. They had quarrelled many times before; and every time, it seemed to Martin, he had given ground, hating the subtle cleverness with which his brother needled him, fearful of the sullen moods which Francis used as refuge when he felt himself in any way outdone. But last night – that was different somehow. For the first time Martin had seen his younger brother as a man, not as a child to be protected or indulged. He had sensed, at last, a dividing of the ways, had felt in last night's confrontation all their past hostilities and all the bitterness to come.

Their quarrel had been trivial enough – at first. The usual sequence: Martin reading by the light of lamp and candles in the room they shared; his brother late to bed and restless, bored, determined to make Martin angry if he could. His laughter, mocking Martin as he turned another page.

'I can't think why you bother! A farmer shouldn't

read – not if he's farming properly. You know what Mother always says: a farmer's work won't wait, tomorrow isn't good enough, you have a duty to the farm . . .'

'*You* read!' Martin had reminded him. His tone was mild – he was used enough to this, had no wish to be provoked.

'Of course – but interesting stuff. On rocks and minerals, scientific things. Not airy-fairy poetry – the sort of thing that Harry gives you. Or the sort of thing he writes, with his fancy Oxford friends.'

Francis leaned across from where he lay outstretched on the far side of the bed. He flicked with his fingers at the finely-printed page. A movement calculated to annoy . . . 'Such a waste of time! You're supposed to be the practical hard-headed one, the one who runs the place – no time for this romantic rubbish –' He was watching Martin, waiting . . .

'Harry Trenaman's a scholar and his poetry is good – a damn sight more important than your wretched bits of rock. As for his fancy friends, they're more intelligent than Margaret's horsey lot, and at least their conversation isn't limited to hunting and the price of wheat!'

'Well wheat, my brother, is your destiny – not mine!' Francis paused dramatically. Then, satisfied that Martin had been roused, went on, 'And you may criticize my bits of rock but I can tell you they'll be useful to me – pretty soon. You can stick to ploughing, cattle, sheep – the farm! Because I won't be here for long. I shall be going in the spring!'

He turned his back on Martin and, deliberately, blew across the chimney of the lamp. 'So now you know. And I want some sleep – there's a meet tomorrow morning and I mean to go. Mother will think I'm gone to market, and Father doesn't give a damn. And I promised Margaret – at least she's got some sense, she doesn't care what Harry thinks.'

In the semi-darkness Martin's hands were turning –

with mechanical rapidity – the pages of the book. The poems meant nothing to him now. His mind was conscious only of his brother's words, of the shock and fury that he knew he must suppress . . .

'I reckon,' Francis murmured, 'maybe Margaret would do for me. She's pretty, in a fairish sort of way – and not too stupid like the other women in this godforsaken place. In fact, she's always been in love with me –'

A sudden scattering of pages as his brother flung the book across the room. A flickering of candles as he seized a blanket from the bed, kicked back the door. And a barely intelligible oath – unusual for Martin – as he swung it shut again.

The cold air of the passage sobered him. But he lay awake on the hard spare bed till dawn, still hearing Francis' voice, still hurt by the unexpected note of malice in his final words. By the time he left the house, in early light, the quarrel seemed to Martin to be part of something more. A separation more far-reaching, more decisive, than any difference they'd had before. From now on he would sleep alone. He needed peace from Francis, more than anything. The closeness they had shared from childhood – physical proximity that reassured and comforted, unquestioned until now – had been shattered, somehow, by the painful implications of it all . . .

He was near to the summit of the hill. Though his breath came hard his pace had slackened to a steady walk. It was impossible, he thought with sudden weariness, to drive all that away, to force it from his consciousness by tiring his body out. Behind him across the valley, Ash Barton was still there, grey stone hidden by the greyness of the rain. Less than an hour since he had crossed the silent yard, closing the rusted gate and passing between the cattle dozing on the hill. Francis must have heard him leave, had followed him almost to the marsh, had fired their father's shotgun in defiance, out of devilment to will his brother to return. Francis would be waiting for him now at the bottom of the wood below the farm, expecting Martin to go back . . .

He stopped, conscious suddenly of rain-soaked hair and the cold wind on his cheek, of his fingers searching in the pocket of his corduroys for a cigarette, of his body's heavy warmth beneath the dampness of his clothes. Conscious too of the decision he had made.

'This time,' Martin murmured, 'this time, little brother, you can wait!'

The smooth green turf to the west of Jason's Wood was a favourite resting-place for sheep. In the evenings, when he went to check the flock, Martin would often stand there, his cigarette dwindling unheeded till the ash felt sharp against his skin. Even in winter he escaped there, glad of any respite from the uneasy atmosphere at home. His father's passive silence angered him, his mother's daily recriminations were increasingly difficult to bear, and Francis – Francis was becoming openly rebellious now. He seemed to thrive on provocation, needed the drama of their arguments to make him feel alive. But Martin loathed the lack of dignity that arguing involved. He was peaceable and reticent: his anger had a slow long-burning fuse but was terrible when roused – even to himself. Physically he appeared even taller then, but his size masked an inner helplessness, an inability to cope with mental pain. If he felt awkward or unhappy his body looked more awkward, limbs large in the shapeless jacket and heavy woollen shirt, the old-fashioned breeches buttoned at the knee. And yet the well-worn clothes had a kind of harmony about them, browns and duns and green, colours of the land on which he lived and worked.

He would cross the river at the shallows downstream from the bridge, climbing the hill with a speed that caused Joe Pike, who sometimes saw him from the yard, to shake his head and reckon Martin Ford 'ud kill 'isself some day. But the hardness of the earth beneath his feet, the steepness of the climb, the clarity of air as he reached the highest ground exhilarated Martin, giving him the inward stillness he needed to survive. He would look along the valley to King's Nymet, seeing the sun transform the copper spire into a shaft of light among the trees, or watching mist expand into the shadowed space between the curves of High Ash Hill and Nymet Woods. Sometimes he listened to the curlews, or the uneven melody of bells. Always he came away renewed.

This morning there was only rain, driving the heat of summer from the ground, washing dust from birch leaves as they blew about the turf. A north-west wind, cutting like an edge of grass at Martin's hands, fingers smooth from constant friction, palms made hard by outside work, knuckles prominent and taut beneath dark skin: hands which at lambing-time would be so badly swollen and disfigured he would wince to look at them. Francis had their mother's hands, well-shaped and finely made, clever hands for mending things or playing the harmonium on Sundays, fingers which could pick out tunes on the violin their father long ago had ceased to care about. Martin could see those fingers tight and delicate upon the hammer of a gun; he saw again the calm intensity of Francis' look when he claimed, last night, that he would leave Ash Barton in the spring. Words which had echoed all the night in Martin's mind, and followed him this morning like the echoes of the shots across the marsh. Today there would be no renewal of his peace.

The sheep had made for the shelter of the wood. A few huddled in against the bank that rose above a deep lane, an old green road running downhill to the trapper's cottage and the bridge. Martin stood with his back to the wind, checking automatically the number and condition of the ewes, the size of lambs to be sent away before the winter came. The rain had eased a little; when he turned he saw the edges of the cloud, dark lines moving across the valley's end. A scent of wood-smoke drifted in the dampness of the air.

There was a woman on the hill. Even from a distance, she had a commanding presence which made Martin hesitate. He could see her profile hard against the morning light, her long skirt black against the grass; her hair, he noticed almost with a shock, was pale and shining, unprotected from the wind and rain. She was watching him walk across the turf towards her, made no attempt to move away from him. It was as if she were aware of his reluctance, overruling it with a will much stronger than his own.

'This is your land.' The woman's voice was clear, with a calm certainty which struck him as odd.

'It is my father's land.' She seemed not to hear. Even before she spoke again he had the strong sensation that she must know everything about him.

'Ford . . .' she murmured.

'He is Robert Ford, of Ash Barton, across the river there.'

Martin resented the appraising look, the silent confidence making him feel a stranger on his father's land.

'Those are your wagons in the lane?' He could see them now, in below the bank; it annoyed him that they were so well concealed, so close to the place where he went to be alone. The woman must be a gipsy, even if she lacked the manner, the wariness combined with cringing that he'd seen in such women at the fairs.

'They are yours?' he repeated, knowing she could not mistake the hardness in his voice.

'We are not many – I, my children, one old man. We shall not trouble you; we shall be careful of your land. It is true that some do not trust us. But we do no harm if we are left in peace.'

Martin was unprepared for courtesy. It made him conscious of his clumsiness, his soaking clothes and boots, his lack of gentleness. She wasn't begging favours – yet there was something in her look that undermined his effort to be firm and make her go. He wanted to know more of her, to find out who she was.

'You have been here before? You know of us?'

She did not answer him at once, but seemed to be gazing past him, out into the valley and the mist.

'As a child I came. Our people have always come this way. Sometimes I have been with them, sometimes not. We cannot always do as we would wish . . . Yet' – her voice was low, with a bitter note as if she remembered an experience that caused her pain – 'we are not cattle to be herded here and there, to be forced to live in ways we do not choose.' She looked at Martin. 'We did not expect your welcome.'

Suddenly he realized. She must have heard the shots, must have thought that he had been responsible. Francis – the fool, with his dramas and his arrogance, the stupid gesture of self-will. Martin's anger drove away uncertainty. This woman's dignity convinced him. He wanted to tell her that he was ashamed of Francis for alarming her – yet she hadn't seemed in any way afraid. She had seen his feeling: there was a disconcerting expression in her eyes, as if she understood not only this but all the times that he had felt such things.

'You will not be disturbed,' he said. 'You can be sure of it.'

At once Martin wondered why he made such promises. No one ever promised anything to people such as these. No one trusted them.

'You will not regret it.' The woman was speaking softly now, but his apprehension grew that she had somehow read his mind. Her eyes, a slate-dark grey, seemed almost black as she looked at him even more intently. Her hair was pale against the sky.

'May you find the happiness you wish.'

He had been manipulated. Martin was sure of it. She

was using the words that any gipsy woman might have used; words that were empty, without significance. She had fooled him, got his sympathy and would be laughing at him next. Martin felt tired out and strangely disappointed, helpless in the face of her deceit. Across the valley came the sound of someone calling in the cows; the weight of mist had lifted from the marsh.

Grace Penfold stood and watched him go.

The trapper had been out since dawn, checking the gins and snares along the edge of Trenaman's estate. He'd done a lot of work for Trenaman this year; rabbits had been more than plentiful – a pest, in fact, which even the quickly breeding foxes couldn't keep at bay. Today was no exception – half a dozen in as many snares in just one corner of the field along from Barton land. Here too a little feral cat was lying broken-backed beside a gin, one hind leg twisted in the metal teeth. The trapper bent to throw it in the hedge.

He straightened when he heard the shots. They weren't the sharp reports of a modern sporting gun, more like a heavy older-fashioned double-barrelled type. You didn't often see the farmers use them nowadays – mostly they were hung up on a beam above the fire, and maybe only taken down a time or two, perhaps at Christmas or on New Year's Eve. He had seen the sort of gun Ralph Trenaman preferred, duck and pheasant were his kind of sport, but not at this time of the year. His quick eye caught the movement of the snipe across the marsh. He waited, watching, hearing the sound of rain against the leaves. Another movement, closer, at the edge of Barton Wood.

'One o' they gipsies' was his first reaction – the figure was dark-haired, with shoulders broad enough to have considerable strength. But then the trapper saw him move clear of the trees, the gun held loosely at his side; he was staring across the valley and, as he turned to walk back slowly to the corner of the wood, the young man's features were plainly visible above the whiteness of his shirt. The trapper knew him. He was Francis Ford.

Later the trapper passed that way again, carrying his bag of rabbits on his back. Cloud was clearing from the hillside opposite; the wind had dropped. Francis was still there, sitting with his back against a tree, the gun beside him on the ground.

From the narrow path a dozen yards away the rabbit trapper watched, waiting for a movement or a sound. There was none, only the rustle of the dying wind among the leaves, cold light shining on the metal of the gun. The young man's body looked relaxed, his head bent forward on his folded arms. From up the valley came the shouts of Joe Pike calling in the cows; Francis didn't move.

Carefully the trapper laid his bag in the bracken that grew tall beside the path. He stood for a moment, listening again. As he slipped between the trees the smell of bracken, rank and heavy, lingered in the morning air.

3

From the kitchen window of Ash Barton, Mary Ford could see the line of thin blue smoke that rose against the clearing sky above the wood.

'So they are back,' she murmured, her mouth tight with disapproval – which in a woman less precise and well-controlled might have been more openly expressed as anger. Even now, after years of mutual mistrust, the gipsies' effrontery astounded her. She knew they would have set their camp exactly where they always did, on neutral ground between the boundary of Trenaman's estate and Barton land. After dark the tethered ponies would be moved into the nearest field, taking grass that Martin needed for the sheep. Then in the morning the women would turn up on the doorstep with their pegs and baskets, expecting her to buy, looking aggrieved when she would not. The farm was always their first calling-place on their way through the valley to King's Nymet, where they would sell or barter till mid-afternoon, then stock up with provisions at the village shops before returning to the vans. And – Mary didn't doubt – the gipsies would stock up on some game of Trenaman's as well.

'What do you intend to do?'

Martin seemed evasive when his mother questioned him. It was long past breakfast-time, and he had come in soaked. She saw his clothes and hair were clinging to him; she could smell the heat and moisture generated by the body of her son. And, like so many things about him they repelled her, made her speak with a sharpness that he knew was meant especially for him. He was used to it, always expected it – and yet it always hurt. Ignoring her, he looked around for Francis, swore under his breath, and tried to retreat down the passage to the yard.

'What will you do about them, Martin?' His mother was determined, he could tell, to pin him down. He was determined she should not. Usually he tried to please her for the sake of peace – this time something seemed to harden him against her.

'They're only a parcel of women and children, mother. They won't do any harm. Maybe a rabbit here and there – but I reckon Ellis won't be missing them.'

'Ellis has a right to them. The rabbits are his living and the gipsies have no business taking anything at all.'

Mary's features, delicate and pretty long ago, were set in an expression that her son knew well. The refinement, the residual delicacy, made her prejudice more shocking somehow. 'Gipsies are always thieves and liars, worse than vermin – how can you say they won't do any harm? We'll need to lock the doors and keep the horses in – you must be mad to let them stay!'

'There's only one old man, mother – he'll not take a lot. And maybe they won't stay. But if they do they're in the right of it – the lane is common land, not ours nor Trenaman's.' Martin could still see the gipsy woman's face, her fair hair shining in the rain. That strange serenity; her eyes a cool clear grey, eyes that in spite of everything compelled respect. Her voice had been per- suasive and yet proud. Why had he felt she was deceiving him – why had he said they would not be disturbed? Why had he promised anything at all?

His mother's eyes were blue, looking at him now without affection. Only Francis could arouse emotion of that kind in Mary Ford. Martin hated her indifference – it hurt him more than anger or reproach could ever do.

'One gipsy or a dozen – they are all the same! And like as not their men are lying in a ditch on Nymet Hill, dead drunk and capable of anything as soon as they come to. Or likely they'll be down to Exeter before the judge, and plotting mischief when they get back on the road again.'

'Mother,' Martin said, 'if you would like to take a walk to Jason's Wood, and have a look at them yourself, I'm not preventing you. And if you want to get them turned away, then go to Trenaman or get your friend the minister to back you up – I'm sure that preacher Passmore would be glad to have another axe to grind. But I'll have nothing more to do with it – until those people prove themselves to be a nuisance they can stay. And they are welcome to the rabbits – they're a bloody plague, in spite of Ellis and his traps!'

His mother stared. She was too astonished to produce the easy tears, a weapon which she knew could always weaken him. In that instant, for the first time ever, Mary was afraid of him. His height, his eyes – a blue much darker than her own, yet just as hard – intimidated her; she felt too old to fight against his youth and certainty.

'And if Francis ever bothers to come in, then tell him I'll be fencing in the middle field. It's time he did a bit of work!'

Something had happened to her son, something Mary Ford could not define. He was gone, leaving behind him the aroma of the rain, the leaves, the grass, like a presence in the neatly ordered kitchen that was her domain.

She could hear the sound of voices in the yard beyond the open door; the clash of metal buckets and rush of running water at the pump. Soon there would be the slow tread of boots along the passageway, cold air clinging to her husband's muddy clothes, to the roughness of his hair and beard, both prematurely white.

For some minutes longer she stood in silence by the

window, looking out across the valley at the wood. Then, decisively, she pulled the heavy casement shut.

'Well, Robert?'

There was contempt, and challenge, and a hint of weariness in Mary's voice as he came into the room. Then a look of unrestrained dislike for the man with whom she had – unwillingly – shared thirty years of married life.

News travels quickly in the valley. Scarcely a cottage child was sent to bed that night without the usual cautionary tales of gipsies ringing in his ears. Even the nursemaid up at Nymet House (who not so long ago had been a cottage child herself) issued warning of the fate that might befall the little Trenamans if they didn't hurry up and do as they were bid: ''Tis the little chillern they likes best, my birds – comin' to get you in your beds they be if you don't watch out. Some says they eats us ordinary folk for their dinner if they can – they magicks 'em and makes 'em fall to sleep wi' potions made from berries and such-like. They witches horses, too – you'll never see a horse stand quiet when a gipsy's in the yard, bolt as soon as look at 'n it will. And my cousin Lily Snell as lives to Barnstaple, *her* says a gipsy woman put the evil eye on her, so just you be good chillern now . . .'

For more than a week the gipsy camp was undisturbed. The nights were cold and still, the days warmed by a sun whose waning cast long shadows on the marsh. Deer grazed each evening along the western edge of Jason's Wood; moisture deepened the colours of the trees, and the margins of the river Aish were thick with willow leaves.

Alice Penfold heard the barking of the hounds. Then, much nearer, the sound of horses' hoofs, the crack of a whip, men's voices echoing along the lane. The lurchers, chained to the back of Grace's wagon, whined and leapt in frustrated reaction to the noise, while the two small children ran down from where they were playing on the grassy bank. Stiffly, the old man got up from where he had been dozing by the ashes of the fire. He walked with difficulty, Alice noticed; as he rubbed his eyes with the back of his hand she saw with a shock how thin his wrist and fingers looked – frail as the dark attenuated twigs that lay about the grass. Like herself, he had grieved since they came away from Bridgwater a year ago . . .

He was looking apprehensively along the lane, then gestured that she should go into the van. Alice was reluctant, yet obeyed him all the same: he wouldn't want her stared at by the *gorgio* men. He might be old and ill, but she respected him and hated it when Charlie laughed at him.

There were four riders, two men up ahead of about a dozen dogs, a third man and a woman following behind. To Alice, watching from the window of the van, it seemed as if their shouts and movement overwhelmed the silence and the stillness of the lane.

They halted by the verge where the old man, apparently unnoticing, now leaned against the *vardo* step. The tallest and most impressive-looking of the riders reached across and said something to his companion – a neat round-shouldered figure with the air of an habitual horseman, eyes quick and staring in a weathered face. In response he shook his head emphatically, glancing to where the tethered ponies grazed some twenty yards away.

'How many more are there?' He indicated them with his long whip, and watched the old man closely. The gipsy shrugged his shoulders, but the dark fingers tightened and his expression was more wary.

'There must be more than just the two, sir. Shall I take a look behind the hedge – it's a common trick these people have, hiding their horses till you're gone.'

'Go on, Luxton.' The other spoke with the decisiveness of a man used to giving orders and expecting them to be obeyed. He waited with obvious impatience while the hounds – all of them young and evidently being exercised – milled around the wagons and the two small canvas benders set against the bank.

Alice could hear the dogs' coarse bodies bumping against the *vardo* sides, the yelps of excitement as they sniffed about, the vicious growls of the lurchers tensed and pulling at their chains. She imagined how it felt to be a quarry of such beasts – a hare hiding for its life in the dank haven of a ditch, a hind running and panting till it reached the deepest thickets of the wood. As a child she had seen a gipsy family driven from their tents by men with dogs and guns and whips; she had grown up used to the violence of such evictions – and she dreaded it now, longing for Grace and Charlie to come back. But they must be miles away by this time, they had gone to market with the boys, it would be dark when they came home again. Alice pulled the children more closely to her side.

There was laughter from the youngest man; he was holding the hand of the girl who sat near to him on a large bay horse. The gipsy still leaned silently against the wagon step. The huntsman had returned.

'Nothing, sir – not on your land nor on Mr Ford's.' He looked disappointed – he would have liked the chance to catch the gipsies in the wrong, but they were cunning devils, nearly always one ahead . . . 'They could be in the covert there – shall I make him go across with me?'

'No, Luxton.' Ralph Trenaman was getting bored. 'We've wasted enough time here as it is. Move the hounds on, then cut through and take them down as far as the bridge – they'll soon flush out anyone or anything they've hidden in the wood. Go ahead with Francis, and I'll have a word with this fellow myself. I must say –' there was no mistaking the annoyance in his voice '– I must say, Francis, from what your mother said I thought we'd find a dozen wagons here. You can tell her that I'll keep an eye on them, or Luxton will – but there's nothing more that we can do. Of course, if we find them trespassing or causing trouble for the hunt . . .'

He moved his horse across to where the gipsy stood.

'Do you understand? Any sign of trouble and we move you on. I'm a magistrate and know the law: if you break it, I shall use it, is that clear?'

The old man stared in front of him. He had lived through such moments many times before: the sudden shattering of peace, the search and questioning; the suspicion and contempt he'd seen so clearly written on the huntsman's face. Sometimes there was a farmer who might let the ponies have a bit of grass, who would give the gipsies casual work when the harvesting was late – but there was never any certainty, and the old man would have been surprised had Trenaman been kind to him. Now he could see the woman watching him. She had a pretty face, brown hair plaited down her back, her eyes were bright with energy and eagerness – but when it came to it, the gipsy knew, it was often the women who were worst.

He looked at Trenaman. It was a steady, weary look which only reinforced the magistrate's distaste for what he had to do. Already Mary Ford's request had angered him: Trenaman could see through all her ladylike pretence, perhaps because he was at heart too radical to be a country gentleman. He had always sympathized with Robert Ford – a good farmer gone to waste, he often thought; and Francis had the makings of an enterprising man, once he'd knocked around a little. But there was something too fanatical in Mary Ford; in matters such as this he would rather use his judgment, acting only when the time was right. He'd been a wanderer himself, long before he settled down at Nymet House: he'd seen a lot of travellers – this one looked genuine enough.

'What is your name? And where do you intend to go?'
He knew the gipsies had their routes and territories; their
movements might appear erratic but they seldom were.

The old man hesitated: a gipsy is always reluctant to
be named. But there was something different about
Ralph Trenaman. Maybe it was in his voice, the persuasive Cornish intonation that lessened his severity.

'I am Isaac Penfold. There are others of our people
down to Crediton, and we will go to them perhaps. My
son's woman and her children are with me – and we are
not tinkers, sir, we are *Romani* folk.'

It was a distinction Trenaman could understand. But
he was not entirely satisfied.

'Your son – why does he not travel with you? Does he
follow you?'

At once the gipsy's expression changed. Sorrow, anger,
hatred flickered in his eyes; then his face became im-
passive once again. Trenaman marvelled at his self-
control.

'My son was William Penfold. He is dead.' He looked
down, folded his arms across his chest, and waited for
Ralph Trenaman to go.

It was Alice, watching from beside the *vardo* door, who
saw the magistrate's reaction to her father's name. For
an instant, he stared in disbelief. Then, recovering, compressed his lips and seemed about to question the old
man again. But he evidently changed his mind: abruptly
gathering his horse's reins, he turned away and, with his
daughter following, rode off in the direction of the
bridge.

It was late in the afternoon. The old man slept, curled
like a grey-black snake in the warm shade beneath the
bank. Alice had said nothing to him of her fears; he was
exhausted after Trenaman had gone. But now the silence
of the lane oppressed her. Every day she longed for the
freedom of the Moor: this valley with its deep enclosing

31

woods seemed to hold her spirit in its hand, depriving her of light and air. Soon they would go even further from the hills. Charlie and the old man would talk of moving on, to the wider country in the south, looking for company and warmth to pass away the winter months. All that Alice wanted was the high cold moorland space, the sound of streams and the hard wind blowing from the sea.

Francis startled her. He was standing not far from the *vardo*, watching her. He was only a little taller than herself and yet, because he had approached so silently and stood so still, she was at once afraid of him. For a moment she did not recognize him as the young man she had seen that morning, when his careless laughter echoed in the lane; then, her fear had had a different cause. Now, though he had no hounds with him, carried no whip, she felt as if he had pursued her here; and, having found her, held her, as the valley did.

She could hear the children calling to each other as they gathered brambles over by the wood. The old man moved a little, murmuring in sleep. She looked again at Francis and saw that though his features were more finely made, his hair and eyes were very dark – nearly as dark as her brother Charlie's were. Francis might almost have been a gipsy; and Alice, with her long bright hair, a *gorgie* girl.

'Why have you come back?' she said at last. 'What is it that you want of us?'

'I am Francis Ford. Something has been stolen from Ash Barton farm.' His voice was hard, not with accusation but with a determined certainty that added to her fear. She waited.

'I believe your people may know where it is . . . I am looking for a gun.' Then, to her astonishment, he used a word that she knew well. 'On the barrel of the gun there is a mark – it is *rupeno*, silver. If I see it, I shall know it, do you understand? It is my father's gun.'

4

Alice was certain, even before she looked at him again, that this was a man she did not wish to know. Everything about this *gorgio* threatened her. His coming there so silently – as silently as any gipsy would; the forcefulness with which he spoke, the strength of will that seemed to cancel out his youth. Most of all, the shock of his invasion of her private world. She had been taught that the language of the Romany was not a possession to be shared: it was something an outsider must not understand. *Rupeno* . . . however he had come by it, the *gorgio* had no right to use a gipsy word.

He was standing with his foot upon the *vardo* step. His boldness angered Alice. Suddenly she did not fear his closeness any more: she could see that in spite of all his confidence he was no more of a danger than her brother Charlie was. She had grown up in the company of boys; her father had been strict with her, as he always was with Grace, but she had taken it as part of the protection that he gave. She had never been afraid of any man, excepting one – a tall Welsh gipsy who had tried to rape her as she waited for her father in the shadows by a public house. Will Penfold, always quick and violent, had almost beaten him to death. Only Grace's intervention had saved Alice from a beating, too: if she encouraged any man or acted wantonly, her father said, she would bring shame upon them all. Now, the thought of him increased her resolution. As she gazed at Francis, willing him to go, she could almost feel the presence of her father at her side.

There was heat in the dusty shafts of sunlight that struck across the lane, illuminating the serrated edges of the hawthorn leaves, deepening the crimson berries where they swung and rustled with each movement of the arching hedge. Behind the girl, the brass and brightly coloured paintwork of the *vardo* gleamed. From where he stood, Francis could see that the interior was neatly kept and clean: it made him curiously reluctant to begin his search, as if he were intimidated by that unexpected glimpse of femininity and calm. He had been convinced, talking to Luxton as they waited by the bridge, that the old man had been hiding something – but he hadn't reckoned, then, on dealing with a girl . . .

She was unaware that she was beautiful. Her laughter, musical and clear, had been heard too little since her father died. But her eyes, though often sorrowful, were still expectant, still untouched by disillusion or despair. Their colour, Francis saw, was strange, the golden-green of moss; but it was the colour of her hair that was more striking, its richness softening the angles of her gipsy features and the heavy texture of her clothes. An impulse made him want to reach and take it in his hand, she was near enough for that – part of him longed for the kind of gentle warmth that he had never known . . . He had forgotten, in that instant, all about the gun.

Alice, maybe guessing his intention, sensing something in his gesture and his look, ran swiftly past him down the *vardo* steps. She pointed to the open door. Her voice was low and fierce.

'*Hokki!* See, we do not have your gun! Look for it, if you please – and if it's there, then take it. But you will find nothing silver in this place, nor anything of gold. *Nai men yag-engri 'cai, nai kooro-mengro, yago-mengro 'cai: mendi panomengri, tatcho Romani. Beng te lel toot – gorgio rye!*'
She turned her back on him and walked across to where

the old man lay; then she sat protectively beside him, almost as if she were a mother, he a sleeping child.

Her final words, so passionate, were unmistakably a curse. Francis was shaken by it, by the sudden transformation of her beauty into ugliness, the gentle warmth to something alien and hard. He knew that he had caused the change in her – and he wished, too late, that he had not.

'How can you possibly have *lost* a gun?'

Francis was shattered by his brother's disbelief. Martin had always listened to him, shielded him, explained away his absences or his neglected work. This time was different. Martin was dismissive; and he seemed remote, as if he had already washed his hands of anything that Francis did.

'It's true, I tell you. I searched the woods for hours. Then I thought you must have come that way and found it, brought it home with you – I guessed you would be angry when you knew I'd taken it. But in any case' – Francis felt aggrieved – 'I can't think why the old man would never let me use it. He doesn't care about his guns, he never looks at them – unless he's drunk, of course!' He was intolerant, as always, of his father's weaknesses: neither son had much respect for Robert Ford.

'I've told you more than once, there's something not quite right with it, the spring is unreliable, he says. And you know it's Mother who sets store by it, she's the one who kept it when Sir Jocelyn died and Father said he should have sent it back. But she wanted a keepsake of the Penningtons, it's got the silver mark and Mother likes such things – though God knows why she ever thought so much of old Sir Jos, he never did the Fords much good.

'Anyway, you have *lost* it, little brother – and if I were you I'd find it pretty quick!' Martin's laughter had an edge to it. Clearly, it was useless to explain to him.

35

Francis had been woken by the mid-day sunlight on his face. He lay there for some minutes, feeling the stiffness of his body in the half-dried clothes, remembering the quarrel of the night before, the hurt in Martin's eyes when he told him of his plans. Disloyal, Martin thought him, and a fool – even to consider the suggestion Captain Trenaman had made ... Mechanically, he reached out for the gun.

Even then, when he knew that it had gone, Francis couldn't quite believe it possible. Returning home, he half expected he would find it in its usual place, among the lumber of the dusty room their father once used as an office, later as an extra harness-room and a repository for guns. There were more than a dozen here, some of them relics of the days when Robert Ford had been a single man, working as apprentice to his uncle in King's Nymet at the gunsmith's trade. All he had brought to his marriage were his guns and a reputation for philandering, both passions he indulged in till the day his only daughter died. Thereafter he became withdrawn, morose: blamed hisself for what had happened to the little maid, the valley said. And he had loved her more than he could ever love his wife and sons, without her he cared nothing for the land. One day, Martin would have Ash Barton: all that Francis would inherit was his father's way with women, and his guns.

It was in the office, as they called it still, that Martin found his brother sitting in their father's high-backed leather chair; he looked exhausted, and was staring with resentment at the empty grate. A dog lay at his feet, its ears and eyes alert, as if it sensed that Francis in his present mood was unpredictable, and not to be provoked. There was a smell of soot and damp. Dust lay on the heaps of papers and the mildewed record books, and an engraving of the young Victoria, placed centrally above the wooden mantelshelf, was marked with mottled brownish stains. The only other decoration on the walls, a

36

fox-mask mounted on a plaque, gazed mockingly at Francis with its eyes of yellow glass. *Killed Ash Barton Farm, December 1896*. He could remember watching with his brother from the gate, hearing the increasing high-pitched cry of hounds, the sudden silence in the wood. A little early snow had fallen, clinging to the hardened fields and naked trees, heightening the tension of the dull mid-winter afternoon. The boys had stroked the severed head and brush when their father and sister reached the gate: Eleanor had laughed at Francis when he hesitated – now her face had faded from his mind, but her scorn had not, and her clothes still lay in a linen-chest upstairs. He remembered the flecks of blood that mingled with the whiteness of the snow; and how, at six years old, he had feared the stiffened head when at last they put it on the wall.

Yet the room, where he helped his father with the winter evening ritual of cleaning guns, had been his favourite. He was fascinated by it all: the intermingled smells of powder, oil and grease, the feel of polished wood and metal beneath his hands, the complex mechanisms of the different kinds of gun. These days, reflected Francis bitterly, the only ones they bothered with were those that he and Martin used – those, and the one that had belonged to old Sir Jocelyn Pennington.

'Someone must have got the blasted thing!' He spoke his thought aloud, then glanced at his brother in despair. He was certain he would never find it now. The gipsies had been his only hope – and he didn't like to think how that had failed.

'Then you will have to find out who it is.' Martin's calm reply infuriated Francis.

'And if I don't – you wouldn't care a damn! Now you know I'm leaving home you've given up on me: little brother's in a hole, and the last thing you will do is help him out!' He stood, thrusting away the heavy chair and giving the dog a vicious kick that sent it running to the corner of the room.

'You think because I've promised Trenaman I'll give his scheme a try that I'm a traitor to the farm – all *you've* ever thought of doing with your life is staying here. It's all that you will ever have to do, because it's yours! You needn't even wait till Father's dead: he's half into his grave already, only another year or two and he'll have drunk himself to death. And then the place belongs to Martin Ford – with little brother as an unpaid hand, and Mother always there to tell us what to do. That's how she's always wanted it, and you've accepted it – because you're part of it, and the land is part of you. Look at any farm around and it's the same old trap – but I intend to go before I'm caught!

'As for the bloody gun, my life won't be worth living when Mother knows it's lost. I might as well leave home tomorrow and have done with everything.'

Martin was silent, leaning with his shoulder hard against the door. He could tell, from the almost desperate note in Francis' voice, that this was the moment when he ought to try and make the peace. Unlike last time, this attack had been unplanned – and part of it, he admitted to himself, was true. Yet some ugly stubborn instinct – something he could no longer keep in check – was urging him to let his brother pay, at last, for all the times that Martin had protected him. Francis was irresponsible, too much influenced by Trenaman – and if he wanted freedom he could take the consequences, now.

'I expect you'll get away with it,' he said. 'You always have – and I suppose you always will.'

Francis had expected criticism, anger even – but this cold hostility was something new. He felt helpless in the face of it. When he spoke again he looked and sounded very young, his long brown fingers tightly clenched, his eyes very dark and large, with an expression of appeal that Martin recognized – and this time intended to resist.

'Listen – every day for the last two weeks I've searched

the farm, the marsh, the wood. Every day I've gone through hell expecting Mother to come in here and notice that the gun has gone. No one from the village would have stolen it – that only leaves the gipsies, and if they took it they'll have hidden it, or taken it away to sell. Luxton reckons they're a cunning lot – he says he found the carcass of a hind last week, down below the Middle Wood. He reckoned someone would be coming back for it, and he waited half the night, went off home to get his gun – and the hind was gone when he came back again.'

'That doesn't prove a thing.'

'No, but it means that someone in this valley's after game – and they could have got the gun. And a night or two ago there was a gipsy up at Nymet, in the tap-room at the Globe. Played his fiddle, drank a tidy bit, and soon as Luxton came in through the door – he was off, so Luxton thinks that he's the one to watch. On the other hand' – Francis sounded doubtful now – 'I didn't see him when I went to Jason's Wood: there was just an old man, and a girl . . .'

'A girl?' Martin's voice was sharper than he realized. 'But I saw an older woman up there – she was in the market at South Molton, too, a couple of young lads with her.' And he suddenly remembered a black-haired gipsy walking at her side, carrying a violin; later, he was playing and taking money from the crowd of women gathered round the pillars of the market hall. Children she had with her, she'd said that morning on the hill: so *had* she lied to him? And – in the light of what had happened – had he been a fool to let them stay?

'Maybe I should try the gunsmith in South Molton,' Francis said. 'Someone could have tried to sell it there. And maybe you could go to Jason's Wood again, you might have better luck than –'

Martin turned on him at once. 'No, I don't intend to do your dirty work for you! And I don't believe those gipsies have the gun. Luxton's always too damn quick to try and pin things on to people that he doesn't like – he'd have half the village lads in court tomorrow if he could. And he'd have them hung for poaching quick as ninepence, like they used to do. If he was a married man with a family to feed he'd see a different side of things – there's a lot of people short of work, and short of money, too: any one of them would poach a bit of venison and not think twice about it.'

'For heaven's sake – that's not important now! I've got to get that gun back, and all you do is preach at me. If the gipsies haven't got it, someone else has – and why the devil won't you help? *Why* won't you tell me where you think it's gone?'

Suddenly the room was very still and cold. The odour of the soot was strong – Martin felt that he could hardly breathe. He saw, behind where Francis stood, the dark line of a crack that stretched across the chimney wall. It started at a corner of the fireplace, which had been blocked in some twenty years ago, and it extended up past Queen Victoria, beyond the staring fox, right up to the blackened beam that bore the rafters' weight. Looking at it Martin felt light-headed, as he knew he would when he drank a lot of cider the night of the Harvest Supper at Ash Ford. Francis seemed far off, his anger and distress were not important any more. The moment of rejection, Martin knew, had come.

'I think,' he said unsteadily, 'that you are on your own in this. I think you've been a careless fool about the gun: you've either lost it, or you've damaged it and won't own up to it. Or, just possibly – though I'd rather not consider it – you've hidden it away and mean to sell it when you can. After all, neither of us ever has much cash, you're always borrowing from me – and if you go as far as South America, or whatever godforsaken place the Captain wants to take you to, you'll need a little bit of money in the bank. No, I haven't finished yet –' He was altogether sober now, determined to make his brother hear him out.

'You're eighteen, Francis, and you think that you're a man: well prove it, and find the gun without my help. And go with Trenaman, if that's what you decide – but don't expect a welcome when it's turned out wrong and you come running back to be a farmer after all!'

Quite slowly, Francis walked across the room. His face was close to Martin's when he spoke.

'You are jealous of me, as you've always been. Because Mother's always favoured me, and because I'm cleverer than you. Because I get on well with Trenaman, who's richer than you'll ever be; maybe you thought you'd marry Margaret and get a bigger farm – but it's me she cares about, not you. And I tell you, her father didn't sit around and wait for land to come to him: Trenaman worked hard for everything he's got, and I shall do the same.' Fiercely he pushed his hair back with a hand which, Martin saw, was not as steady as his voice.

'You think I'm a traitor and a fool – and possibly a thief. If any other man had called me that I'd have killed him: as it's you I'll prove you wrong and make you suffer for it later on. One day, *brother*, when I come home rich, you'll wish you'd not been born. And,' Francis added bitterly, before he left the room, 'I'll never turn to you for help again. I shall find that gun without you, since I must.'

Late that evening, farther down the valley, near to where the river Nymet runs into the Aish, the lights were on in an upstairs room of Nymet House. Ralph Trenaman, his grey hair still unruly from a long and solitary walk, was sitting at his desk. He was studying a map.

5

Alice had discovered High Ash Hill. Here, lying in the bracken, listening to the fine-spun song of larks, she was at rest. There were heather patches, milkwort blue and white, clumps of rough-leaved wortleberry, even the little stars of moorland moss, dark green and shining in the damp depressions of the highest ground. She could see Exmoor from the hill, a series of uncompromising curves against the northern sky, beyond the ragged top of Jason's Wood, beyond the lesser moors of Nymet Ridge.

Eastward, on the valley's curve, lay the village of Ash Ford – a twisting uphill lane, a church tower squat among the elm and beech, heavy with gold and brown. With the steady fall of leaves, the shapes of buttresses and branches would become more visible; already swallows gathered on the slate roofs of the chapel and the lattice-windowed school. Soon, as gales from west and north stripped the valley bare, the triple arches of the bridge – built by the Earl of Portsmouth to appease his neighbour Pennington – would be battered by the swelling waters of the Aish. Downstream the spate would drive its wreckage hard against the smaller, crooked ancient bridge, spilling across the disused road and leaving lines of mud along the trapper's cottage wall.

Sometimes Alice saw the trapper but he never spoke. His lean ungainly figure, carrying a dirty sack or a string of rabbits dangling from a heavy stick, would vanish into a damp and evil-smelling shed beside the path. Later the river bore away the blackened blood and heaps of entrails from the carcasses the trapper paunched – ready for the carrier to take them to the nearest railway junction, in the valley of the Taw. From the hilltop, when the wind was right, could be heard the far-off whistle of the train, its reckless rattle as it steamed from Barnstaple to Exeter with crates of chickens, wagon-loads of clay, or heavy-booted passengers to the livestock markets held in station yards along the line. Often, waiting ill-at-ease alongside tweeded gentry or the weekend fishermen, were bright-complexioned village girls – sent off with shabby bags and hard-won railway fares to the cities, to relieve their parents' poverty at home. Victorian prosperity had scarcely reached the isolated valleys of the West; now, under Edward, it was clear that the long-established fabric of the country hierarchy had worn dangerously thin. Even Alice knew, from the way the gipsies were received at farms and cottages, that times were getting hard. At Ash Ford, in the Pennington, at King's Nymet in the Globe, there were rumours that the landlord's agent was a worried man. Already the Earl had left his mansion by the river Taw – gone up-country, so they said. They spoke of Portsmouth properties that might be coming up for sale, their tenants anxious after generations of commitment to the land.

One night at Nymet, Charlie Penfold said, he'd heard the huntsman Luxton reckon Trenaman would buy Ash Barton Farm . . .

She looked down at the farm from High Ash Hill. Three tall black firs behind the house, a group of graceful ash trees by the gate; a square of buildings with a long high leaning wall of cob that sheltered yard and linhay from prevailing winds. With its heavy russet-coloured cattle browsing on the open shoulder of the hill, its orchard steeply sloping to the edge of Barton Wood, it looked serene, untouched. Alice had no understanding of the lives within its walls, no premonition of the years to come.

'*Dinnelesko si!*' Charlie had laughed when, after a day of hesitation, Alice told him about Francis and the gun.

'You got the better of him then – it serves the *gorgio* right! *Givengro si* – he's a farmer, after all: he thinks a man can't be a man without a gun. But I can catch the *bauro chericlo* more easily than that. I can take a fish without a line, a stag without a horse or a pack of hounds. And if he'd done you any harm, my sister, I'd have killed him with my naked hands.' Cheerfully, and with contempt, he spat into the hedge. She knew he meant exactly what he said.

'But listen now, *mi pen*,' – this time Charlie didn't laugh – 'the huntsman – he's the one that hates the gipsy folk. You must be very careful: if he comes again, you must tell him it's only hedgehog and nettles in the pot. But with any luck he'll be too late – only another week and we'll be on the road.'

The young man was impatient to be moving on. But Grace would not listen to his arguments: while the roads were dry, she told him, and their food and fuel easily obtained, there was no need. And though Alice said nothing of it to her brother, she was sure there was some other reason why Grace did not choose to leave the valley yet. For when, remembering that Captain Trenaman had seemed to recognize Will Penfold's name, the girl herself had urged that they should go, her mother had refused. *It is not time, my daughter*, Grace had said. *We must wait – it is not yet the time.*

So far the huntsman had not troubled them again. But as the gipsy women walked the lanes and bridleways they saw the brothers – Martin driving sheep or carting loads of straw, Francis riding with the pretty girl from Nymet House.

Francis ignored the women when he passed; but once when Margaret Trenaman remarked that he was being very dull, he astonished her by a sudden burst of anger. Later he apologized; but, still preoccupied, refused to stay for croquet on the lawn, claiming he was needed back at home. It was the truth – but Margaret knew him well enough to realize that something was amiss: maybe he was having second thoughts about her father's plans . . . He reassured her, promised he would come to tea tomorrow, and escaped, relieved to be alone. He had discovered long ago that he could flatter Margaret Trenaman, though she was older than himself; she liked it – and he thought the less of her for that.

Margaret had been in love with Francis since their childhood days, when he had charmed and teased her, confident that she would wait until he chose to take the honour that she offered him. He had been right, of course. Her social world was full of Reginalds and Henrys dressed in well-cut tweeds or dashing riding-gear, young men languid and impressive in their motor-cars that terrified the cottage children, staring as they roared past on their way to Nymet House. Margaret had despised them all. True, she danced and flirted with them at the hunt balls, rode with them to local meets; but she would not marry any of them and the Nymet people thought it strange – most of the village girls were well established in their cottages with steady husbands and a child or two before their teens were past. As for Francis, the valley judged that he were always proper wild. 'I shouldn't like to let 'n near my maidens, that's a fact,' the Ash Ford blacksmith said.

The gossip didn't bother Francis. But he was determined he would never let a woman dominate him as his mother dominated Robert Ford. Sometimes Margaret's possessiveness annoyed him; beneath the graceful figure and the charming smile he sensed a ladylike aversion to the kind of love he knew, already, he would need.

Maybe she would suit his brother after all – Martin was a callous devil and deserved a woman who would give him hell. Martin's accusations burned within his mind; and somehow, each time Francis saw the gipsy girl his bitterness increased. It wasn't just the gun: that hardly seemed to matter any more. But the thought of Alice's contempt, the way she turned her back on him, still shamed and angered him – he remembered the autumn colour of her hair long after she had passed him on the road.

Francis should have been the elder son. Martin had believed it as a child, from the moment when, in an impulse of comparison, he held his own rough, clumsy hand against his brother's neater, more assertive one. He felt more respect than envy; later his size and innate gentleness made possible the strong affection binding them, the fierce protectiveness that lasted longer than his brother's need. Francis Cheldon Ford: he had been named for Mary's father, as if she were determined that he would inherit all the drive and mental power of the Cheldon men. She would always think of Francis as a Cheldon, rather than a Ford: Martin – she was in no doubt – was his inferior in all but years.

Yet Eleanor, their father's favourite, outshone them both. Even after death she would come first with Robert Ford. Martin would remember her vindictiveness, so quickly turned to tears or smiles when anyone came near; her radiant pleasure when he brought things to her – flowers, butterflies, a fledgling bird. At first he had adored and feared her, then he drew more close to Francis and avoided her, aware she had grown away from him. It was Martin, finally, who found her – as he went, one summer afternoon, to fetch the cows: she lay pinned beneath the staid old cob their father rode about the farm and had, indulgently, encouraged Eleanor to ride. As always she had tired him out, this time driving

46

the horse beyond endurance of the heat until in desperation he had leapt the hedge and fallen, broken-backed, on top of her. Martin was used to death – a calf aborted in the yard, lambs frozen by a late-spring blizzard on the hill. But Eleanor was part of him. When he saw her twisted limbs, her black hair tangled in the grass, he knew she was destroyed – like the wild unwitting creatures that the trapper caught.

Martin's childhood, too, was gone.

When the gipsy women stood aside to let him pass, Martin always greeted them – a quick grave glance at Alice, a murmured word to Grace. His courtesy surprised the girl; she was wary of him, and she was conscious even in such brief moments of a strange expectancy, an unvoiced questioning between her mother and this man. Yet when Alice, learning who he was, protested that he would surely harass them as Francis had, Grace answered sharply, 'No, this *gorgio* will not break his word.' She recognized the doubt that troubled him, despite the firmness of his voice; but she knew instinctively that there was something more – that Martin was torn apart by doubts which had a different, deeper cause.

One morning Alice saw him in Ash Ford. While her mother took the children to the Rectory, she walked along a narrow path and through the lych-gate to the church. No one seemed to be about, but the heavy door was open wide. At the porch, Alice hesitated, remembering how the cold damp air of a little church in Somerset had made her shiver as she stood beside her mother and the boys. Her father, who had laughed and sung and played the fiddle all night long, who called her *tikni chericli*, his little bird, and kissed or beat her with the same wild spirit that was part of all he did – now he was a withered empty thing, no more to those who loved him than the dead leaves on the flagstones at her feet. Sometimes, on the top of High Ash Hill or watching the river's steady flow beneath the trees, she felt close to him again: here, she knew she was alone. And yet, like many of their people her father had respect for places such as this, a reverence for sacred things . . . Alice went into the church.

The air was warm and sweet. Sheaves of corn were heaped against the pillars and the chancel steps. Bunches of drooping oats and rich bright cottage flowers – purple daisies, marigolds, chrysanthemums – were tied against the darker richness of the carved oak screen; before the altar rail, along the window-sills, lay polished apples, red and green in alternating rows. Sprays of hazelnuts and blackberries and fronds of golden fern adorned the pulpit and the granite font; and on the white cloth of the altar lay a single roughly fashioned loaf of bread. To Alice, moving slowly past the empty pews, beneath the faded sky-blue plaster of the wagon-vaulted roof, it seemed that the pale hard stone had blossomed into life – and the freshness of the fields and woods drove out the taint of death.

But to Martin, watching from the shadows near the vestry door, it was the gipsy girl who brought new life and colour to that ancient place. The way she moved – so tentatively, yet with ease. Her crimson shawl, the brown folds of her skirt, the rich abundance of her flowing hair: a natural harmony, outshining all the nature that surrounded her. He didn't fear her, as he feared her mother on the hill; Grace had compelled him with a power he could not understand. But Alice roused in him a kind of awe, a sense that she belonged to something older and more innocent than Martin's world. Perhaps it was the look of wonder on her face – an open uncorrupted quality that made him think of all the new young creatures he had found and cared for in his life: already she was part of everything familiar and loved – and yet she was unknown to him, a mystery. Whatever ambiguity the future held, his first and purest impulse was of deep emotion, certain, clear as light.

48

It was as if he'd gone alone into an empty room and, glancing in a mirror, saw not darkness or despair but all the bright fulfilment of the flowers – the culmination of an unadmitted dream. When Alice reached the chancel step and turned and looked at him, he knew that here, among the ripeness and the imminent decay, she promised spring.

Between them lay the white and gold of sheaves – the harvest Martin's family had won in dust and heat from the reluctant land. To place it there, before the altar of the parish church, had made him proud: he felt that Francis had been right – he'd never wanted more. For centuries the valley had been farmed by Cheldons and by Fords: as tenants of the Penningtons, their fortunes had been linked since the days of civil war, when they had fought together on the manor ground of Middle Aish, not far from where the gipsies set their camp. Often they had tilled the land without reward; sometimes, prudently, they made dynastic marriages, uniting farm with farm. Now there were Cheldons at Nymet Barton and at Forda Mill, and at Ash Leigh above the village on the northern side. At Town Farm, nearest to the church, and at Ash Barton, there were Fords. They might not own the land, but they thought of it as theirs, and worked for it: when times were difficult, a younger son might leave – always, the elder sons remained. For the men and women of the farms, the valley was the centre of the world.

But Alice Penfold was a wanderer. The presence of her family was seen as an intrusion in that ordered place, a threat to moral decency, to all that was secure. From the moment Martin saw her in the church, he knew his life must change.

He was silent as he drove the wagon home.

'Who was that girl?' his mother asked. 'That girl – she had no right to be in church. She was staring at you, Martin, when I came to find you – she was a gipsy, wasn't she? You must tell the Rector, Martin; you must speak to him tonight!'

Later, at the harvest service in Ash Ford, he thought of Alice still. Her startled glance towards the vestry door, her quick light tread, the rustle of her skirt. She had gone – sudden as the deer at dawn on High Ash Hill . . .

He said nothing to the Rector and, ignoring his mother's fury and the valley protocol, made a point of sitting down to supper with Joe Pike. By the time the evening ended, Martin and the cowman were – to their mutual satisfaction – comfortably drunk.

Between the lych-gate and the corner of the village school there is a low stone wall, surmounted by an iron fence that separates the churchyard from the cobbled path. In autumn, spiders weave a second wall against the leaning rusted uprights of the rails, which shine deceptively above protruding tufts of grass and captured leaves. The cobblestones are always treacherous with moisture rising from the clay beneath or dripping softly from the branches of the overhanging trees.

The sound of children's voices, chanting steadily, reached Alice as she stood beside the wall. She scarcely knew how she had come there, nor at that moment could she understand the fear that had impelled her, like some hunted creature, from the church. The woman standing at the vestry door: her sharp command, her anger – palpable as knives – had entered Alice's awareness and destroyed her dream. The silence had been broken, warmth and fragrance dissipated, an enchantment gone. Yet she remembered Martin's look: never until then had Alice seen, in the eyes of any man, such steady longing, or so deep a need. She saw him still, a king among his harvest, and the sunlight shining on the sheaves . . . She was filled with an intensity of loss – as if on reaching out to touch a flower she saw its colour fade, its petals fall to dust.

The chanting of the children ceased. A sparrow pecked between the cobbles; mist was drifting round the branches and the cottage roofs. She knew that she should wait for Grace; she was afraid to stay. Briefly in the church her spirit knew the freedom that it sought – but here, once more the valley hemmed her in.

An old man came along the path. At first he reminded Alice of her grandfather, his movements were so slow. But he was not so very old – beneath his shabby coat his back was twisted and one arm hung useless at his side; his hair, though white, was cared-for, unusually thick and long. She recognized him: they had seen him once or twice upon the road. Grace knew that he had been a culpritcher – a peddler of books around the villages, a singer and musician too until a carriage ran him down and crippled him, depriving him of speech. A clever man, Grace said, and some folk were afraid of him because he had the reputation of a scholar once. Alice noticed that the pocket of his coat was stuffed with papers; in his hand, a small and well-worn leather book.

She pitied him – until he stopped beside her and she saw he was a man for whom respect was more appropriate. His eyes were dark, deep-set, intelligent, their gaze was humorous and keen; the mouth, a thin pale line above the bushy beard, unmarked by bitterness in spite of all he had endured. His smile was unexpected, kind. One day, when she had need of friends, Alice would remember it, and how of all the villagers he showed her least hostility. Now, already, she had guessed that he was not an Ash Ford man.

He seemed to wait for her; and, glad of any reason not to linger, Alice walked with him until they reached some steps beside the schoolhouse wall. Here he hesitated. Seeing that the steps were steep and slippery with leaves, she offered him her arm and helped him to the path, which continued past the backs of cottages and through an unfenced corner of the graveyard to the Rectory: she would find her mother here. They walked on at the cripple's pace, aware that though there was no speech between them there was yet communication – an affinity that Alice was unable to define.

Whether he had come that way by chance, or by premeditation, she would never know. But as the old man left her, where another flight of steps led down into a cottage yard, he gestured to a headstone leaning at an angle to the path. Alice watched him go – then, curious to know what he could mean, she bent and looked more closely at the grave. It had been neatly kept, unlike the others that surrounded it. The letters on the stone were clear. *Euphemia Penfold.* And below the name in smaller letters: *Thomas William, her infant son.* There was no date.

But by the headstone someone had placed flowers – purple daisies, yellow marigolds, their colours fresh and bright as those the girl had seen that morning in the church ... From the school, as Alice stood there, came the high sweet sound of children's voices, practising a harvest hymn.

6

The Reverend Michael Pennington was getting old. Stiffly, with deliberation – almost as if the effort might prove more than they could bear – he uncrossed his gaitered legs and stretched them to the comfort of his study fire. The curtains were not drawn. He could see, beyond the shining copper beech whose leaves were drifting onto uncut grass, the rotund shape of his Exmoor pony, hunched and stubbornly unmoving in the lightly falling rain: like the Rector of Ash Ford, he looked unwilling to give up his solitude. The outside world, the trivia of others' lives, were irritations, best ignored.

A timid half-reclusive bachelor, the Rector could not be described as a religious man. Like many younger brothers of the country aristocracy, he had accepted his vocation – with its perquisites of an enormous chilly rectory, some unproductive land, and a status only slightly less respected than the squire – as a chance to keep within his social class. He had fulfilled his duties reasonably well: he spent the greater portion of his time in studying geology and other natural forms, and only interfered with his parishioners when their affairs became too troublesome to overlook. He knew the cottage children by their Christian names – though he got their second names confused. His housekeeper, a penniless acerbic gentlewoman widowed early in her life, reminded him of christenings and funerals, and the Rector muddled through – becoming vaguely conscious as the decades passed of an unchecked slide to Nonconformity among the villagers, and the distracting sound of rival hymns from the neat square building just a hundred yards along the lane. Here, as elsewhere in the West, the strong-voiced chapel preachers with their simple texts and promise of redemption for the poor had made their mark.

But the Rector had not forfeited respect. Old women bobbed their curtsies as they'd always done, the men helped out at hay-time or with cutting winter wood. And the farmers, in this isolated parish, were not yet so rich or powerful that they could break their ancient ties with landlord or with church. The days of old Sir Jocelyn Pennington were gone, his properties reverted to the Earl of Portsmouth a quarter of a century ago: but his younger brother was the Rector still, and more a squire than Trenaman would ever be . . .

Everyone had liked Sir Jos. Women would remember how he gave them surreptitious kisses when, as little girls in borrowed boots and stiff-starched petticoats, they went up for their prizes at the Sunday School; their husbands, how he always treated them to cider at the village feasts, joining their procession to the church and reading lessons in his powerful baritone. His accent was as broad as theirs, his clothes well-worn; his hounds and horses the best for miles around. He hunted, with impartial zeal, the stag, the fox, the otter and the hare – across terrain which was well known to be the roughest, least rewarding in the whole of Devonshire. But the thought of travelling to London daunted him – and he refused to see his lawyers even when the terminal complexities of his affairs demanded it. Unwisely, he had quarrelled with his richer relatives, the Portsmouths and the Poltimores; and he had been too open-handed – which in part accounted for his local popularity. Sir Jos was happiest among the people that he knew: the dealers in the markets where he bought and sold his stock regardless of the cautions of his bank; the tradesmen of King's Nymet, who could never quite believe the rumours of extravagance and debt. And the men who farmed his land – like Francis Cheldon who, though a tenant, was his closest friend.

Once, the family estates extended from Ashreigney – Ring's Ash – in the south above the Taw, as far as Rose Ash to the north. In the shelter of the highest ridge between, the first Sir Joclin Penyngton had built his manor house at Middle Aish, and settled a dispute between two yeomen. – John of Cheldon and his neighbour Richard Forde. Later, when the villages were torn apart by civil war, the Royalist Sir Jocelyn watched the manor burn. He saw his brother Jason, who supported Cromwell, die – trapped in an ambush on the hillside by the margin of the wood. For their loyal part in this affray, he granted Thomas Cheldon tenancy of Nymet Barton, and to William Ford the freehold of some cottages at Forda Mill. In the quiet years that followed, the Penningtons were prosperous and safe at Nymet House. But by the time the last Sir Jocelyn died, all that he could leave his only heir, a daughter, was her childhood home – and the doubtful honour of his name . . .

The Rector spread his long white fingers to the blaze. His hands were smooth, refined, and veined with bluish-purple threads like those that marked the marble mantelpiece – where, ranged with great precision, stood the formal sepia photographs in heavy frames, the candlesticks of silver, and the carriage clock of brass. The symbols of an ordered way of life, a heritage that Michael Pennington had venerated, set upon an altar long grown cold. A heritage his brother Jocelyn had betrayed.

The Reverend Michael Pennington had hated Jos. With all the silent fervour of a lonely man, he condemned his brother's recklessness, despised his charm. He envied him his domesticity – the gentle wife who died too young, a daughter whose devotion eased his middle age. But most of all he blamed him for the changes that had come about: the loss of status and security, the loss of kinship with the land; the rise of opportunists like Ralph Trenaman.

Childless, the Rector centred all his passion on the past. The family heroes were his gods – those feudal lords who could dispose the lives of lesser men, command allegiance, even kill a brother for the future's sake. Lords who ruled the land, who owned its woods and fields, its very blades of grass; the streams that watered it, the rock beneath. The country lords whose time – at last – was running out.

For over forty years the Rector had suppressed his hatred of his brother – conscious that he could not preach of charity while burdened with such sin. When Jocelyn died he gained some peace of mind – but even that was marred by the conviction that he was respected only for the old squire's sake, not for his own. Too late, he looked back at a life that had been self-absorbed, a slow progression to an unlamented death. His day – like the glory of the Penningtons – was drawing to its close . . .

The clock showed almost five. Time to light the lamps. The Rector's hands were cold, his fingers trembled as he reached to touch the bell. And hesitated, putting off the moment when he ought to send for Mrs Hannaford, remember practicalities – this evening's sermon, the arrangements for the parish supper afterwards . . .

Each year it was the same. Each year at harvest-time – more than at any other season – the Rector's mind was troubled by his memories of Jos. As he grew old, there were the sharp inevitable apprehensions that he might himself not see another winter through; there was the pain of knowing that, but for his futile anger, his brother might have been a much-loved friend. And there were other matters buried in the past – unsettled matters which, more even than his anger, Michael Pennington had prayed he might forget. With every autumn, fear had been renewed; as winter closed the valley in, he felt secure.

This year it was not so. The harvest, this year, would not end . . .

That morning, when he saw the gipsy woman come into the yard, the Rector knew that there was reparation to be made. Although her hair was pale as wheat and plaited close about her head, where once it had been long, luxuriant and black, he recognized Grace Penfold – recognized the woman's height, her bearing and, as she approached, the knowledge in her eyes.

He had not spoken to her. Mrs Hannaford had dealt with her of course. There were children with her, and while she was talking with the housekeeper another gipsy came along the churchyard path and waited silently beside the wicket gate. This girl, the Rector saw, re-sembled Grace.

And yet to Michael Pennington she was not Grace nor Alice but another gipsy girl from long ago. A girl whom he had seen in those unhappy months before his brother's death, an infant in her arms, a look of desperation on her face. There was a sound of rushing water and of baying hounds; the flash of harness, and the heavy breath of horses in the early mist. Far off, a strange discordant music; and at last, the weeping of a man beside an open grave . . .

The women with their baskets, the children running on ahead, had gone. The Rector, sitting by his study fire, could not forget. He did not doubt that soon Grace Penfold would come back.

In church that evening Mary Ford was waiting for her younger son. Beside her, Robert, looking frail and bothered, fumbled at the buttons of his stiff black suit. Martin was preoccupied and still, remote from Mary as he'd always been. Beyond him, a place for Francis: he had left the farm that morning, and had not returned.

They were surrounded by the families they knew. Three of the Cheldon brothers had arrived; of the remaining three, the eldest had long ago rebelled and joined the chapel at King's Nymet, and another would be sitting with his dogs and bottle by the fire at home. Tom, the youngest and his sister Mary's favourite, was riding fifteen miles from Rincombe where he farmed alone, high up on Anstey Moor. He would almost certainly be late. The Ash Ford labourers – the Pikes and Snells, the Endicotts, the Parrishes – relinquished chapel loyalties at harvest-time. Only the more militant of Methodists would keep away: the blacksmith Roger Braund was one of them – he was the preacher Passmore's right-hand man. Most villagers, too poor to risk their livelihood, preferred a middle course.

The organ sounded, hesitant and sweet. Its music was as always punctuated by the breathing of its bellows, pumped – with no great regard to rhythm – by a thin old man. His single arm, protruding like a scarecrow's from his jacket, did the work; from time to time, he paused to wipe his forehead with his other, empty sleeve. The light of lamps and candles flickered on the polished apples, on the glowing flowers, the eerie shapes of sheaves that stood like shadow men along the aisle. The Reverend Michael Pennington was speaking of the seed that fell on barren ground. Above his head the plaster angels mutilated in the time of Cromwell looked enlarged, grotesque. The congregation prayed. In well-bred careful monotone the Rector blessed the fruits of earth, and all who laboured on the land.

In the pew reserved for Barton families, beneath the brass memorial to old Sir Jos, the place for Francis Ford remained unfilled.

Along the valley in King's Nymet church, among the tradesmen, publicans and gentlefolk, Ralph Trenaman was singing heartily. His deep bass voice, his steady gaze, the confidence with which he read the lesson or responded to the prayers – all testified to his conviction that he was established in this place as squire. His wife was by his side. Their daughter Margaret and other white-clad ladies were to sing a harvest anthem, specially prepared; the parish supper would be held at Nymet House.

But his mind was not entirely on the hymns. He was thinking of another church, set in the shadow of a mountain-side five thousand miles away. The quiet nuns who tended it, the ringing of its single mournful bell. The Indian women with their children standing curiously by; the black lace shawls and high-piled hair of Spanish women – remnants of the Old World aristocracy who once controlled the town. A dark-haired girl in a flowing many-coloured gown, attended by a small *mestizo* boy . . . Beyond the church an arid ochreous plain, from which rose narrow chimneys and the tin-roofed buildings of a mine, surrounded like a fortress by a high white wall. Within it, the steady beat of engines, built by Cornishmen to pump the water from the once-neglected shafts; and the chanting of the Indian miners as they waited, naked in the sunlight, for their dangerous descent to darkness and the veins of silver hidden in the rock. Above the town, a sky intensely blue. And always, the purity of air that deepened every colour, sharpened every shape, and brought the massive presence of the mountains close.

A place to which Ralph Trenaman was planning to return.

He had been nearly forty when he married Laura Pennington. She knew little of his early life. 'Her's twenty-five, and her must be getting desperate' the Nymet gossips said: they had forgotten that Sir Jos's daughter was bound to be not only democratic but determined to ignore advice. Her relatives, like Michael Pennington, believed she had betrayed her class; yet they were glad that Trenaman was rich, and would relieve them of responsibility for Jocelyn's child. To those among the congregation who had known her as a girl, she seemed to have retained in middle age her mother's gentleness and calm patrician looks. Yet Laura had her father's charm, his legendary common touch – which had done more to smooth her husband's path than he would ever know. To Trenaman, success as squire – success in anything he chose to do – was due to merit and hard work, to the strong-willed Cornish character that knew its worth.

Even as he sang, there was about Ralph Trenaman an air of energy compressed, a power that reached beyond the rows of village people and their narrow lives, the valley gossip and the petty boundaries of land. It was this quality that had attracted Francis Ford, whose instinct was to drive a pathway out, to find what lay beyond the closeness of tradition, the routine that bound a man or woman to a patch of earth. In Trenaman he recognized the outward-looking vision that his father, even his brother Martin, lacked: a vision which for Francis would become more necessary than the duty to a farm, or ties of blood.

. . . The boy had promise. Headstrong maybe, but intelligent and practical – exactly what was needed if he were to make his way, to deal with men who could be brutal yet would never suffer fools. He must go to Cornwall first, he'd learn the basics of the mining business pretty quickly there. Then Mexico, and southward to Peru, Bolivia perhaps . . .

As he leaned back in his pew, Ralph Trenaman thought of Francis, wished – not for the first time – that his own son Harry weren't so sensitive and bookish, or that Margaret had not been born a girl. The little ones, still in the nursery, were far too young; and even Laura didn't comprehend his need – his need for the light and space he'd found in Mexico, long before he came into her life. He'd been glad at first to be domestic, settled. It had been a challenge, buying the estate, putting it to

60

rights. The house had been neglected, land run down: Ralph had made it all his own, leaving the mark of his self-educated taste, his gift for absorbing all that was socially required. Now it was complete – and he was restless, bored.

Margaret, glancing at him, recognized his mood. She could tell – with the quick intuitive knowledge of a man that a daughter, rather than a wife, will often have – that Trenaman in spirit was far off, in places she would never see. Sometimes Francis was the same. That was why she loved him, she supposed. Because he was like her father; because his wild enthusiasm captured her imagination and his daring startled and enthralled her. She could never be like that: she was like her mother, static, bound to home. But one day, she was certain, Francis – and her father – would return, and come to rest. So Margaret would wait.

But she was hurt that he hadn't come to church. She tried to concentrate, look at the carving on the screen, the coloured fragments in the chancel window – she could only think of him. He had promised. 'I shall come and hear you sing. Of course I will.'

Why hadn't Francis come?

Rose Ellis, the trapper's daughter, was returning home. She knew each variation of the path, each rise and hollow of the ground. She knew where to look for early daffodils, for the last pale flowers of honeysuckle, faintly scented, or the hidden tracks of deer. When she came to where the path divided – up the hillside to Ash Barton, or along the river and the margin of the wood, she took the downward turn. As she half expected, Francis waited for her there.

He took her hand and led her to an empty cottage, deep among the trees. The thatch was green with moss, the windows boarded in. And here, where they had come as children, he made love to her, at dusk, among the withered leaves.

7

There were more gipsies in the lane. While the valley
worshipped, church or chapel, and while Rosie Ellis lay
in Francis' arms, two carts heaped high with shabby
canvas, rope and pots and a miscellany of odds and ends,
turned in from the Ash Ford road. Late that night, when
the mist had cleared and a sharpness in the still air
indicated frost, the glow of several fires was seen and a
wilder irreligious singing echoed on the hill above the
Aish.

The travellers were Smiths from Dartmoor, on their
way to Somerset. When they spoke of it to Grace, she
glanced at Alice, guessing what her thoughts would be.

'You might go with them, my daughter,' she said
when at last they were alone.

The girl was silent. Was her mother testing her? Or,
with her powerful insight, had Grace perceived a change
in Alice – a change so new and subtle that the girl herself
could scarcely understand how it had come about . . .

'No, my mother,' Alice said. 'I shall not go.'

'And where's Sir Jocelyn's gun?'

Mary Ford faced both her sons. She could tell, from
their silence and the swift exchange of looks, that she had
caught them out. The heat from the kitchen stove seemed
more intense than usual, yet Robert – leaning close
against its metal bar as if looking for support – could not
control the shaking of his hands.

'I suppose you thought I'd never know. But I'm not blind. Francis, mooning in and out of Father's office like a cat that's lost its kits. And you' – she turned on Martin – 'as ever, trying to cover up for him. You're cowards, both of you, you only want to put off trouble and prevent me finding out. Well, this time it hasn't worked – I've known the pair of you for long enough.'

'Mother,' Francis said, 'we'll get it back.'

'Oh yes! From wherever you and Martin lost it, I suppose. The yard or the river or the wood, wherever you've been looking for it all this time. Joe says –'

'Curse Joe!'

'That's right, curse Joe – because he's stupid enough to tell me when I ask him what's been going on.'

'The gipsies could have taken it.'

'Well if they have you can blame your brother for it: he's the one that wouldn't move them on. Trenaman's as bad – he says there's nothing he can do. And the Rector's useless – old and past it all. He wouldn't listen when I told him there's another lot up there. Wherever gipsies go there's trouble, that's what I told the Rector – and it's true.'

'I don't believe they have the gun,' said Martin quietly. He was certain of it now. Since seeing Alice, all his doubts – even his fear of Grace – had become irrelevant, unreal.

'You're hardly likely to. You won't hear anything against them, as we know.' Mary laughed unpleasantly. 'But if it's any comfort to you, I don't think they'd take it anyway. I may be a woman and a fool, but even I know that a gipsy wouldn't use a gun. And if they tried to sell one anywhere round here, they'd pretty soon get caught. So you'd better think of another story, hadn't you?' She looked at Francis; her scorn was unexpected, clear.

'It's just an old gun, Mother.' Francis, goaded into saying it, was sure – as soon as it was said – that this was something Mary Ford would not forgive.

'And Sir Jocelyn Pennington was *just* the squire! And just a man a woman could respect, which is more than I can say for any one of you. Sir Jos was like a father to me – it was because of him we got the farm. And that gun just *happened* to be his!'

Her contempt had turned – too readily – to tears. And Martin – pale, distressed, and like his father, longing to escape – felt bound to intervene.

'That's why we couldn't tell you, Mother, don't you see? Because we knew you'd be upset –'

'But you forgot that when you took it, didn't you?' Mary's accusation, her assumption of his guilt, cut Martin – leaving him, so easily, without defence. It had always been like that . . .

'It wasn't Martin, Mother,' Francis said. She stared at him. 'It wasn't Martin,' he repeated, holding Mary's gaze, determined she should know at last that he was not afraid of her – had never been afraid as Martin was.

'I lost the gun, and I shall find it,' Francis said.

His cool assurance irritated Martin and alarmed him. He had seen that look – quite unmistakable – in his brother's eyes before. Whichever girl it might have been, the confidence of sexual conquest had made Francis reckless. He was enjoying being centre stage, had almost laughed at Mary when she asked him why he hadn't been to church. And now that she had guessed about the gun, Francis didn't seem to care. Martin envied him his self-possession; yet instinctive caution told him that in challenging their mother over anything connected with Sir Jos, Francis had gone too far.

Martin glanced at Robert, wishing – beyond all reason – that his father would assert himself to keep the peace. Why was he always so detached, so self-absorbed? He was slumped in the battered chair beside the stove, his once substantial frame looked uncoordinated, like a shapeless toy from long ago. Once, Martin thought, he must have been like Francis – confident and brash, a man their mother wanted, even loved . . .

He saw that she was ominously calm. They were waiting for her, all of them. It angered him that she must always dominate, must forever be allowed to call the tune – yet he knew he didn't have the nerve, the underlying strength that Francis seemed to have.

'I suppose,' said Mary, 'that you thought you had a right to take it – as you seem to think you have a right to everything.' She spoke to Francis with the coldness usually reserved for dealing with her elder son.

'And I suppose you think I'm like your father – weak, and that I don't care whether you neglect the farm, or that you're always sneaking off to Nymet, running after Trenaman. I suppose it's Margaret's money that you want. Well, you'll never get it, that's for sure – her father's not a fool.'

'But Mother, Trenaman's –'

'I know a lot about Ralph Trenaman.' She's jealous of him, Martin thought at once – she's never cared for Francis' going there. But she'll never stop him now . . .

'And I can tell you, Francis, that there's only one thing Trenaman wants out of any of us here. He wants to buy this valley up. He's always after land – we all know that. He'll never be content until he's got back everything Sir Jocelyn lost – then he can really be the Squire. But he's just a jumped-up Cornishman, a foreigner, he'll never be Sir Jos. He can try and squire it over all of us but it won't get him anywhere – not now. I'm telling you, he'll never do it now!'

She spoke with an air of triumph, of excitement, that disturbed them all. Even Robert had aroused himself, was gazing at his wife with a look half anxious, half intent.

'We've made our minds up, all of us. Your Uncle Richard up at Nymet has told us what to do – he's already bought his farm, he's free of landlords such as

Trenaman. And when the Portsmouth sale comes up, the rest of us will be the same. While you were mooning after Margaret or playing with Sir Jos's gun – some folk have been deciding what to do. I went to see the agent while your Uncle Tom was here, and Webber said that the tenants will be offered first. It's the usual thing when estates are broken up, and he reckons that the prices will be low – it's what we've all been working for for years.'

'But the money, Mother?' Francis was the first to speak.

'We Cheldons will stick together, as we've always done. It's the only way. How else do you think we've managed all this time, while the landlords have been on top? We've been waiting, see. Tom hasn't any family and he'll help me out. And when the Rector passes on, your Uncle Philip means to buy up Town – he won't have long to wait. Us won't let the Cornishman buy up our valley. If he wants my farm, he can wait until I'm dead!'

In the silence, Martin turned to Robert Ford. He was sitting with his hands spread on his knees, fingers gripping at the fabric of his breeches, worn with age. 'Father? . . .'

Robert Ford said nothing, simply stared. Then, unsteadily, he stood, walked across the kitchen and out into the yard.

'You can see how much he cares! He thinks I haven't noticed – it's as much as he can do to get as far as the cider barrel now. He tears his guts out making all that stuff, then rots himself with drinking it. He's finished – anyone can tell it now.' Mary's voice was bitter; there was no love or pity in her look.

'You two are all I've got. Between us we shall run this farm without your father if – or rather when – he's gone.'

Martin could not respond. He was shaken by it all, hurt that Mary trusted him too little to confide in him.

Even so, she was doing exactly what he'd longed, for years, to do. He feared the implications – there was Francis, they would need him now. Yet how could the two of them work together after all that had been said – after Martin had rejected him? He knew then – as he waited for his brother – how he wanted it to be . . .

'Mother,' Francis said, 'there's something you had better know.' His eyes were dark with determination. Martin could tell he was making up his mind – yet surely it wasn't possible that he would go. Ash Barton would be theirs . . .

'Mother,' Francis said again, 'you'd better hear me out. You must buy the farm if you are able to – I hope you will – but not for me. Martin's the eldest, he'll get it in the end. So buy it. But I won't be here.'

He could see the shock in Mary's face. Whatever else she might have known, she hadn't guessed at this. And he saw – not without a sense of satisfaction, and of power – that Martin was appalled.

'I didn't mean to tell you yet. But it's all arranged – with Captain Trenaman. He is sending me to Cornwall in the spring, and then to South America, to Mexico. He says I can make a lot of money there – in mining, it's what he did himself . . .'

Francis was hesitating – as if he'd had it all by heart, as if he'd planned it but was running out of words. Martin wondered suddenly if along his brother meant to burn his boats – he was in trouble, it was one way out . . . But a heartless way, a blow their mother would find hard to take. And himself? He needed Francis now!

'So that's why you – why Trenaman . . .' Mary was speaking softly, almost to herself. 'He wants my farm, and he takes my son as well. But he has his own son – why can't he go instead?' Fiercely, she turned to Martin. 'Why Francis? Why must Francis go?'

'I don't think Harry cares for mines and money, Mother.' Martin answered as gently as he could. 'He's never wanted to be like his father – when he leaves Oxford he'll be a writer, for the magazines. That's what he always wanted. Captain Trenaman –'

'Captain? He's not a proper captain, everybody knows it!' Mary's anger had returned, and she looked at Francis, at the son she loved, as if he had been made unclean by his association with the man. Even so, Francis stood his ground.

'He was a captain in the mines in Mexico – it's an important job, a powerful one. He had estates and servants, everything – as I intend to have.'

'I see,' said Mary Ford. She stood beside the window, looking out, yet unaware of the valley she had always known. When she spoke it was as if she were another person, not herself.

'If that is what you mean to do, then do it. Do it. Go with Trenaman,' she said. 'But don't come back.'

Francis, his face without expression, did not hesitate again. He was as cold, as hard, as she had always been.

'In that case, Mother, there's nothing more to say.'

Mary, left with Martin, fingered at the patterned oil-cloth on the table. He could see the trembling of her hands, and sensed – though this time he could not have borne to see – the inevitable tears. Compassion almost overwhelmed him, made him want to take her in his arms, be all she had ever needed in a father, husband, son. She had always seemed to stand alone, but never so much as he knew her to be now. Yet he also knew, with compelling certainty, that he must not play into her hands.

She looked at him. And he saw in her not the woman who had always seemed to hate him but the girl she once had been. For there was no reproach, no anger, only questioning. He could not answer it at once: deep down, Martin felt that this time if he acquiesced, it would not be for the sake of peace or for his mother's sake, but for reasons of his own.

'And you?' her look was saying.

'No,' he answered. 'I shall stay.'

In the cottage by the bridge the trapper was at work. He was mending snares, and cleaning up his gins. So far the season had been good; he was making money – more than most – and he whistled softly as he worked. Like any craftsman – even one whose life was spent devising death – he was pleased when his skills were in demand. The cottage windows, stained with dust and the marks of river slime, let in little light. When evening came he lit a lamp; the air was thick and moist with fumes of oil and the smell of skins that he was setting out to dry.

When his routine work was done, the trapper stood and listened by the open door. There was only the rush of water and the movement of the wood. But the trapper was a cautious man. He waited – knowing that in quiet places silence may be as dangerous as any unexpected sound. Satisfied at last, he shut the door.

He crossed the room to the fireplace, empty since his daughter went away to work at Nymet House: she came back rarely now, and the cottage hearth was cold. From inside the blackened chimney he took down Sir Jocelyn's gun. With care, he cleaned it, noting that the spring was slack. But he primed it all the same and returned it to its place behind the chimney beam. He would have a use for it, the trapper reckoned, very soon.

8

Why Francis? Why must Francis go? That question, more than any other, haunted Mary's mind. The continuing presence of the gipsies, even the loss of old Sir Jocelyn's gun, became as nothing to her as the days passed by, each cold bright morning a renewal of the pain her younger son had caused. Her grief at his indifference, the shock of his desertion of the farm, consumed her utterly.

She could not appeal to Trenaman. Pride made that unthinkable – to beg a favour from an incomer, a man who bought himself into the place as squire; the man who lured her son away with talk of profit and who coveted her farm. Once, as a girl at Nymet Barton, Mary had been close to Laura Pennington: together they had nursed Sir Jos before he died, their children had grown up as friends. But that early closeness had been undermined – eroded by the painful contrast of their married lives; by Mary's jealous vision of the future Laura's children would inherit while her own sons worked – as she had always worked – on someone else's land. She had taken refuge in her dream of ownership, had centred all her hopes on Francis, had believed the two of them together would control the farm. She had not discounted Martin: but she saw him as the willing horse, dependable and dull, while Francis – stronger, bolder, more intelligent – would always be the one who made her life worth while. All that was gone. Destroyed by Trenaman – whom Laura, once her friend, would not oppose.

A week went by, with Francis leaving early and returning late; a week during which his mother waited for a
change in him – yet knew he would not change. Now
that his plans were known, he made no secret of the
books and papers he brought home from Nymet House.
In the room which once the brothers shared, his lamp
burned on into the night – as if, thought Mary, Francis
meant to show he had a purpose, and would keep to it.

At last, worn down by that week of silence, Mary
went to him. She felt, as she climbed the stair, a resur-
gence of authority, of anger – and a sudden certainty that
if she talked with him he would see reason, be her son
again. But as she hesitated in the darkness of the passageway, she knew the hope was false. She heard his
quick firm step across the room, the noisy rattle of the
bolt as Francis barred the door. She waited, spoke his
name. It was no use. His will was stronger than her own.

Next morning she was blind to Martin's troubled
looks, his small attempts at tenderness, his quiet determination that the daily work – whatever the upheaval
– must be done. He guessed that even had she seen his
efforts Mary would have scorned them as a weakness, a
reminder that like Robert he could be too easily destroyed. Yet he persevered. His brother had meant everything to her. And if Francis would not change his mind,
then she must turn to Martin – not through love, but
through necessity.

Increasingly, he thought about the gipsy girl. Martin
did not feel, as yet, the lover's fierce impatience to
possess. It was enough – as he went about the yard or
walked the hill – to think of her. He could not seek Alice
out. But her image stayed with him, as clear as when he
saw her first – and he watched, across the valley, the thin
smoke rise above the top of Jason's Wood.

The buildings at the centre of King's Nymet overlook an
open cobbled space which – though irregular in shape –

is always called the Square. It seems, on summer days, enclosed and intimate, a place for desultory gossip, old men watching from a bench beside the iron pump, young women eager to prolong escape from home by staring in the small crammed windows of the shops. Fore Street, East Street, Mill Street. Market Street and Chapel Lane. The names of narrow roads converging there are timeless, functional, repeated county-wide in other villages and towns – and scarcely hinting at a past more prosperous and self-contained, when King's Nymet was a stopping-point for London mails and famous for its live-stock fairs. For the romantic-minded visitor it has a quiet, antiquated charm. To the realist – the farmer, tradesman, labourer – it is too far from the markets and the railway line, cut off from turnpike traffic by its steep surrounding hills. A dull, neglected, fast-decaying place.

To Francis, crossing Fore Street on a dark October night with an east wind funnelling across the Square, it offered nothing more than the temporary comfort of the Globe. And even that, he thought with a sudden access of dislike, he would be glad if he never saw again. He was feeling tired, dispirited – as though the strength of will that until now had fuelled his rebellion had drained away and left him empty, cold.

He had spent that day with Trenaman. They drove early to South Molton, hired a pair of sturdy ponies from the George and rode on up to Heasley, to the edges of the Moor. For hours, in the autumn brightness, they studied maps and plans, tracing the disused workings of the mine. As they walked among the fallen buildings, following the banks and culverts that ran between the shafts, Francis had a curious sensation of belonging there, of knowing deep within his bones why men became obsessed by minerals, by earth and rock – a life that lay untouched and secret, waiting to be found.

'Iron, copper, haematite. And even – in the fifties – there was talk of gold. There were over a hundred miners here in those days, they came across the Moor and from the villages. And some were Cornishmen. All finished. Gone.' Ralph Trenaman was angered by it even now: Francis was learning a lot about this man.

'How could it fail?' he asked.

'Greed – and lack of confidence of course. Some of the tributers became corrupt. And the owners wanted bigger, quicker profits, looked for them up-country or abroad. No one likes to take a risk so near to home: if a mine fails several thousand miles away you need not feel the consequence. You lose your money but you don't see the miners starving on your doorstep, or lose your seat in Parliament because of it. Or get assassinated – as you might in Mexico.' Ralph Trenaman had smiled and looked at Francis. There was a hint of challenge in his glance – but he saw at once that the boy was not alarmed. He seemed fascinated by it all, and Trenaman was pleased.

'There's a thousand years of mining here,' he said. 'Even the Saxons knew about these hills. And one day we might need it all again.' Especially, he added silently, if there's a war in Europe, as they seem to think . . .

'Someone has been here lately,' Francis said. There were marks of wheels in the soft ground near the lane, the ashes of a fire beside the river Mole. 'Just travellers,' he said.

They rode down to South Molton in the dusk, along a grassy tramway which, for a few unprofitable years, had linked the mines of Exmoor to the railhead and the outside world. The ponies pushed through trails of bramble, clumps of clinging furze; they passed by broken wagons, twisted metal, heaps of spoil. The river ran below them, fast and pure. A heron rose, its harsh uneven cry a judgment, Francis thought, of so much effort, so much waste. He could feel in the pocket of his coat a lump of green-veined rock that he had picked up from the mine. His hope lay in that rock, in Trenaman. He could not give it up.

He had dined at Nymet House. The women there were gentle, sympathetic – they guessed how things had been at home. Yet a certain heaviness of heart had stayed with Francis – almost a sense of dread at the changes he had set in motion and could not control.

Now Luxton was waiting for him in the Globe. There would be talk of hunting prospects – tomorrow, hounds were meeting in the Square. Francis knew he didn't want to think of it. All he wanted – it was inadmissible but true – was to go back to Ash Barton: not to his mother but to Martin, who had been beside him all his life. There was something in him, after all, of the boy that he had been. He was still too young to be entirely confident, too emotional to be without regret.

The lights of the public house were golden and inviting, spilling a glow of warmth into the shadows of the Square. Was his future, which had seemed so clear, a bright illusion that would fade when morning came? Francis cast the thought away, and went into the Globe.

Until lately Francis had preferred the Ash Ford pub, the Pennington. Though his mother disapproved, he enjoyed an evening playing cribbage with Joe Pike. Or sometimes Reed, the culpritcher, came in – he couldn't speak, but liked a drink or two and was a skilful hand at cards. The Cheldon cousins might be in there, or the Fords from Town. In winter there was Rose's father, silent in a corner, drinking steadily all evening when the weather was too rough for setting traps: a surly man, who'd rarely greet you though he'd known you all your life. In the Pennington, the locals' past and family affairs were always talked about – with an accurate recall and acid wit that would surprise a stranger, who might wander in believing he was in the company of yokels, barely literate village folk. There, Francis knew he would be watched, sized up, and in his absence torn apart.

Tonight he would feel safer in the Globe. He ignored

the crowded tap-room and went straight into the snug. Luxton wasn't there. 'He'll be in,' the landlord said. 'Be in d'reckly.'

Francis laughed and went to the settle by the fire. 'D'reckly' might mean anything between a minute and an hour. He waited, hearing the hiss and bubble of the ash logs as they flared: the sound was soothing, distancing him from the mental turmoil of the day. Idly he watched the flames.

There were gipsies in the Globe. From beyond the black oak panelling between the tap-room and the snug came a sudden burst of laughter, voices raised; a pause, then, sweet and clear, the sound of a fiddle being played.

He listened. First with all the arrogance of youth, the certainty he could have played the tune himself. But as it gathered force he heard in it the rushing waters of the Mole, that tumbled past the hollow mines and echoed through the valley where he rode with Trenaman. He heard in it, as it grew gentle, plaintive, Rose's voice, her cries of love as they lay among the leaves. And Francis heard at last a song unknown to him – of wilder stranger things, of distant places he would one day find ... A song he would remember when he came, in time, to face perplexities of pain and fear, the truths of war and death. It was music only a gipsy could have known.

It seemed to Francis that the man and the music that he played were one. Yet he was young, with careless laughing eyes in a heavy-featured face; and with a height and slenderness that marked him out from the shorter, broader-chested local men. Taller too than the gipsies standing by him: they were ragged, coarser-looking – and as the young man put his fiddle down he glanced at them, then turned away. As Francis watched him from the tap-room door, he recognized that look, that movement of the head. He saw again – even before the gipsy came towards him – Alice Penfold's anger, her passionate contempt.

'Young devil!' Luxton was at his side, and staring at the gipsy as he crossed the room.

'The Captain should've whipped the lot o' them – sent 'n packing long ago. I can't think why he don't. Asked 'n yesterday again – just leave 'em be, he says, just leave 'em be.'

'Has his reasons, I expect,' said Francis. He disliked the huntsman suddenly. And he was watching Charlie Penfold, remembering the girl. Her voice, and the colour of her hair . . .

'Bold as foxes – till you catch 'n. Then they'm cowards, see!' Luxton looked and sounded venomous. The gipsy had caught sight of him. Without any change in his expression, only the slightest squaring of his shoulders, he walked away to where an old man leaned against the tap-room wall. 'See?' said Luxton.

'Cautious, more like.' That's not a coward, Francis thought. Nor was the girl. He wouldn't trust them – there was still the matter of the gun. But he was glad that Luxton didn't know of it.

'The old Squire would have seen them off, I'm sure o' that. He couldn't stick the Penfolds. Always said they poached the deer. And the Smiths are just as bad – Ellis says they're taking rabbits from his wires. Now if Captain Trenaman thought more about the hunt –'

'Will the hounds be drawing Nymet Wood tomorrow?' Francis asked the question pointedly. The huntsman had a nerve, to criticize the Captain in that way. As for the gipsies, he would judge them for himself.

Luxton took the hint. But as Francis listened to him, he noticed the gipsies had gathered in a group. The air was thick and hot, and above the general noise he could hear Charlie Penfold's laughter, the harsher voices of the Smiths. Even before they left, with a crash of the heavy outer door, he guessed they were quarrelling among themselves.

They passed the uncurtained window. Shouting

echoed and receded in the Square. Then he heard, beyond the hum and movement of the crowd, a high thin cry of pain – like the distant scream of a creature in a trap.

Luxton was watching Francis carefully. 'They'm all the same. They turns against each other – worse 'n rats. Never did get on, the Penfolds and the Smiths . . .' His small hard eyes were gleaming – killer's eyes, thought Francis, hating him.

Another cry, more piercing and persistent, stilled – for a shocking moment – the indifferent murmur of the room. The landlord stared uneasily. Then laughter from the snug, behind the panelled wall; a resumption of the tap-room noise.

'Reckon I'll be going,' Francis said.

'Let 'n be, boy.' The huntsman touched his arm. 'Just get on home. They'm vermin, gippoes be!'

'I'll see you in the morning,' Francis said.

The old man lay on the cobbles of the Square. His body, black and shapeless as a fallen crow, was visible within the patch of light from a single lamp at the corner of the lane. He'd crawled there maybe: there was blood on his forehead and his hands, as if he had dragged himself across the stones or had been flung against the roughness of the wall. Even with limbs outspread, he looked no larger than a child.

Francis might have left him. Though he resented being warned, he had an instinct for self-protection, a reluctance to become involved: a countryman will always watch or comment, rarely intervene. But Francis saw once more the old man sleeping in the autumn sun, the girl protecting him, her tender look. Her curse still echoed in his mind, with the closer echo of the gipsy's cry. He felt shame again, and pity, and a fiercely rising anger at the memory – so fresh – of Luxton's callous eyes.

The Square was quiet now. With the exception of the Globe, windows were darkened, doors were firmly shut. No sign of Charlie or the Smiths. The old man's clothes were thin, the east wind cutting at Francis' back as he stripped off his own much warmer coat and, with a murmured oath as he stumbled on the stones, carried the gipsy to the step beside the pump. Maybe, then, he saw something of his father's frailty in him; maybe, in the gentleness with which he washed the blood and dirt from the old man's face, there was some remnant of a feeling long denied – his childhood love for Robert Ford. For he felt no revulsion, no unwillingness to touch the matted hair, the hard brown skin, the jacket stiff with the grease and smoke of many fires. 'Dirty gipsy,' he remembered, they had cried at school at the ragged child who came in winter for a month or two, who sat so patiently and learned to read in spite of all they did. Francis had jeered at him with the rest, repeating the theme of 'dirty gipsy' he had heard at home.

Yet later when he went to Bampton Fair or the Taunton races with his Uncle Tom, he had watched the gipsy dealers, drawn by their vigour and astuteness, their skill with the ponies he'd seen roaming wild up on the Moor. He'd listened to Tom Cheldon bargaining, using the language of the Romany: Tom taught Francis all he knew about the travellers – but made him swear he would never let his mother know. Then, last year, on a warm September night, a woman had seduced him at the Fair at Barnstaple – calling him her *pireno*, her darling, making him cross her palm with silver in the time-honoured gipsy way. A coarse-haired laughing creature, much older than himself, she had flattered his virginity away with a heady mixture of determination and cajolery which afterwards had angered him. And she sent him off with empty pockets, which annoyed him most of all. Next night he turned the tables on her – and reckoned by the time he'd done with her that the conquest was his own. Francis felt, when he got back home, much older than his brother, far more worldly-wise: Martin would never find himself a woman, he was too fastidious and slow . . .

The thought of Martin hurt him still. All he'd longed for – only an hour ago – was to go back home; to renew the tie – he was not ashamed to call it love – that had always been between the two of them. Yet as he waited in the silent Square, feeling the faint unsteady beat of the old man's heart beneath his hand, Ash Barton seemed remote, his childhood done – and his desire to go with Trenaman not merely a gesture of defiance but a part of something greater, a purpose he could not define. How far, he wondered, had this gipsy travelled in his life, what places had he seen? Without possessions, had he felt released from the restrictions binding other men? There must be a sort of freedom in such rootlessness – a freedom of the body and the mind . . . Francis had recognized it, surely, in the music Charlie played . . .

He was startled, then, by the suddenness with which the old man moved, pushing away the arms that held him, forcing himself to stand with a strength of will that seemed impossible in one so thin and small. He would have fallen, even so, had Francis not supported him again; and he was shaking – whether from cold or anger Francis couldn't tell, for he freed himself with a violent gesture and some muttered words of Romany.

There was laughter from the shadows. Charlie's voice: 'You are living then, *mi puro dad*!'

'No thanks to you! Why the devil did you leave him here?' Francis was shocked by the young man's unconcern – maybe Luxton had been right about him after all. 'He could have died! If those friends of yours had come back here and found him – if I hadn't seen him first –'

'Not friends of mine! Nor yours if they'd caught you helping one of us just now . . . But it's true, they might have killed him if I hadn't taken these . . .' Charlie held out both his hands, and by the spreading lamplight Francis saw the gleam of metal – two short knives with narrow finely sharpened blades.

'Those Smiths should learn to hold their drink – then they wouldn't part with things so easily.' The gipsy bent and dipped them quickly in the water-trough beside the pump. It hadn't been that easy, Francis thought: he had seen the blood, and the cuts on Charlie's hands. He could respect the young man's coolness now.

They stood together, watching Isaac Penfold as – without any word of thanks – he pulled his jacket close and moved unsteadily away into the dark.

'He's tough, that old one – stronger than he looks. And he doesn't like to have a *gorgio*'s help. He is proud – too proud to think that I must take him home. So I'll follow him, in case he walks into the Smiths . . .

'But I thank you,' Charlie said, retrieving Francis' coat and handing it to him. 'You're a brother to us – even if you are too friendly with the magistrate!'

He turned away and Francis thought he'd seen the last of him. But in a moment he was back, speaking with unexpected urgency. 'Brother, you should be careful where you go!'

Francis guessed he meant the Smiths – but then he added, 'There are tricky people at Ash Ford. So be careful, even close to home.' Francis felt him lightly touch his sleeve. 'I shall see you, *chal*!' He was gone.

It was late. The wind cut still more keenly now. Francis saw, as he left the Square to walk down Nymet Hill, the thin spire of Saint Mary's Church, a hard black line against the speeding cloud. He thrust his hands more deeply in his pockets – and could feel, beneath his fingers, first the roughness of a wooden handle, then the smoothness of a blade.

He knew at once who'd put it there. But it seemed, when he stopped and touched it carefully, that such a knife was strangely out of place – unnecessary here, in the valley where he'd been a boy, where he knew every-one and everyone knew Francis Ford. Yet – there was Charlie's warning ... He put the knife back in his pocket, thinking, as he made for home, that he might be glad of it some day – in Mexico.

9

Autumn had never seemed so powerfully beautiful. Even high summer – June in its glory – was pallid in recollection. Now, beneath the rich intensity of mid-day light, the almost weighty blue, the valley burned. As if the shortness of the days, the chill of night, lent urgency to every moment's heat; as if with each leaf's fall fresh brilliance was added to the trees. And it seemed, before each cutting frost, as if the flowers late-blossoming by cottage walls had never glowed so bright, or smelled so sweet. The slope of High Ash Hill was hard, and warm with reddened bramble leaves and bracken rust. Between the slowly changing woods the Aish flowed gently, clear, still innocent.

It could not last long – this strange premonitory calm. Martin felt it was becoming almost thunderous, ominous. And he knew that time was running out: he must see Alice soon. Some of the gipsies had already left the lane. Making trouble in the pubs Joe Pike had said – took off 'n went as sudden as they came. The Penfold wagons had remained. Yet the stream that ran through Jason's Wood must be getting dry: Martin had seen the barefoot children dipping buckets in the pool beside the bridge. There could be little grazing left; lately the ponies had been tethered on the wider verges of the Nymet road – even there, the grass would soon be gone. The young man had been at Molton market once or twice, but of the women there had been no sign. They were making preparations, Martin guessed. Before the weather broke, before the onset of November storms, the gipsies would be moving on.

Narracott Water runs into the Aish at Forda Mill. The tributary marks the eastern end of Ash Ford parish – and a change in the nature of the land. The tops are cold and barely tillable, the valley sides precipitously steep. Here and there, where stone is quarried, water drips incessantly; bright curls of fern, young birch and willow spring from fissures of the rock, which gleams and alters with the light – through silver, shades of grey, to black.

The Mill itself is built of stone: a range of cottages and barns, the tall square house where once the mill-wheel turned. The buildings rise – or seem to grow – against a wall of rock; and a muddy path, perpetually shadowed, runs between, on a level with the small square upper windows and the moss-encrusted edges of the roof. Green water-meadows, sunlit narrow strips beside the Aish, are the only fertile ground. But now, where cattle used to graze in summer, there is empty marsh. The leats and locks are silted up and overgrown with nettles, weirs and pools are gone.

A Sunday afternoon at Forda . . . Martin, as a child, had feared and longed to go. Nervous of his Cheldon uncles – tall men, the two of them, with rough red hair, impressive shoulders, heavy hands. Enchanted by the noisy wheel, its constant spray that flew and bounced like anvil sparks against the blackened wood and stone. And conscious always of his desperate awkwardness before the gaze of Mary's mother, Sarah Cheldon – who, as girl and matriarch, had dominated Forda Mill. Martin never pleased her: his brother was the favourite. In old age, even, she preferred men to be handsome, quick of mind – and attentive to herself; she was lively and tyrannical and must, when young, have been a good deal like his sister Eleanor, so Martin thought.

He could believe the tale he had been told. How Sarah Blake, the miller's only child, was courted by Sir Jocelyn Pennington, who rode along the valley from King's Nymet every day – until at last she told him she loved Francis Cheldon, tenant of Nymet Barton and his dearest friend. Much later, as a widow, Sarah had turned toward Sir Jos – there were rumours he would marry for a second time. But maybe they had quarrelled: she had suddenly – capriciously, it seemed – gone home to Forda, leaving Richard, as the eldest of her sons, to run the farm. She had not seen Jocelyn Pennington again.

'Yet I know he asked for her – he wanted her to go to him,' said Mary Ford. 'And Laura Trenaman once told me that he asked again to see her, just before he died. But Mother wouldn't listen when I came to tell her that Sir Jos was ill. She wouldn't let me speak of him . . .'

Martin had heard the bitterness in Mary's voice. Yet when he glanced at her she seemed entirely calm, dispassionate – as if she spoke of strangers rather than of Sarah whom she'd openly disliked, and of Sir Jocelyn who had meant so much to her. It was shortly after Sarah Cheldon's death, and they were walking home one Sunday from the Mill; he'd noticed how his mother had been happier while up at Forda – almost as if the death of Sarah had released her in some way. But it hadn't lasted. Mary's customary hardness, and her inability to speak to him of things that mattered, had returned. Martin had forgotten how she'd been that day . . .

Until this afternoon. Another autumn Sunday, as he walked – this time alone – along the river path to Forda Mill.

'I can't think why you have to go to Forda now, today. They're not expecting us – there isn't any need. Besides, Tom won't be there. He's coming down next week to talk about the farm – you'll see him soon enough!'

If I want to see him, Martin thought. Unlike Francis and his mother, he didn't care for Tom. He didn't wish to think his uncle's money would be used to buy Ash Barton – there was sure to be some trouble later on.

'And you haven't been to church since Harvest Supper – Rector will be wondering –'

'The parson never notices a thing. He only wants to get the sermon done and be off home again. Joe's wife says Mrs Hannaford reminds him every time. And in any case I thought you'd turn to chapel now – it's what you always said you'd do.' Martin didn't care if that annoyed her. Mary had been evil-tempered all the time since Francis told her he would go.

'Well, Passmore *is* a better preacher – Richard thinks a lot of him, and I shall go to chapel when the farm is ours and there's no need to bow to anyone. It's a poor thing, anyway, if the Rector can't remember when to go to church! But I intend to go this morning – and your father isn't fit . . .'

'Then you will have to go without us, Mother – and put up with it!'

He hadn't meant to be so sharp – but wouldn't wait to see her disbelief, her outraged piety. The days of patient tolerance of all she said and did to hurt him – times when Martin saw his father driven out to find a quiet corner where he'd sit and smoke his pipe until she called him in – quite suddenly became too much to take. Within an hour the morning's work was done; and he had crossed the river near the trapper's cottage, by the crooked bridge.

Now, as he walked beside the Aish, remembering, he felt he understood. Why Mary couldn't bear to be held back by Robert Ford – so easygoing, unambitious, sensitive. Why she detested Trenaman, the knowledge that a son of hers was patronized by him. And of course – why she had disliked her mother so: a woman who held back from marrying the Squire, establishing the Cheldons firmly in the ruling class. Mary hated seeing Pennington estates bought up by strangers, rather than by families to whom the valley rightfully belonged. Her mother's marriage to Sir Jocelyn could have changed all that. For Sarah Blake had been strongminded from the start: she would not have let a husband gamble an inheritance away.

Yet why had she at last rejected him? Or had it been Sir Jocelyn's fault – the disagreement that divided them? Perhaps, reflected Martin, there was something else – that his mother hadn't known, or Sarah hadn't told . . . He knew, at least, that the dislike between the women had been mutual. It was quite clear, from everything his mother said, that Sarah had been jealous of her only daughter and – with open prejudice – had spoiled her sons. Yet she had kept her family together, ruled them all from Forda till her death.

The Cheldon brothers were a formidable lot. Maturity or marriages or even quarrels could not – when it really came to it – destroy the unity that Sarah had decreed. As a small boy Francis had admired them. Martin feared their size, their belly-laughs, their massive presence in a farmhouse kitchen after some collective effort – harvesting, a shoot, or dipping sheep – at Nymet Barton or Ash Leigh. The pair who worked the Mill were bachelors, and always kindest to the boys; while Tom, the youngest of the six, was believed to have a wife in Bampton even though he lived alone up on the Moor. He took advantage of his status as a kind of family god – could do no wrong as far as Sarah or his sister were concerned – but had a meanness that his nephews had grown wary of. Tom was reputed to have shot too closely at a neighbour who'd looked hard at him across an auction ring one Thursday and had spoiled his bid: if there were other grievances between them no one knew, but Philip Snell was seen to limp as a result of Tom's unlikely aim – which had somehow missed a snipe in Forda Marsh.

There was a curious closeness between Mary and her brother Tom. An intimacy which for Martin could not be explained by the resemblance in their looks or the nearness of their age. It made him feel uneasy even now to think of it. Of how his mother always seemed to show a tenderness towards his uncle, and a strangely youthful eagerness, whenever he appeared or when they went with her to Rincombe for the sheep sales or for Bampton Fair. Francis hadn't noticed it – he was exhilarated by the journey to the Moor in their uncle's ancient trap, by his tales of gipsies, poachers, witches or the customs that he knew. He told the boys about the mines, the rush for gold at Heasley and the silver up at Combe. Francis was enthralled. But Martin never quite forgot those evenings by the fireside, when he saw Tom Cheldon close to Mary, and the touching of their hands . . .

There is, where the valley narrows downstream from the Mill, a pathway leading to a quarry, long disused – save when in summer tramps or other wanderers set makeshift tents, or light their fires. In late October sun, a silent sheltered place – still sweet with honeysuckle, gold and faded green.

A buzzard, feathers almost white beneath its wings, made curving shadow as it turned above the rock. And there were deer slots, sharp and recent in the softer ground where water trickled, darkening the dust. Martin had noticed movement on the hillside as he left the Forda track: a stag, he didn't doubt – he'd heard one only yesterday in Barton Wood. A young one, probably. It would lie up in the bracken through the afternoon, then cross the river, following the hinds. He would see it, maybe, as he walked back home at dusk: a heavy body delicately poised and subtle-coloured on the autumn hill, the antlers winter-sharp against the sky.

His mood was calmer now. He'd needed this – a long slow walk to get his thoughts in order, ease the tensions of the past few weeks. Ash Barton – everything – had grown oppressive: he had never in his life felt so alone. He had rejected Francis at the very moment when they should have worked together, built the farm to something they would never lose . . . Martin somehow hadn't quite believed in Francis's decision – not until last week, when they had spoken to each other late one night. He'd heard his brother in the passage, waited while he threw off coat and boots; and thought, as soon as he saw Francis, that he looked worn out.

No quarrel this time, just a brief exchange of words.

'Where have you been?'

'To Heasley.'

'With –'

'With Trenaman. To look at Bamfylde Mine.'

'You mean it, then? You mean to go?'

That quick dark look. The brother Martin loved!

'Of course.' No more.

Since then he'd swung between determination and despair. His silences and flares of anger had alarmed his mother, made things even worse. She hadn't wanted him to go to Forda yet: her brothers would have questions, criticism, good advice. Mary could never turn to them as readily as she would go to Tom. But Martin might. He'd always liked and trusted them. They weren't expecting him – but they would quietly sit him by the fire and let him talk as much, or as little, as he chose.

It made him feel more resolute, to think of them: how they and their part of the valley scarcely seemed to change. Their bodies had become more bent, their red hair sparser, greying to the colour of the stone – and yet their roots, like willows at the gate, were stronger, deeper-set, each year. There was a kind of peace, perhaps, to be found in knowledge of a place, its weaknesses and strengths: a certainty that made his uncles what they were. Even without Francis – Martin knew it now – his life could be like theirs. As he'd always wanted it to be . . .

He was standing on the Forda track, by the turning to the quarry, when he saw again that sudden movement on the hill.

Alice had seen him cross the bridge. Decisive-looking, shoulders back, a dog at heel. Too quick to have noticed Alice at the corner of the lane. Too angry still to slacken pace or turn to glimpse her hesitation at the Ash Ford road, where Martin crossed the Aish a second time and took the path toward the Mill. And too absorbed in thought to see her slip between the birches high above the river – though he walked more slowly then, a tall long-striding figure clear against the smoothness of the meadow grass.

He changed direction suddenly. Near where a narrow wooden footbridge spanned the Aish, he climbed a fence beside the track and moved away into the shadow of the trees. From the hillside Alice watched. She saw a buzzard rise and turn above the quarry face. Martin was gone – and the impulse that had driven her to follow him was spent.

It had been as though the sight of Martin made her conscious of the empty days since she had seen him in the church, the hours spent dreaming up on High Ash Hill, the melancholy moods that made her chafe at everything familiar and dear. The *vardo* walls confined her; while the children's play and teasing, even the old man's care, distressed her constantly. Often she had longed to leave the valley, longed to stay. Now, the urgency with which she followed Martin had compelled her to ignore the steepness and the roughness of the ground, the stones and thorns and stems of fern that cut her feet and hands. Alice hardly knew how she had come there – only that a weariness of spirit far beyond fatigue of body overcame her, draining her of strength. She lay, as if discarded, in the bracken on the hill.

It was here that Martin came to her at last. He was

breathless from the climb, all memory of Forda far behind. Despairing in the moments when he thought that Alice must have gone. But then he saw the russet colour of her skirt, the golden-brown of skin, the flame of hair that burned more brightly even than the hill. He was exultant in his certainty.

For an instant only, when his heavy frame seemed dark against the birches – silver-frail and almost stripped of leaves – the girl imagined Francis, would have fled. But it was Martin's voice, more gentle now than when she heard him greet her mother on the road. His touch, more powerful than anything she dreamed of when alone. And Martin's look – as it had been in church, that harvest-time . . .

Above them, black against the deepest blue, the buzzard poised and curved, alone. Beyond the valley, and beyond the western Moor, fine cloud began to drift before the wind. It gathered, bringing rain.

10

I won't be afraid of being happy, Martin thought. I will lie here and soak it up, like a flower soaks up the sun, stretches its petals, breathes in the light. Maybe it fades soon, is gone before morning. Yet it's worth it – worth the pain of knowing that your time is passing, soon to be a drift of petals fallen, scattered on the grass.

He reached out a hand, picked up the coloured scarf that she had left, in her forgetfulness. He turned the faded silk in his hand, wondered idly how she came by it – hardly something a gipsy girl would find in the hedgerow, after all. Stolen, for all that Martin knew. Did he care? He had been brought up to think that thieving was immoral. Gipsies and vagrants of any kind were not allowed to enter through the narrow gate his mother guarded with such pride – the gate of virtuous religion, Sunday neatness not just once a week but every day. Each day there was a text of righteousness to set her on the safe path through the petty tasks; each day she tore off, first thing in the morning, yesterday's leaf from the calendar above the kitchen sink. And read aloud – like some ritual incantation – the new day's text: not always taken from the Bible, Martin had discovered, yet each one a part of Mary's pious certitude.

'*Remember thy creator in the days of thy youth.*' How that had haunted him in childhood – the notion of an unseen power overlooking all he did. Until, he remembered wrily, he had realized one morning that it was only the first sight of those texts that had such impact on him: look at them in a day or two, or a week or fortnight later (Mary kept them faithfully, stuck into one of those thin bits of wire with a vicious point that tore into the butcher's bill or the boldly printed date) – and their significance was gone. They were only words on cheap scraps of paper after all. They had no power to erase the things that mattered – the sight of a hare on the hilltop in early morning, the sense of possession Martin felt as he walked alone through misty fields . . .

Just as now his mother's words of warning – 'Remember, you have a duty to the farm!' – could not destroy the image of a laughing girl, the brightness of her hair against his hand, the inward certainty that she was only there for him. Alice, when he found her on the hill, was all that he remembered. Only this time not remote, part of a dream or vision that would vanish at his mother's voice. This time – a gipsy girl in dusty clothes; the murmured words he could not know, and yet had understood; the shock and joy of recognition in their love.

Yet even to be content – as Martin must be now – was to commit rebellion, defiance of the daily imposition of his mother's will upon his own. It was not the work itself: often its monotony had soothed his spirit, could assert a silent old-established strength outweighing that of Mary Ford. She was convinced that Martin, like her husband, must give in – or seek a refuge from the level piercing look, the silence of reproach through which her anger spoke with more effect than words, or even tears. But always, later, those would come. Later, in the afternoon, when Martin came in with the dog for a moment's warmth beside the stove before the milking must be done, he would be driven out with words which had been festering all day. Or tears which he ignored by putting all his mind into the rhythm of the evening work, moving from barn to yard with straw or hay, feeling the steady breath of standing cattle, heat of muscle, skin and hair against his hands, a chilling blast of air as his father came in through the shippen door. Theirs was a different kind of silence, broken only by sounds that held no threat or inner meaning – cows shifting their bulk against the stalls with a dull rattle of chain; a murmur of agreement as to this one's yield, another's feed; the distant noise of dogs, alert in the darkening yard. Here, with the heavy blackened door barred firm against the wind, Martin felt secure; at one with his father in their warmer world, at peace.

. . . A different peace from this. Another world – which must soon encompass Alice, who was part of him. Tomorrow he would face perplexities, the implications of it all.

Martin had watched her go from him. Along the ridge and through the trees, barefoot across the river; out of sight. He held the coloured silk between his fingers. It would be enough, to be content. Today.

He would not go to Forda now.

'Tell me now, my mother,' Alice said. 'Who was Euphemia Penfold? Why is she buried in the churchyard at Ash Ford?'

The questions Grace had known must come. For a moment she was silent. Then, with a gesture of affection clear enough, she touched her daughter's arm, looked into the strangely apprehensive eyes.

'You must know it all,' she said. 'And I shall tell you all – but you must wait a little longer, till we go from here. When we have left this place, my daughter, you shall know.'

Grace could see that Alice was distressed. She had returned to Jason's Wood an hour ago – and as she held the youngest child beside the fire she seemed once more the eager girl who danced and sang in Somerset, before her father's death. But when the children begged her for another song she had refused; then withdrew into the *vardo*, where she sat alone.

It was almost dusk when Grace went to her. The air had suddenly gone cold. The girl spoke urgently – yet Alice did not ask the question that her mother feared the most. Grace knew she must forestall that if she could.

'Euphemia was your father's sister – youngest of them all. She loved a *gorgio* once. But I shall speak of that another time, I promise you. There is another story – you must know that first. I should have told it to you long ago.

'For there's good *gorgios* and there's bad, my daughter, don't forget. My grandfather Jacob – Black Jack they called him – he was wedded to a *gorgie* girl from Somerset. My own mother's mother, Janet was – and many Roms would be ashamed of it but none would ever dare to say it to my face. And when I was a little thing he told me how it came about. For he was proud of it – a fine wife she made him though she gived him trouble enough in the beginning of it all.

'He was walking into Somerset from Dulverton one day, and he had sold some horses and their colts at Bampton Fair – and he was pleased with the deals he'd made that day, but he wasn't pleased with the pony that he had. As he was walking he came to a fine park with a great house standing fine and white upon the hill. There was deer in the park, he said – small ones, not like the Exmoor deer at all. And he was standing looking at them, thinking they would make a meal or two (for he was living on his wits and playing his fiddle at the fairs and had a small tent all his own) – when he sees this lady on a horse, a white mare, white as milk it was with a long mane and tail and plenty of spirit. She was dreaming along all gently when it saw him and his pony, and of course it shied and bucked a bit. My grandfather took his chance and asked if she would like to sell it – knowing of course that she would not but thinking he would like the chance to speak with her, she looking very beautiful with long gold hair, just the same as mine it must have been ... But she spoke proudly at him and moved the white mare on, flicking at it with her riding-whip which caught him on the arm as he was standing there. That made him mad of course – he was a fine young man and used to having his way with all the girls.

'So Jack upped on to the pony and made it gallop after her along the forest path, faster and faster till he caught up with her. But she only spurred *her* pony on and hit at him again, her hair all streaming in the wind and her eyes all bright and flashing. On they went till they came to the open moor – but she would not give in and nor would he. At last he caught her, right up in the moor at Lanacombe – near where the river widens out and there's a little heap of rocks beside an elder tree. There he caught her up at last, and she was angry still and bade him leave her be. But it was getting dusk by then, and he was more anxious for her than he let her see – he didn't want to harm her after all.

'Then he took his fiddle from the pony's neck where he always kept it tied, and played a tune for her, thinking it would calm her tears, and so it did. For it's said that a gipsy fiddler can get his mastery of any woman – for his music has the ancient magic in it. So he didn't take her back, leastways not to her own house but to his tent instead, and there they lived together happy as the birds. For she was married to a rich old man and there had been a child that died, and that had grieved her more than anything. She could have been a rich *rawnie* when her husband died because he begged her to go back. But she would not – and not a penny of his money did she get.

'Janet became a gipsy woman, right enough. She dyed her hair with juice of berries and her skin got darker every day, so her own mother didn't know her when they met by chance one market-day at Dulverton. My grandfather Jacob was a Lovel – a true *Kaulo Camlo* – blackest of all the Romany, they say. But he wanted the

95

lady and he got her, and the horse as well. And every word of it is true – for that's the very fiddle that your brother Charlie plays, and there's none so sweet in the whole of Somerset.'

Alice listened silently. She had been told a little of Jack Lovel's story long ago – but Will had never liked to hear of it. He had spoken sharply to her mother; later Grace refused to tell her more. Like all the Penfolds Alice feared her father's rage – yet sometimes when her mother looked so very tall, her hair worn like a coronet about her head, the girl had feared her even more. Secretly, perhaps, Will Penfold too had been afraid of Lovel pride, had envied Grace the black blood running in her veins: for the *Kaulo Camlo* were indeed an ancient race, their name a noble one among the Romany.

Now, Alice wondered what her father might have done if he had known she loved a *gorgio chal*. He would have been ashamed of her: it grieved her just to think of it. And yet today with Martin, on the hillside, she had felt no guilt or shame. Her joy had lasted till she took the youngest of her brothers in her arms – then wondered suddenly what could have happened to that other Penfold girl, Euphemia, and who had been the father of her child ... An Ash Ford man, she had already guessed; her lover too had been a *gorgio*, Grace had said – and that was all that Alice could be told. She had been back to the churchyard several times; once, she saw John Reed, the culpritcher, again. But he had seemed reluctant to acknowledge her, had hurried into church. She was disappointed, went to see the headstone on the grave – and found it yet again made bright with flowers. Who was it that remembered her – Euphemia, a gipsy like herself? And why would Grace not speak of her to Alice now?

The *vardo* had grown dim. The girl could scarcely see the polished brass, the colours of the china plates and cups so carefully arranged. Her mother had not lit the lamp; Alice felt the wagon, which had always been her home, was chill – the warmth of childhood gone. If Charlie, who had always shared her thoughts, should guess where she had been today, with whom, his anger would be worse than Will's. He had his father's temper, and she could not bear to think how it would be if Charlie ever met with Martin now. Though he laughed and flirted with the village girls, he'd never think of wedding any but a proper *chi* – one of the many Penfold cousins, Alice didn't doubt. She knew already his opinion of Francis: Charlie, like so many gipsies, scorned the farmers with their ownership of land, their use of guns. And once, when Grace reminded him that Martin had permitted them to stay, Alice saw the fire that came into her brother's glance. He said nothing to her afterwards; but she had felt his censure of the man she loved, had waited for the words that did not come . . . It would be better for them all, thought Alice bitterly, to leave the valley now.

But Grace had read her daughter's heart. Even before the girl herself had understood, the woman saw it all. Saw all that had come about – as Grace had known it must, that morning when she first met Martin on the hill by Jason's Wood.

Now, as then, she knew that nothing could be changed. That any warning, fears or anger came too late. With Alice – as with Jacob Lovel – passion was instant and complete. Already, she belonged to Martin Ford.

As the bells rang out for evensong, Grace left the gipsy camp. She went alone, and without her customary basket on her arm. And, as she intended, reached the wicket gate in time to meet the Reverend Michael Pennington – who, like a thin-legged fragile bird, was hurrying from church.

Within an hour she left the Rectory again. It was too dark for anyone to notice that she carried in her arms a small plain metal trunk, of the kind most commonly in use among the working class. It was loosely tied with fraying cord, and from time to time as the woman climbed the old green road she set it down, as if what it contained was of considerable weight. Once, before she stooped to take it up, Grace hesitated: maybe she had thought to open it, but changed her mind. In spite of her increasing weariness she did not stop again until she reached the top of Jason's Wood, where she surveyed her burden and, beneath the starlight, smiled.

A bargain had been made.

Next morning when, as had become his habit, Martin looked across the valley to the wood, he saw no smoke. And knew, with a weight of sorrow in his heart, that there would be no gipsies in the lane.

The rabbit trapper, too, was on the road. His work for Trenaman was done. Usually, this time of the year, he went to keep his contract with a farmer in the valley of the Taw. He had shut up his home beside the bridge: his daughter Rose would know where he had gone. If she ever bothered to come back – he reckoned she'd found better ways of spending any time that she was free of Nymet House . . .

He stopped when he reached the summit of the Ash Ford hill, and looked across to Barton Wood. He was thinking of the empty cottage there – and the trap that he had set the night before. The last thing he had done: a simple trap, the kind that keepers used to set for poachers in the olden days. You had to be quite certain of the path your quarry took – and then, a hidden wire, a loaded gun. A fitting trap for vermin – of the human sort. And by the time that it was sprung, he would be well away.

The trapper raised his head and sniffed the air – a creature of the wild. It would be winter soon.

PART TWO

A man, naked to the waist, works in the centre of a field. Around him lie the tumbled sheaves, awry and shapeless like the harvest houses children make – and then destroy. He is bent and sweating with the effort of his work, the August heat, yet he is now the pivot upon which the future of his acres turns.

REGISTER OF BAPTISMS
solemnized in the parish of Ash Ford, county of Devon

1909   September 10   Philip John Ellis
                     father —
                     mother Rose Ellis   spinster   Narracott

REGISTER OF MARRIAGES
solemnized in the parish of Ash Ford, county of Devon

1909   October 4
          Martin Robert Ford   24   farmer   Ash Barton
                  to
          Alice Joan Penfold   17   housemaid   The Rectory

           Witnessed by: J. Reed   colporter
                        M. Hannaford   housekeeper

           Signed: M. J. Pennington   Rector

1

Alice went back in the spring, alone. As she stepped down from the train at Nymet Junction she appeared like any other country girl in search of work – wearing a neat but obviously altered jacket and a serviceable skirt, and carrying a battered metal trunk. Only the darker colour of her skin and bolder features showed her gipsy blood; her hair, with its distinctive brightness, was drawn back and, like her mother's, plaited close about her head.

They were Euphemia Penfold's clothes. When Alice had protested Grace had silenced her. 'You must become a *gorgie* if you are to marry one – as much as Janet Lovel made herself a gipsy *chi*. When you go to Martin Ford you shall take clothes and some money of your own: his mother shall not say you go to them for charity! Euphemia should have been a *gorgio*'s wife – and her clothes will fit you when I've done with them.'

The trunk – Euphemia's, too – was heavy. Alice tried to lift it by the cord. The station porter stared, but was not unkind. 'You can leave the luggage, miss – there'll be someone going up the village later on. And it needn't cost you nothing,' – he mistook her hesitation – 'us'll send it safe now, don't you fret.' He watched her cross the line towards the Ash Ford road. A pretty thing and frightened as a tiddy-mouse, he would tell them later in the Globe. He was a cousin of Joe Pike.

She walked between high hedges. Rain and primroses

and earth – their freshness drove away the taint of town, the noise and dust. Exmoor was hidden by low cloud as Alice gained the ridge. The chimneys of Ash Barton lay below. For an instant, from a gateway, visible – then gone.

There was no welcome at the Rectory. The Reverend Pennington was not at home. Yet as soon as Alice showed the slip of paper Grace had given her the woman changed her mind. She knew the Rector's signature and later when the old man told her to prepare a room she thought she recognized the girl. But Martha Hannaford would keep her counsel, as a servant of long standing ought to do.

That night, between cold sheets, Alice wept for the *vardo* she had loved.

'If you must marry him, you must, my daughter. But remember – he will own you, just as he will own his cattle or his land. And often men destroy the thing they love the most.

'*Givengro camo-mescro, si tatcho camo-mescro!* The farmer is your lover, truly. But a lover cannot always see the way – he's like a mole, a *puvo-baulor*, in the dark, then in the light. Too blind to see the trap – the *pando-mengro* – till too late. *Cam si merripen ta merripen si cam*: love may be life, it may be death – and we cannot know which it will be.'

Martin had found them in the gipsy camp – a hostile, strangely independent place. A damp, low-lying field on the outskirts of the town, between the river and the railway line. Tents and wagons, flat-topped carts, the tethered ponies picking at the frozen turf; here and there a blaze to warm the old men sitting silently, the infants wrapped in coloured rags. Snow lay on the hardened mud, small children ran and screamed, their thin legs red and blue from bruises or the biting cold. The litter was unpleasant, noise and smells a shock to Martin, used to an ordered farmhouse and the quiet fields. He had felt cut off from Alice, longed to come to her – but he hadn't thought of her as part of this . . .

The Penfold women saw him – tall, in working clothes, bareheaded in the icy wind that cut across the country from the east. He was standing – clearly hesitating – on the track that led into the camp.

'If the *gorgio*'s looking for his gun then he can go back home!' Charlie had seen him too. 'And I could tell him where to find it quick enough!' His tone was odd – regret and satisfaction. Alice would remember it one day.

'But it isn't that he's wanting, is it now? A girl he's after this time, isn't it, *mi pen*?' His hand was gripping at her shoulder. She could feel his fingers' pressure even through her heavy shawl. Ever since they left the valley Charlie had been rough with her, seemed to watch her all the time. It was New Year now and he was drinking hard – but he'd known that it was Martin straight away. Alice was certain he had guessed . . .

'Let her alone!' Grace intervened. 'Alice, you must go into the van. I shall speak to Mr Ford – without your brother's help.'

'You can speak to him – and he can have her if he's fool enough, but she won't be my sister any more!' Charlie pushed the girl towards the *vardo* step. 'And I can tell you, little bitch – if the *gorgio* hadn't got a brother of his own I'd cut his throat. I would rather kill him than let him have you in his bed!'

His anger, and the grief it hid, hurt Alice more than any beating that her father ever gave. She scarcely saw her brother go, or heard when Martin spoke to her. The joy of loving had so quickly turned to pain.

'Alice!'

But when Martin spoke again, so urgently, it was as if the weeks of waiting, moments of despair, had vanished as the snow would melt in spring. His hand touched hers, she saw the need and passion in his look, her doubts were gone. She had not doubted that he loved her – but she had a gipsy's sense of time, which holds no certainty except the passing moment and excludes the unreality of hope. Now, Martin's presence gave her courage. Alice faced her mother and, for the first time in her life, defied her openly.

'I will not go in! He has come to find me, Mother, and I shall not give him up whatever Charlie says. You were right – this *gorgio* doesn't break his promises. You told me so yourself. And if we are to marry then my place is here with him, not in the *vardo* while you bargain with him just as if he were a gipsy man. I will do whatever else you tell me to – I'll go with him or wait for him, whatever you decide. But I will not leave him now when he has come so far!'

She turned to Martin. And he knew at once the answer to the question he had asked himself so many times since the day he found her on the hill.

'I am not afraid of loving you – though I hate to hurt my brother and to make my mother sad. I'll be your wife if that is what you want. If not, I'll never love another man – and I shall never change my mind!'

Alice spoke the truth, as he had believed she would. He too had suffered since he saw her last – he had felt winter closing in, the distancing that can destroy the happiness so briefly found and gone again. There were days of indecision, fear of taking Alice from her old life to a stranger's home; and other days when thoughts of her had been the only brightness, love for her his only hope. But this day – even in the bleakness of the gipsy camp – he felt her certainty and strength, which both of them would need. Martin did not see her as a girl but as a woman who would be beside him always in the valley that he loved.

'There will be difficulties –' Martin hesitated. 'I would be lying if I told you otherwise. And one thing in particular –'

'I know it!' Alice said. 'Your mother will not want me there – how could she want me for her son? But I will try –' She was suddenly uncertain, thinking of the woman she had seen in church . . .

'She knows nothing of you yet.' He too remembered, was afraid for Alice – yet he could not give her up! 'We must wait until the spring,' he said, 'when my brother Francis has left home. She will be more ready to accept you then.' And, he thought, she will have bought the farm by that time: surely Mary would not risk the loss of both her sons?

Grace listened, watched them. If she had foreseen the sorrow that would come to them, she could not say. But it seemed to her they had no way of choosing what might happen to them – only the illusion of a choice.

And yet, what Alice said was true: whatever else Grace feared for them, she had trusted Martin Ford. Already he had proved that he would not merely use a gipsy girl and then discard her, as Euphemia had been abandoned long ago. He was surely worth the love her daughter showed so openly – and Grace was proud of Alice now. She could see in her Will Penfold's spirit, and the daring that made Jacob Lovel seize his chance and take a lady for his wife . . .

'You will always be my child,' she said at last, 'whatever you may do, whatever may befall. But there will be many miles between us, and for a little longer you will stay with me. There are things that only I can teach you – things you must know before you go to him.

'And you' – she turned to Martin – 'you will need to be her father and her brother, too. She will have no man but you. It will be hard – yet if you suffer for each other that will make you strong. But you must understand: she will not be able to come back to us. When a gipsy leaves her people she must go for good. It is a death, there is no going back. Our people can be just as unforgiving as you *gorgios* are!'

106

In winter light, beside her painted *vardo*, and surrounded by the squalor of the camp, Grace seemed to Martin as remote and unapproachable as when he saw her first at Jason's Wood. Then – he could acknowledge it – he had been afraid of her, had recognized her powerful insight, and held back from her. This time he felt her caution as a challenge and her wisdom as a threat. Perhaps, deep down, he sensed that she was testing him. He didn't care – he answered her as forcefully as he had answered Mary Ford, when he refused to make the gipsies leave.

'How could I want her to come back to you – to this! How could I ever want to lose what I have found?' Martin's voice was steady, yet in it they heard anger – almost scorn – that made him seem much older and more resolute. 'When Alice comes to me it will be as my wife – and if she ever leaves Ash Barton she will not go alone!'

'I believe you.' Grace was satisfied at last. 'It is not your goods or money that my daughter needs, but help and love.'

She told them then about Euphemia – how she had gone, some thirty years before, to be a servant to the Penningtons at Nymet House. She had been ruined by a local man, Grace said, and lost her place; but when she went in desperation to the Rectory they had refused to take her in. Later, when Will Penfold learned that she had died, he was beside himself with grief and threatened to get even with the Penningtons.

'Your father was as young as Charlie, then, and just as angry that his sister loved a *gorgio* man.'

'But, Mother,' Alice said, 'who was the father of her child?'

'Will knew it, but he would not speak of it to me. He loved her and refused to name the man who had dishonoured her and caused her death. He said it would be dangerous for me to know – and he was certain that Sir Jocelyn Pennington would get the gipsies driven out.

'So now you know as much as I can tell. And if you still wish to marry Martin Ford, it shall be your choice.'

'Mother,' Alice said, 'I can do nothing else!'

'In that case you shall go to Ash Ford in the spring. The Reverend will be expecting you and will provide you with a home. He owes a debt to us for keeping silence all these years – he will not wish it to be broken now. And you – you must forget the past. All that matters is that you should learn to be as like a *gorgie* as you can: you must prove to Mistress Ford that you can be a farmer's wife!'

Martin had guessed that Grace was keeping something back. He waited till they walked together to the lane that led up to the railway and the town. Then he asked, 'Why are you so afraid for Alice? Surely you don't think that even now I –'

'No, not that! It isn't you I fear. You have the will to care for her. Yet you are hurt too easily – and those who feel too much are often weakest when it comes to helping others through the world. No –' Grace paused, looked keenly at him. 'I believe your valley is an unforgiving place. Our people have discovered that – and I fear the same for her, for you. That is why you must be married, and have the protection of your church against the evil you may find. I can do nothing more than I have done. The land itself – you are a farmer, you have seen! – the land itself is hard, and it has made the people hard.'

Martin was silent. He couldn't want her to be right – and surely evil was too strong a word. The gipsies could be superstitious. Ignorant, his mother would have said . . .

'I know – it is your home, and beautiful. A part of you –'

He stared at her. Then laughed. 'Another thing,' he said. 'How did you know my name, that day?'

'Your father did a kindness to my husband once. A gipsy won't forgive an enemy, but he won't forget a

108

friend. And we see much more than others do. Will told me that your father was too peaceable – perhaps you are the same. But I must tell you this. The evil in your valley killed Euphemia. I cannot tell you how, but it was so!' She saw his shock, and added swiftly, 'Do not speak of it to Alice. She is young – she will have enough to bear!'

Grace took Martin's hand and looked at it, then shook her head. 'There is nothing more that I can do. May you find the happiness you seek.'

She had said those words before – but her meaning had been hidden from him then. And even then, she seemed to understand so much. Had she seen everything, he wondered, as he slowly walked away. Could there be anything Grace Penfold had not known?

In her attic room at Ash Ford Rectory, through long slow hours when Alice could not sleep, she would re-member how she watched them cross the frozen field – the man she loved, the mother she would leave. How when she saw against the reddened sky the smoke and sparks from the train that carried Martin home, she felt that part of her had gone with him. Already she had weighed the life she knew against a future that she could not see. And had guessed that in the spring when it was time for her to go, the Penfolds would be moving on.

Before she left, old Isaac had called Alice to his tent. He was sitting with his body hunched against the wind; his face and hands looked stiff with cold – yet it was April and the air was mild. To her surprise he held her hand in his – she knew that he was fond of her, but it was the first and only gesture of affection he had ever shown.

'I had a daughter once,' he said. 'Like you she was, and knew her mind, the same as you.'

'She was Euphemia! My mother said –'

'Your mother knows a lot, but she doesn't know it all.' The old man sounded sharp: there had been many disagreements, Alice knew. 'There's things I haven't spoken of – maybe I should, but it's too late. And you'll be going – to the farmer, Ford?'

'I shall,' said Alice. 'It is settled. I'll be going soon.'

'I loved that girl – there were others but I loved my 'Phemia the best. Your father did as well – and because of it he died. Maybe your mother guessed it, maybe not – we never talk of things like that. But I was with your father when they found him – on the quay and right beside a fishing-boat he was, half in the water, nearly drowned. And drunk they said he was, but I knew better, see. For he could talk a bit, and making sense he was . . .' The old man seemed to lapse into a dream, his eyes half closed – and Alice was afraid to speak, afraid to move. She waited, hoping that her silence would encourage him to tell her more . . .

'It's true enough, I was with Will before they took him to the hospital, before he died – and he reckoned it was Ash Ford folk that got him in the end. It wasn't one of our lot, that's for sure – though he'd been fighting like he always was. And something else there was. Don't never trust a Pennington, he says – and if he'd had the chance he would have told the law, the *poknish*, how my 'Phemie died. The one they call the Captain, he's the *poknish* man, he came that day –'

'But you told him who you were – and he knew my father's name! My mother said that it meant nothing –'

'Maybe it meant something, maybe not. Who knows – and maybe it's too late. But you saw it – I was right, and he didn't turn us off. And you'll be going there again, my girl –' the old man stared at Alice. She could tell that there was something more behind his look, his words – a purposeful malevolence that she had never seen in him before. 'You'll be going there, and you must listen, you must watch. And perhaps you'll see the Captain too. And you won't forget that you're a Penfold even when you're married to a Ford!'

'I – won't forget!' She couldn't help but promise him. He frightened her with his insistence – but she thought of Will, the father she had lost . . .

'You're a good girl, Alice, and you've watched for me when others didn't care, or hadn't time. I'll be sorry to leave here without you – but I shan't be sorry to be on the road.'

Isaac was thin, and through the winter he had coughed incessantly. Alice saw the talking must have weakened him. He almost whispered to her now. 'There'll be something for your wedding day, but never tell a soul. Not all the *gorgios* are as bad as they are painted – there are gipsies that are worse, I'm sure of that!' His fingers touched the scar – still rough and ugly-looking – that his face had carried since his trouble with the Smiths. Since then, he hadn't seemed the same . . .

Alice kissed him. But she knew that he would not see Somerset again.

2

Alice longed for the *vardo*'s intimacy now – the breathing of the little children as they slept, her mother's sighs; the growling of the lurchers, all the harsh noise of the camp. The Rectory was echoing and large, its rooms half empty, most of them unused. The unaccustomed privacy felt isolating, cold – she missed the constant closeness of humanity. The knowledge that she was so near to Martin made her loneliness more bearable – but Alice could not go to him, must wait until he sent her word.

Soon the Penfold wagons would be moving slowly through the springtime lanes, beneath the newly opened leaves, the brightness of the April sky. Birdsong all the day; at night the sound of wind through branches, rain against the *vardo* roof. Yet here – it seemed to Alice there could be no moon, no stars, only the oppressiveness of walls. She had never in her life been so confined. And through the darkness she was haunted by the story of Euphemia. In daytime, when she wore the altered clothes or touched the metal box she thought of her – and wished, even in spite of Martin, that she hadn't come. It was as if by coming to the valley where she died, and living in the household that rejected her, she had become that other gipsy girl . . . She seemed to hear her desperate knocking at the door, her gentle voice, her baby's cry . . . What right had Alice to be here? – Euphemia had been turned away and could not rest . . .

It was impossible to tell the Rector or confide in Mrs

Hannaford. Apart from Mrs Pike who came each day to do the heavy work there was just one other servant – she was elderly and rather deaf, and suspicious when she realized Alice was to stay. And they were strangers. Only a gipsy – Grace or Isaac, even Charlie – might have understood her fears.

Late one night, only two weeks after she had reached Ash Ford, she left the Rectory. There was a side door to the garden; it was rarely locked and Alice had discovered, at the far end of the grounds, an iron gate leading to the village and the lane. The moon was hidden, but high cloud and the intermittent light of stars enabled her to find the way. She wore the heavy skirt and gipsy shawl she had concealed – on the morning that she came away – among the clothes her mother had prepared. Before she left the house she went into the kitchen, where it might have been supposed she found provisions for a journey – yet she took, from the heavy earthen crock upon the larder shelf, no more than one small piece of bread. Alice placed this with some other articles, safe in the pocket of her skirt.

It was long past midnight when she reached the top of Jason's Wood. She had not intended to come quite so far – but the thought of Martin, just across the valley in the sleeping farm, encouraged her and kept her dread at bay. For Alice knew exactly what she ought to do. And it was – there could be no doubt – what her mother would have wished.

The old green lane was silent, shadowed, moist with heavy dew. Not far from where the wagons rested last October Alice found a bank of primroses, which even in the darkness seemed more fragrant than the Rector's garden flowers. With the knife she always carried in her skirt she carefully removed some plants, and then some moss from higher up the bank; all these she wrapped within her shawl. For some minutes afterwards she stood and listened – as she used to do so often, months before –

to all the gentle unseen movement of the night, in hedge and field and wood. And far below, yet clear, the murmur of the Aish.

There was moonlight when Alice came down to the cottage by the bridge. Here all was quiet – not even the expected barking of the trapper's dogs. Stones and mud and branches left by winter floods were heaped against the doorway, while the door itself was partly open, hanging by a broken hinge. No drift of wood-smoke from the chimney, only the smell of something rotting in the nettles by the wall. The cottage must be empty – but Alice hurried past, remembering with sudden horror how one morning she had seen the trapper standing there with fresh blood on his face and hands.

She reached the churchyard as the clock struck two. Euphemia's grave was just as she recalled – beside the path and with a leaning stone. But there were no flowers this time – only the scattered fragments of a jar. Alice shivered as she touched them with her hand – perhaps, she thought, Euphemia had grieved when someone had forgotten her at last . . .

With her knife she quickly dug away the grass and earth beneath the headstone, exactly where the autumn flowers had been. And here, when she had made a deep enough depression in the ground, she placed the contents of her pocket: lace and ribbon from a gown Euphemia had worn, a silver coin from the money Grace had given Alice when she left, and the little piece of bread. Finally, with fingers stiff from cold and apprehension, she unclasped her heavy silver ear-rings. These were her wedding-gift from Isaac Penfold and, so he had said, had been intended for Euphemia . . . Alice placed them on the grave.

The primrose plants, the earth and grass, the pale moss from Jason's Wood: all carefully arranged in spite of haste, and her fear that someone from the nearby cottages might be aroused. As Alice left the churchyard she could almost have imagined that she saw the bent form of the culpritcher – but it was just a shadow cast by yew-tree branches near the iron railing in the wall.

Back in her attic room, for the remainder of the night she slept at last. And woke to hear the song of birds beyond the open window, and to feel against her face the freshness of the air. She knew she had been right – the spirit of Euphemia would be at peace. For Alice, still a gipsy, had done all she could. Now she must prepare to be with Martin. She would learn, for him, to be a *gorgie* and a farmer's wife.

She hardly saw the Reverend Pennington. She was aware of him – a slight-built grey-clad figure who would often seem to hover like a moth beside the window of his study, watching Alice as she walked along the gravel path or crossed the unkempt grass towards the paddock where his pony leaned against the rail. Sometimes she heard the Rector's voice, precise and clear, as he gave the housekeeper her orders for the week; but apart from their first meeting – when he merely glanced at her and sent her off upstairs with Mrs Hannaford – she had not met him face to face. He was a scholar and a busy man, of course: she heard the housekeeper explain to callers that the Rector was at work and must not be disturbed. 'Engaged upon his history of the Penningtons, he is – it takes up all his time, except for sermons on a Saturday.' When Alice, after several days, had enquired if she might speak to him, she had received the same reply.

Mrs Hannaford felt sorry for the girl. Whatever reason her employer had for keeping Alice here, it was quite clear that she felt ill at ease. She was silent for the most part – did as she was bidden and was learning quickly all the household duties she had been assigned, but only seemed content when she could wander in the garden on her own. And even here the woman sometimes saw her pacing, staring out beyond the paddock rail and the enclosing trees – a white bird in a cage of summer green. One morning, long before the Rector had come down, the housekeeper caught sight of Alice running barefoot out across the garden to the field – and running even faster there beside the pony, with her rich hair loose and gleaming in the early light.

'No trouble is she, Mrs Hannaford?'

The Rector's sudden question, coming in the wake of his instructions on a Monday late in May, took the woman by surprise.

'Why, no – no trouble, sir. In fact – no bother, sir, at all. Except –'

'Except for what?' He didn't wait for her reply. 'Quite happy is she, Martha, would you say?' His gaze was more direct than usual – he was generally inattentive, vague.

'I think so, sir. It's difficult to know . . .' Impossible, she meant – the girl was such a puzzle, everything about her strange. As for her being happy – it wasn't like the Rector to be interested in a person's feelings . . . Martha Hannaford had learned that long ago, and had suppressed her own.

'I really cannot judge –' she broke off suddenly, this time quite mystified.

The Reverend Pennington, with an agility she had not known he still possessed, had hurried past her, through the study door and down the stairs. Some minutes later she could see him at the far side of the garden, talking to the girl. Then, together, they were passing through the wicket gate, and walking down the path between the yew trees to the church.

The pair of them had been too far away for her to note the look of joy, the tears of gratitude that transformed Alice from a wistful solitary girl into a woman filled with an intensity of love – so pure and undisguised that even Michael Pennington was moved. He had been so long an adept at the art of hiding what he felt that he appeared to Mrs Hannaford to have no personal involvement in the girl's affairs. Yet they were absent from the Rectory – the housekeeper would readily have sworn – at least an hour: the Reverend Pennington, so punctual as a rule, was late for lunch.

Before that morning Martin had seen Alice only when he went to church. She was so much more like Grace than he remembered – yet so changed. Tall, and slender in her plain white dress. Or perhaps it was her hair – so neatly braided now and hardly visible beneath the borrowed hat, which Mrs Hannaford insisted she must wear on Sundays when she had to sit – exposed to village scrutiny – beside her in the Rectory pew. And she was wearing gloves: they hid the long brown fingers that would always seem to Martin far more beautiful than those of Margaret Trenaman, or any other woman he had known.

Alice's composure had astonished Martin. How could she possibly remain so calm? He was painfully aware of how his own hands might betray his nervousness. His mother stood next to him. Surely she must sense he wasn't concentrating, hardly heard the music or the words of Michael Pennington, while all his thought and feeling reached out to the unknown girl who sat with Mrs Hannaford.

And what would Mary think of her? Martin had to speak of Alice soon – he dreaded it. Grace Penfold had been right, of course: he'd always known he was too peaceable, that Francis was the one with courage to carry out his plans however furious their mother proved to be. Yet he'd borne the brunt of Mary's wrath, had shielded Francis – surely his back was broad enough for anything? Last winter had been the worst that he had known, but he'd survived. Since March, when Francis left for Cornwall, Mary's temper had improved – she hardly mentioned him, had scarcely seemed to care that all they'd heard of him was a brief report from Captain Trenaman. And when – again through Nymet House – he had requested that they send his books, she had remarked, 'Thank God for that – I'll be glad to see the back of them!'

She *must* accept the girl. Martin would only wait till Mary was accustomed to the sight of Alice, till he was certain the Rector wouldn't break his word. Grace had been sure he would agree to marry them – but in the valley the old man had a reputation for capriciousness. He was frequently evasive when approached by his parishioners: 'A tricky sort o' chap the Passon be – you'm never sure what 'n be thinkin', like.' Martin had often heard the village people say such things.

But how could Alice bear it, cooped up in that gloomy house with a couple of old women and the Reverend Pennington? He could imagine nothing worse, almost hated Grace for having thought of it – yet what else could they have done? At least she would be reasonably safe from prying eyes; and Mrs Hannaford was kind enough beneath that prim expression, that uncompromising stare with which she looked around the church before she settled to the singing of a hymn . . .

'I must say,' Mary whispered, 'I'm amazed at Martha Hannaford.'

Martin didn't ask her why. It was clear enough his mother meant a reference to Alice, for she had been gazing at the girl throughout the service, with an overt curiosity that had alarmed and angered him. Then she was watching closely as they left the pew – the housekeeper with head erect and silk dress rustling as she walked, Alice with the graceful movement he remembered. He could scarcely keep himself from saying something as she passed – her sudden closeness was a shock, the sense of separation so unbearable that he could hardly breathe . . .

'You'd think, if the Rector needed servants – and it seems extravagant to me – that he'd have made sure

Martha Hannaford would pick a village girl. I shall tell her when I get the chance – and she'd have done much better with a plainer one, the handsome ones are always troublesome!' His mother had compressed her lips and shut her leather prayer book with a snap. But it seemed she hadn't recognized the gipsy girl . . .

Mary had said nothing more that day to Martin and, so far as he could ascertain, did not go to the Rectory or speak to Mrs Hannaford. He reckoned even if she did her criticism would be wasted on such stony ground. The housekeeper, as everybody knew, could be formidable when crossed: in a village like Ash Ford – so small that the scope for power was limited – a meeting of such strongminded women rarely ended in a compromise. Mrs Hannaford would take the Rector's part in everything. And Martin saw, in the way she glanced encouragement to Alice as they left, that she might prove a useful ally in the weeks ahead.

For he had decided then, as he followed Mary out of church. He'd endured it long enough. It was time to speak to Michael Pennington.

Sunday 9 May 1909 Today the young man came to me. He had sent me several notes which I ignored – being in that frame of mind when anything to do with the affair depressed me. I am getting far too old to wish for anything – in these last few months remaining to me – but to be at peace. I had intended to refuse to see him – nothing good can come of it. The Penfold woman's threats amount to blackmail, no one but a tired old fool would have been influenced by them – now, it goes against the grain to let this thing develop further than it has already gone. The girl has a good position here and so long as she behaves correctly she may stay. But as for my conniving at a marriage such as is proposed – I cannot think my obligation need extend so far. I have said as much to Ford.

I think I have a duty to advise him not to marry such a girl. His mother's family is good – I doubt if she or any

of the Cheldons could approve; and his father is a drunk-
ard, hardly capable of giving him advice. I have told him
he should give the whole thing up. I shall have no more
to do with it.

The Rector had been sharp with Martha Hannaford
when he returned from evensong that night. And he did
not seem to be himself. Refused to dine – complained of
indigestion, very rare with him – and went upstairs
before his usual hour.

She watched him closely in the days that followed.
Michael Pennington, to her, was the lover she had lost,
the child that she would never bear: she would have
gone through fire and water for this withered un-
responsive man. She believed she knew him, through
and through.

Sunday 16 May 1909 Today, Martin Ford insisted that he
speak to me again. He was forthright – almost rude; I
myself extremely firm. I refused to let him see the girl.

For the second Sunday in succession Michael Pennington was late from evensong.

Sunday 23 May 1909 I cannot help but be impressed by
Ford's persistence. He is, I do believe, an intelligent
young man. I have agreed – albeit with reluctance – to
his meeting with the Penfold girl. But I have made it
plain it must be brief and in the vestry here: I cannot
tolerate such things beneath my roof. And this must be
the last of it – after tomorrow morning I shall wash my
hands of this affair. To let these gipsy women have their
way would be a grave mistake: who knows where it may
end. The girl is quiet enough, but deceitful I don't doubt
– they are all the same.

I regret I was not more firm this time with Martin Ford.
God knows I am exhausted by it now – and I have surely
paid enough in an unquiet conscience all these years . . .

As the Rector locked his private journal in the vestry safe, he wished that with it he could lock away the past.

For him she *was* the past.

Whenever Michael Pennington saw Alice, he remembered. As she went about the house or walked alone beneath the trees – she seemed to him to be that other gipsy girl, whose name was written in his mind as clearly as he had inscribed it in the Register so long ago. She was Euphemia – whose infant son he had baptized. Whose voice and look remained with him years after he'd forgotten all the nameless, faceless ones for whom he had performed the Christian rites – long since become perfunctory and meaningless.

He had seen her three times only. When she brought her child he had condemned her sin with words he always used to young women in disgrace. Weeks later, when the Rector heard her frantic weeping at his door, he had – reluctantly enough – told Martha Hannaford to bring her in: then lectured her again and sent her off into the dark. And the last time – when they pulled her from the Aish. The sodden clothes, the features swollen and the child wrapped tightly in her shawl . . . He saw her still. Her eyes, her sweet expression – and Alice was the same.

At first he would not admit it to himself. But even in the safety of his study and surrounded by the documents relating to his work, he could not escape the truth. For his task was to write a history of the Penningtons – and here he thought of Jocelyn and his hatred of the Penfold clan. A hatred that could only be explained in terms of something personal, something his brother Jos had wished to hide . . . of which, as a Pennington, he was ashamed. For reasons of his own Sir Jocelyn – though a magistrate – had not made public all the circumstances of Euphemia's death. Grace Penfold had been right: the Rector did not wish the silence to be broken after thirty years.

Yet he must face another truth. This time, if he failed, there would be no second chance. Michael Pennington would bear the burden of his conscience to the grave – and now, that could not be far away . . .

That other girl was dead and gone: for her, it was too late. Alice Penfold was the present, not the past. And this time – Michael Pennington admitted it at length – it could not be the same. Euphemia, as a woman, had meant nothing to him then. But Alice had, unwittingly and by degrees, aroused in him a feeling he'd thought buried long ago. Not physical – the Rector had been too long celibate, was too fastidious for that. Her presence drew from him a sudden tenderness – the kind he'd felt in boyhood for the creatures he had found in hedge or field. And a longing he had felt in manhood when he'd envied Jos so bitterly: the longing for a child.

Her astonishment and joy at seeing Martin moved the Rector – yet he concealed it well. Next morning Alice brought into the house a sheaf of flowers, bluebells from the little coppice by the lane. She put them in the Rector's study, on his desk, to Martha Hannaford's amazement – it was sacrosanct; and in the dining-room, upon the polished table where he always took his meals alone. And if the housekeeper had been perturbed by his behaviour of recent weeks, she was confounded now. For her employer walked with Alice in the garden every day. Gravely, and with hands that shook, he pointed out his special – long neglected – plants; and each time Alice asked a question he responded with a courtesy that was a relic of his youth, a charm that had preceded all the disillusion of maturity.

In his journal, at the end of June, Michael Pennington would write: 'I have agreed to marry Alice Penfold, after harvest-time, to Martin Ford.'

3

The tallet door was open wide. Lying in the loft, among
the new-cut hay, Martin could hear the gentle desultory
sounds of summer – pigeons calling to each other from
the swaying firs behind the house, young sparrows in a
nest below the shippen roof, the restless movement of a
horse against a stable door. He lay there drifting, dreaming, forming in his mind the shapes of words, the poems
he would never write. As so often when the body was
exhausted, limbs too stiff and sore to move, his thoughts
were quick as swallows darting through the rafters overhead.

. . . a field of tall thick gently-moving grass, small
flowers between the blades, the drying heads of seed. A
smell of clover crushed against his mouth – the sweetness
and the bitter after-taste. A girl with long bright hair,
unbound at last. Her fingers brown and cool against his
face.

. . . a day when heat and dust drove cattle to the
shadow of the hedge, when may-flies danced like sparks
across the surface of the Aish. And Martin's heavy horses
shook the water from their fetlocks as they climbed the
stony path above the ford. While Alice watched them
from the bridge, her laughter echoing.

. . . a month of meeting Alice secretly, unnoticed, sometimes unexpectedly. Times when the moments slipped
away too quickly, suddenly – and yet the hours of
absence held a promise and a certainty more meaningful

to Martin than anything he'd known before. He worked as hard as he had ever worked, but now with stronger purpose, fiercer energy. With Alice at the centre of it all.

The hay was in at last. This year, a long slow awkward business with the weather playing tricks. No Francis here to share the labour with him – his exhilaration as the wagons carried home the loads, and weary satisfaction at the sight of empty fields. If it hadn't been for Harry, home from Oxford for the summer, Joe and Martin would be at it still.

Today Martin had Ash Barton to himself, a few hours' peace. He'd sent Joe off to help out Robert's brothers with the hay at Town; while Robert, under protest, had gone with Mary to King's Nymet – there were papers to be signed for the purchase of the farm. Martin believed his mother would have gone alone – she thought of it as her affair; but the agent, Webber, wouldn't stand for that – he had a reputation for disliking women when it came to making deals. At Michaelmas, possession of Ash Barton would be theirs. And by Michaelmas, the Rector would have called the banns in church . . .

'You may meet each other,' Michael Pennington had told them. 'You may make your plans, as far as possible. But you must be discreet. This parish has been mine for half a century – and there are things that do not change: if there should be a scandal, your marriage will never be accepted in Ash Ford. And as to whether I can marry you – you shall have my decision in a month.' In spite of their misgivings, he had kept his word. They knew now that the Rector had agreed. And whatever happened, Martin thought, however fierce the coming storm, they had had those weeks of summer calm . . .

He heard the gate swing to, the barking of the dogs, shut in till milking-time. Voices; silence; a knocking at the door. Ann Pike should have answered – she was doing his mother's dairy work this afternoon. Martin listened, then rolled over to the open window of the tallet. From there he could see out across the yard –

124

'So that is where you're hiding. Come on down! Harry – Martin *is* here, after all.' They waited till he joined them by the steps.

'Mother wanted cream, you see,' said Margaret, out of breath and dusting down her skirt. 'But she didn't care to come herself. Your mother has been – well, so very strange of late. I mean, since Francis went away –' She paused, embarrassed – then she laughed. 'But nothing's really altered, has it? *We're* the same as usual!'

Margaret smiled uncertainly and looked at Harry, who (as ever, Martin thought) was cheerful, unperturbed by the complications that his sister seemed to find in everything.

'We've been lunching at the Rectory. For once our reverend uncle felt hospitable – I can't imagine what's come over him. We're *never* asked. Though I must say Father has some business there before he goes to Cornwall next – it's something geological I should expect. Uncle Michael is the expert in such things. So we've left them to a deep discussion while we walk back home. And I thought,' said Harry, 'that there might be tea. After all, you can't be making hay . . .'

'And there's a letter for you – Francis sent it. Father will take an answer if you like. He'll be going down again next week.' Margaret held the letter out – and Martin saw her glance at it a little sadly. Maybe Francis hasn't written to her yet, he guessed. He's a brute, she doesn't see it though. And she is charming still . . .

'I wonder if he thinks of coming home before they go to Mexico. He's doing very well at Camborne, Father says.' She sounded wistful yet resigned. Martin felt protective suddenly. He was realizing now – with the clarity of mind that comes when one is at a turning-point – how close their lives had always been.

Sometimes, as a child, he had resented Laura Trenaman's officiousness, her patronage, that had persuaded Mary Ford to let her sons have lessons up at Nymet

125

House. Much later, when he understood his mother far too well, he saw that her ambition for her younger son outweighed her jealousy – she hadn't known that Francis would be drawn away, seduced into another world. And she surely hadn't seen how Margaret, for a time, had eased the loss of Eleanor – how Martin found in her the sister he had loved. But today, as Margaret stood there in the sunlit yard, her brown hair streaked with gold from riding hatless as she insisted she preferred, he knew he cared for her for Harry's sake much more than for her own. In manner – if in little else – they were so alike, with that open eagerness which often seemed to contradict the innate coolness and self-confidence, the hallmarks of their class.

'Of course you must have tea, and I'm sure there'll be some cream. I'll see about it afterwards.'

Joe's daughter Ann, round-faced and silent, served them in the kitchen. Shadowed, neat, it was so much Mary's place – and one day Alice would be here, among them all. Martin wanted it – and yet, he was enjoying this. It was as it used to be. Himself, the Trenamans; a break from the monotony of work and Mary's watchfulness, her impulse to destroy whatever pleased her elder son. 'Unmanly' she called Harry's love of books and his dislike of sport – Sir Jocelyn would have been ashamed of him; and she suspected Margaret's unselfconscious charm, though she had come to recognize the strength of will beneath the ladylike exterior. If it came to a battle over Francis, Martin thought, his mother might not win. But Margaret was much too good for Francis – he treated her so carelessly: surely she wouldn't always be so blind . . .

She was at ease now, seated in his mother's rocking-chair, and balancing the flowered tea-things Ann had judged appropriate for guests from Nymet House. When the girl had left the kitchen Margaret looked around with satisfaction, and declared impulsively –

126

'You see, I'm right – it hasn't changed. Oh I am so glad we came! We were talking, weren't we Harry, as we came along – of the things we used to do. And how wicked Francis was! Like the time he put a slow-worm on Miss Matford's chair and she ran off in hysterics, wouldn't stay, and mother had to find another governess. Or when we made our tree-house on the island in the river and we watched an otter hiding from the hounds – you wouldn't let us tell the huntsman it was there. He complained to Father that we'd spoiled the day.'

'I can remember,' Martin said. 'I had a fight with Francis afterwards.'

'And that was the summer when we had our pony race on Nymet Moor. You didn't want to ride but we persuaded you – your pony won and Francis didn't like to think you rode as well as he.'

How I hated that, thought Martin. It was Eleanor, of course – but the others hadn't understood what held him back. He hadn't ridden since . . . and Francis, after that, had set his sights on Margaret.

'But what has happened to old Ellis?' Harry interrupted them. 'He never liked us – said we spoiled his snares, which in fact we hadn't done. His cottage looks to be shut up. We came along the river and we didn't see a sign of him at all.'

'And I hoped we might see Rose. The children miss her so – we often wonder how she is. It was sad, but she couldn't stay, of course. And Mother did her best for her . . .' A tactful pause, while Margaret sighed and reached out to fill her cup.

In that moment Martin glanced at Harry, saw the apprehensive look he gave his sister, the relief when she continued, 'Mother was afraid that Ellis wouldn't have Rose back – he was always very strict with her, and I think she must have hated him. But if he's gone away for good . . .'

'It isn't certain,' Martin said. 'It's just that no one's

seen him for the last few months. They say he had a lot of money stacked away and has gone off on the spree – but I can't imagine that, he's never been exactly sociable.' . . . Rose was lucky – Ellis would have beaten her to death if he'd heard them in the Pennington. Thank God, he thought, that Margaret clearly didn't know about all that! The ribald jokes about the potency of Cornishmen – the speculation that if Trenaman himself were not the father of the child, then Harry must have been. 'Tis true, they'd said, her was a nursemaid up at Nymet House, and it wouldn't be the first time that a squire had tilled his oats at harvest, or a village maiden reaped a come-bichance.

'Rose,' he added quickly, 'is at Narracott. She's with the Snells, my uncles' neighbours up by Forda Mill. Her mother was a Snell, of course – they had the trapper's cottage years ago, till Ellis came.'

'Why – where was Ellis from? I always thought he was an Ash Ford man.' Harry never minded Martin's knowing more than he about such things. Their friendship had survived in spite of separation – school and Oxford even: they knew that it would last.

'The story is that Ellis just turned up one winter night. And no one knew him – only that he'd come from Dartmoor way. But he stayed, trapped rabbits for his keep, then married Rose's mother. He got the cottage too. It wasn't long before her parents left and went back up the valley – they couldn't stand him any more.

'There's something odd, as well, about the way he went last year . . . We didn't even know till Francis found some wire, and those wooden pegs he uses for the snares – he reckoned Ellis must have meant to set a trap and got disturbed, or changed his mind. And when Francis took them down he found the house shut up – yet you'd think if he'd been going to another job he would have taken all his gear, not left the things behind. They weren't where he'd been working but on Barton land, in the wood across from where your father's pheasant hutches are.'

. . . And close to the cottage where his brother had been meeting Rose – though Francis had denied that until Martin made it clear he'd guessed. Now, remembering, he thought how strange it was they hadn't quarrelled over that: they'd both been shaken by the thought that Ellis could have known, and Francis (Martin gave his brother credit for some feeling, if not for common sense) had been anxious for the girl . . .

'Well I hope he won't come back!' said Margaret in her forthright way. 'I used to hate it when I was out walking and Ellis would appear, quite suddenly, and stare – without quite seeing one . . . And the way he moved, in a sliding sort of fashion, silently –' She shivered, then, with a little frown – as if ashamed – stood up decisively.

'How stupid, and on such a lovely day! We had better go, and let you milk the cows or something useful, not chatter on to us. I'll find Ann in the dairy, for the cream – I know the way, of course.'

They heard her footsteps echoing, her voice, the creaking of a heavy door.

'I was right then? Francis, wasn't it – and Rose?'

'I thought you'd guess. You have known him long enough.'

'And he's not exactly facing up to it. His going off with Father *is* convenient, for him at least – you must admit.' Harry looked and sounded cynical.

'Of course – though I don't believe he meant it so. He does respect your father, wouldn't choose to let him down. But it's Margaret –' Martin glanced towards the passage.

'It would kill her!' Harry's voice was low, expression grim. 'And heaven help Francis if she does find out – I should like to wring his neck!'

The heat, as they left the coolness of the house, seemed

more intense, pulsating from the surface of the high cob wall. There was a smell of drying hay, a heady perfume from the yellow rose that overhung the narrow door where Margaret paused, held out her hand. 'I'll walk with you,' Martin said, 'a little of the way.' He was reluctant – for some reason he could not identify – to see them go.

Beyond the wall, across the hill behind the farm, a soft breeze blew. They climbed the path, an ancient trackway smooth with close-cropped grass; here and there a patch of thyme, a flat grey rock, small butterflies, bright blue and brown. At the highest point, where the path curved down from the shoulder of the hill, they stopped. Below, the valley lay enclosed and silent, filled with summer light.

'Look – there!' said Martin quietly. Above the dark line of the wood a kestrel hovered, quivering – then plunged into the shadow of the trees. For a moment, perfect: place and light, suspended motion of the bird. And gone as suddenly.

He had meant to leave them then. But Margaret looked regretful, Harry took him by the arm. Their pleasure in the afternoon had been as great as his. They were persuasive – Martin would walk down to the turning, cut back home through Barton Wood. After all, they didn't see each other often now . . .

It was when they neared the gate, where the path divided, that Margaret suddenly exclaimed, 'I quite forgot! Martin – who *is* the new girl at the Rectory? So very striking, Harry, wasn't she? Oh come' – she laughed at his denial – 'even Father was impressed, and you know you couldn't take your eyes off her at lunch. She was helping Mrs Hannaford, you see,' she had turned to Martin once again. 'Now, do tell us who she is – your mother's bound to have discovered it. We wondered, could she be a relative of Martha Hannaford? Yet she isn't very like – but tall and a little foreign-looking, don't you think?'

In the silence, it was Harry – always sensitive to Martin's moods – who almost guessed.

'I think you've said enough!' He was sharp with Margaret. He had felt Martin's shock at the unexpected questioning. And when Martin drew away from him decisively – thrusting his hands deep into his pockets, tightening his mouth to a thin hard line – Harry knew he was making up his mind. To what, he couldn't know . . . and somehow, didn't care to ask . . .

'It's getting late – we must be keeping you. There isn't any need –'

Martin cut him short. 'I should have told you both before. Today, perhaps – but I haven't spoken to my parents yet. At least, if I do it now you'll know the truth of it, and I would rather that.' His voice was steady, almost too controlled. Yet they heard the strength of feeling in his words, and waited. Margaret, bewildered; Harry with a cool detachment, his defence (perfected long ago) against unpleasantness of any kind, against reality.

'The girl you saw is Alice Penfold. She's not foreign but a gipsy. Her people are from Somerset – up Lydiard way. But this time of the year they're on the road; that's why she's at the Rectory – your uncle has, at present, given her a home.' Martin paused, noted the quick exchange of looks between the Trenamans. Already, they were distancing themselves from him . . . Rejecting him? If so, he had some pride – would make no bid to keep them as his friends. That must be their choice.

'Your uncle has agreed to marry us. In the autumn, after harvest, she will be my wife.'

The room had not been touched since Francis left. Even Mary, it was obvious, had not been in there – everything was dusty and the place had a hollow feel; yet to Martin it was as if his brother had walked out and left it for an afternoon. There were the rocks and fossils Francis had

131

collected, whitened bones from rabbit, sheep or deer; he'd often claimed (perversely, Martin thought) that he found dead animals more interesting than living ones. His relics of the hunting-field – some cast-off horseshoes and an otter's paw, a hoof from the stag they killed one season up at Middle Aish – were ranged along the mantelpiece with his silver-handled whip. The riding-jacket on a chair beside the bed, and boots – well-worn but highly polished – flung in a corner as if he'd used them yesterday. He was always careless with his things – had thrown his books in boxes and left them in the harness-room: Martin had repacked them thoroughly and sent them down to Nymet House. Now there were random spaces on the shelves, a heap of half-burned rubbish in the grate, some papers scattered by the desk the brothers used to share.

Since that night last autumn Martin had slept in the room that once was Eleanor's. Had hated it at first, but came to like the neat white calmness of it, even the texts that hung to each side of the big brass bed – one with bluebirds and a cherub, one with a shepherd and some unconvincing sheep. Faded, meaningless, yet somehow reassuring, part of a long-lost childish certainty. He had a vision, suddenly, of Alice in that bed – her hair against the pillow with its crochet border, limbs outstretched beneath the quilted counterpane. They would be to-gether in that room . . . Their future – children strong and beautiful as Alice, whom he'd always love; a farm to work for, care for, that would one day be their own.

The past with Francis, and the life he'd known before the gipsies came – all that was done with now. Even last year's quarrel – he could hear it, in this room, so clearly – had receded: the beginning and the end of everything. They hadn't found the gun. He had been right about it, Francis wrong. Unless . . . but this was something Martin couldn't bear to think of, never wanted to believe . . . His brother wouldn't steal – a careless fool, and irresponsible, but not a thief. Sir Jocelyn's gun had been mislaid: even Mary Ford, at length, accepted that. It was irrevocably lost.

Decisively he crossed the room and sat down at the desk. The letter Margaret Trenaman had brought that afternoon was still unread – he'd found it on the kitchen dresser after walking home from Barton Wood. Those final moments with the Trenamans had shaken him. The look in Margaret's eyes as she murmured formal words, mechanical and meaningless, then turned away; and Harry's reticence, which Martin knew meant more than anything he might have said. Harry would try to understand, would want to talk about it one day; in the meantime, Martin sensed, the feeling that had always been between them – delicate and undefined – was under threat. Could not, he must suppose, be otherwise . . .

'Don't let Mother see this letter . . .' Martin almost laughed out loud. His brother's secrecy, his evasiveness – that hadn't changed. And nor, it seemed, had his self-confidence. He was accepted now, he wrote: it had been difficult, but he had proved that a Devonian could labour just as hard as any Cornishman. The mines were like another world – he'd never been so tired or dirty in his life, and yet it was exciting, fascinated him.

You'd hate it – darkness, stinking water, all those bodies. Sometimes underground you lose all sense of time, you surface and discover that you've lost your bearings, missed a day or two. It's strange to think of you and Joe and Father working in the fields and I'm below the land – the hay and corn and trees. The men are very tough, some of the villages are poor, with people desperate for work. They make me feel ashamed of the easy time we have at home. [For you, perhaps, thought Martin. Not for all of us!] The fishing's all they have here when the tin and copper fail, so when the mines close down it's very hard – and opening them up again is dangerous. But some,

133

the bigger ones, have been electrified – that's the reason Trenaman is here so much, to see them for himself. He reckons things are much improved, there'll be another boom, he'll make a lot of money out of it. For me, it's just a stepping-stone – I'm learning all I can before we go . . .

And that, wrote Francis, would be sooner than he'd thought. There was trouble in the mines in Mexico. Some of the men he'd met had come back home because of it. Ralph Trenaman was keen to get out there to see his interests were protected.

In Pachuca, where we're going first, it seems it's not so bad. The Cornish have been there for years and are needed still. They've modernized the mines, the owners have a lot of plans which Trenaman would like to see get under way. He knows the ropes of course, and even if the strikes get worse we should be safe enough. But he's said nothing of all this at Nymet House in case the women get alarmed – so don't tell Mother that I've written to you . . .

They would sail from Plymouth some time in October. And before they went he might come home – for just a week or two . . .

How typical of Francis! Martin crushed the letter in his hand. How arrogant and selfish – thinking he could walk into Ash Barton after all those months, as if he'd never made that show of independence, hadn't left them at the moment he was badly needed on the farm. That boasting of how hard he worked – no interest in the place or people he'd abandoned, not a word of all the trouble he had caused. Why should he come back here?

The room felt hot and airless. Martin threw the window wide. A startling sound and gesture that brought home to him the violence of his anger – all the deep resentment he'd thought buried and forgotten, superseded by his love for Alice and his hopes, his plans. October . . . he'd be married then. And Francis might be coming back: the last thing Martin had imagined possible. The last thing he would want.

He wrote his answer. It was short and to the point. It might have been less brutal had he waited, weighed the consequences: Martin rarely acted on his anger, as he did that day. Perhaps his judgment would have been less harsh had he not seen – and hated seeing – how his marriage might affect his friendship with the Trenamans; perhaps he feared that in allowing Francis to come back he risked a further, even more important loss – his future at Ash Barton, his security. In spite of Martin's gentleness his passion for the land, his instinct to possess, was absolute. Last year he would have shared the farm with Francis: now, it was too late.

The answer had been written, sealed. Martin shut the window of his brother's room, replaced the chair beside the desk. He noticed as he did so that among the papers scattered on the floor there was a photograph – perhaps intended for the fire and never burned.

It was of Francis, seated on his horse in front of Nymet House. A girl beside him – Margaret Trenaman, of course. It had been taken not so long ago; last autumn, Martin guessed. He turned it over: on the back it was inscribed – 'Take care, and come back soon. Love M.' How like his brother to accept a parting gift, and something personal at that, and leave it lying there for anyone to see. He might have known it would enrage his mother if she found it; maybe, even, he had done it purposely. Martin meant to put the photograph away – but stared at it again. He'd seen another somewhere, he could not remember when . . . Perhaps it was his brother's likeness to their Uncle Tom – much darker than the other Cheldon men, and with the same slight build that Francis had . . .

But no – it wasn't that. It was the pose: the easy seat

on horseback; and his head – the heavy lock of hair that fell so carelessly across the brow, the air of confidence. The way that Francis always looked when with a woman – conscious of his power. Martin took the photograph, on impulse, back into his own room where he put it safely in a drawer. One day he would find it there again.

The sound of wheels along the lane: his parents back from Nymet and their interview with Webber. It had been a crucial day. Now, Martin felt entirely certain of himself, quite resolute. He'd told the Trenamans of Alice. So tonight, when they discussed the farm, he'd tell his mother what he meant to do – his father would just listen, shake his head, and wander out into the yard. Robert would accept whatever Mary told him to accept.

And ultimately, Martin knew, his mother had no choice. She would protest and weep and, for a time, would give him hell. She'd fight his marriage – he was in no doubt. But with Francis gone for good – and Martin's letter making sure of it – the way was clear. At last, Ash Barton would belong to Fords. To Martin, and his sons.

A hundred miles away, in Camborne, Francis thought of Rose.

4

Several times, in that first summer, Alice saw the trapper's daughter. Once, when Rose was standing with a group of village girls beside the churchyard steps. Though obviously pregnant, she hadn't seemed to care – her laughter echoed, and the sunlight touched the fine gold hair that fell below her waist. Alice recognized her, then, as the nursery maid she'd seen when she called at Nymet House with Grace – and she remembered how the little Trenamans had run to Rose, and held her hands so tightly as the gipsy women passed them in the lane. In those days, with her apron freshly starched and hair confined within a ribboned cap, she looked demure and neat, incapable of immorality.

But – as Mrs Pike told Alice – there were always something just a bit deceiving in the girl. 'You'd see her running down the woods – wild as a hare! And her never went to school, till Mrs Trenaman had words with Ellis, said it wasn't right – her *had* to go. Her father didn't like her working at the House, but Rosie took a notion and her went, without a word of it to him. So now some gurt vool's been and spoiled her and her'll never get another place – the Snells won't keep her long – they'm Methodist, see.' Mrs Pike had paused for breath, looked round as if afraid that Mrs Hannaford might hear. 'Now Joe, he reckons *he* knows who 'twas – and he says that Ellis would've killed the both o' them if he'd've found them out. But there – the poor maid never had a mother that would learn her right from wrong!'

Rose didn't look unhappy, Alice thought. That morning, she had seen her lying in the shade of an overhanging willow by the bridge, near her father's empty house. Her shabby skirt tucked up around her hips, her long legs stretched – as brown as any boy's – across the warmth of stones, her feet beneath the water. There was something self-absorbed, untouched, about her still: an air of innocent repose. To Alice it had seemed impossible – that she should be the trapper's child.

It was early in July, when she met her on the path to Forda Mill, that Alice saw the change in Rose. The girl appeared worn out. Her hair was tangled, stiff with sweat and dust, her delicate complexion coarsened by the heat. She walked with the clumsiness of heavy pregnancy, setting down her basket with a gesture of such hopelessness that Alice longed to speak to her, to offer help.

She would have been rejected. Alice knew it from the girl's instinctive fear – in her eyes, the way she tensed her body, drawing back and clutching at her cotton shawl with nervous hands, as if she must protect her unborn infant from the evil in her way. Even when, at length, she found the courage to go past, while Alice stood aside and waited patiently, Rose kept on looking back – as though she dreaded being followed, threatened by a gipsy's curse.

Alice felt no bitterness. The stronger of the two, she could only pity Rose – so young, without defence. As she watched her cross the Aish by the wooden bridge below the Mill, she thought: She's another like Euphemia – alone against the world. I might have been the same, if Martin hadn't loved me as he does!

Though unaware, as yet, of the link between their lives, Alice sensed – already – her affinity with Rose. What would become of her, she wondered, when her child was born? From beside the river she could just make out the distant figure of the girl – slow-moving, bent and dark against the rough steep track that led uphill to Narracott.

'Perhaps you'll meet the Captain . . .'

Alice hadn't thought that it would be so soon. But he was here – close by her at the Rectory. The man who'd recognized her father's name, whom her father must have known and trusted. Why else would Will Penfold have remembered him in those last dreadful moments, when he'd spoken to old Isaac – spoken desperately as he lay, so near to death, on the deserted quay at Bridgwater? . . . She had tried so hard to put it from her mind – that image of her father's body on the cold wet stone, beside a fishing-boat, at dawn . . . But his words were clear enough: he would have told the magistrate about Euphemia. The *poknish* – Captain Trenaman.

Even here, in the cool high-ceilinged dining-room with its impressive silver and the heavy portraits of the Penningtons, he dominated. Not with any vocal strength: his voice was gentler and more musical than when she'd heard it last. In the lane at Jason's Wood, when Alice watched him from the *vardo*, Trenaman had been the magistrate. Today he played the family man, urbane yet fatherly. Like many self-assertive men he was chivalrous towards his womenfolk, affectionately patronizing with the son who'd always disappointed him: these were his natural satellites, their lives predetermined by his own.

Physically his presence was a force. Next to him Michael Pennington looked ineffectual, dried and faded as a winter leaf. At sixty, Trenaman was handsome, confident – the height and square-set shoulders, powerful lines of brow and jaw. The quick keen glance that seemed to Alice more alarming than the ladies' overt curiosity. She had expected that, had grown quite hardened, in the past few weeks, to feminine appraisal – the silent village women staring as she went about her errands for the housekeeper. Their suspicion, verging on hostility, could not surprise her. They must recognize – more readily than Laura Trenaman or Margaret – that Alice was a gipsy, with no claim to their respect. In spite of Michael Pennington's protection she could have, as yet, no status in Ash Ford. Now, even Harry's interest – unexpected, undisguised – could scarcely trouble her. She had watched him in the fields with Martin, knew her lover was his friend: it was enough. Ralph Trenaman's attention, though more subtle, was a threat . . .

Alice realized it with a shock. As she followed Mrs Hannaford's instructions in the ritual of the dining-room, she longed – with a distracting urgency – to speak to him. And with her quick perception, born of constant wariness, she sensed the recognition in his look – though he had merely glanced at her, and though she knew he hadn't seen her when he came to Jason's Wood. She was sure, and her certainty increased with every moment, that her father had been right. This magistrate was someone she should trust. And yet – Alice felt despairing suddenly, as if the chance she hoped for had been snatched away, might never come again. She must speak to Captain Trenaman today, while he was here – yet she could not.

She saw him murmur something to the Rector as they left the room. The old man coughed and looked embarrassed, stared across at Alice, turned away. But not before the girl had seen the nervous flutter of his hands, the apprehensive gaze . . . If the Captain were to question her or suspect the Rector's motive might be more than common charity, their plans would be at risk. And Michael Pennington had deeper fears. Alice knew no more than Grace had told her – yet enough to realize that the Rector might withdraw his help, disclaim all knowledge of the Penfolds, rather than admit the errors of the past. Although he had been kind and she was not ungrateful, she could not share her mother's certainty nor Martin's confidence: all round her in this place were the reminders that the Reverend was a Pennington. A man of God, perhaps – but he might break his word if Alice spoke too soon to Captain Trenaman.

She had to wait.

'An interesting girl . . .'

Ralph Trenaman was used to weighing people up. As another man might judge a horse or assess a beast for market, he could appraise a person's social standing at a glance – knew when they'd jumped a rung or two, or had slipped from being generally acceptable to being marginally less, or irretrievably beyond the pale. He was accurate in recognizing people's moral worth: as a magistrate it stood him in good stead.

But Alice puzzled him. She had served them competently – Mrs Hannaford had taught her well. Yet there was something that he couldn't quite make out. A quality of quiet remoteness that he felt he'd seen before. She neither looked nor moved like a member of the servant class. And she was half a Romany, at least, he'd swear. He had observed that watchful air, that strange ambiguous composure in the Indian women, long ago in Mexico: he recognized it now. But that sensual passion underlying the simplicity . . . what – in heaven's name – could Michael Pennington be thinking of?

'A story there, I should suppose?' He angled for the information, certain there was something – some compelling reason why the girl was here.

This time the Rector was prepared. He'd guessed that Trenaman would try again. At luncheon – it had been a duty to his niece's family, no more than that – he'd almost let his nervousness betray him. Even, as the meal progressed and he became aware of Trenaman's keen observation of the gipsy girl, he'd been afraid . . . But now he felt a rising anger that this Cornishman – a crudely practical self-seeker – should attempt to ferret out his past, invade his privacy.

They were taking coffee in the library. A shabby well-used room where Michael Pennington could feel at ease, superior to Trenaman – who was of course self-educated and determined to be proud of it, quite unaware of his deficiencies, the Rector thought. But he resented, more than anything, the way that Laura's husband – whom he'd never liked – must always underrate him, treating him as if he were a simpleminded fool. As if his age and frailty made him childlike, biddable, while Ralph could play the magistrate and squire without the benefit of birth or breeding. Money couldn't buy such things – and even marriage couldn't change the essence of the man.

'And not a local girl, I take it?'

The Rector was unhelpful, shrugged away the question.

'Mrs Hannaford is pleased with her. And Martha's usually a judge . . .' His tone was vague, his eyes half closed; fingers shaking as he held the fine white china in his hand. 'But she won't be here much longer. To be married, I believe . . .'

Evasiveness – or was the old man verging on senility? It angered Trenaman to think he didn't know, that the Rector might be playing tricks. When at last, as he had hoped, Alice came into the room, the Captain seized his chance. As she took his cup she hesitated; then she answered him with what he judged to be surprising readiness and total honesty.

'I don't belong here, sir. My people have gone back to Somerset. To Lydiard. That is where my father's buried – in the churchyard there.' She spoke with a depth of feeling that impressed him strongly; and though the words were plain enough he sensed that there was something more behind them – a significance which might, in time, mean something to him.

The Rector, Trenaman was certain, had been listening: he was alert, though one might have thought him half asleep. Alice had been open with the Captain, had said nothing that the Rector could have wished to hide. Yet he'd avoided answering the question, for some reason of his own ... In all these years of living in the valley, being married to his niece, Ralph hadn't ever understood the Reverend Pennington. At times he'd thought the man was wasted here; his intellect had withered, his emotion stultified in isolation – he was not the kind of parson people felt affection for. His life was simple, limited. Or at least had seemed to be. But was that just the surface – could he, all along, have been misleading them? And if so, what purpose might he have?

The girl had gone. The Rector, suddenly communicative, volunteered to find the documents that Trenaman required. Town Farm, the Glebe estate, the woodland and the cottages. All land belonging to the Church, but tenanted by Fords. Ash Leigh – now there was another Portsmouth farm which would soon be on the market. The Captain might have better luck with that one – a pity he had missed the chance to buy the Barton after all. The whole estate as far as Forda Mill had once belonged to Penningtons, of course; the plans were old but everything was clearly marked. The Rector had been using these in the writing of his family's history.

He was speaking with authority – no hint of feeble-mindedness. But a note of malice, almost satisfaction, in that mention of Ash Barton: it annoyed Ralph Trenaman extremely and confirmed his certainty that Michael Pennington was up to something. As for the girl – he hadn't even told them who she was ... While the Rector, with deliberate precision, set the papers out upon the table, Ralph was making up his mind.

He crossed the room to where his son was sitting – in an attitude of not quite languid thoughtfulness – beside a door that opened out on to the garden. It was sheltered from the full intensity of summer heat by trees – acacia, chestnut, lime. The drifting sweetness of their scent, the subtle play of light between their leaves, the flutter of the women's clothes where Margaret and Laura were reclining in the shade: a richer, warmer world, removed by more than that short distance from the chill interior – the formal rows of books, a life of ordered intellectuality. The contrast was, for Harry, more than one of mood or the reaction of the moment. It was part of the dichotomy within himself, a personal dilemma that he felt each time he came back home from Oxford.

Since childhood visits to the Rectory, he had been drawn towards an atmosphere more scholarly, more private, than the practicalities of Nymet House – his mother's parish work, his father's dual role of squire and businessman. In a dusty corner of the library he found the books of poetry and legend that the Rector had abandoned, long ago, in favour of theology. Though Margaret – the elder twin, already dominant and more conventional – had scorned her brother's growing love of literature and his unwillingness to ride to hounds, he persevered. While Martin, even then, had understood. The two boys walked and read together, shared each other's thoughts; when Harry went away to school he sent his first attempts at poems back to Martin – knowing that his efforts would be scrutinized with care, and with a forceful honesty that would have been unbearable from anybody else. But later Harry sought – with a craving almost physically passionate – the mental stimulus of Oxford: for a time its academic grace enchanted, satisfied the quieter part of him – he felt released, impelled to creativity. Then by degrees it stifled him. Frustrated him – to feel his power, in such a place, yet to find it purposeless! The golden walls closed in. He needed Martin, and the valley, even more.

Harry knew where he belonged. He was aware, as soon as he had left the train at Nymet Junction, of a lightening of spirit that increased as he walked home through summer lanes, through softer air. In winter when he saw the waiting glow of lamps in mist, and heard the voices – country voices that he'd always loved and understood; and then the sound of hooves and wheels along the darkness of the road. But there was more than this – much more than the nostalgia of the voluntary exile. He had heard the politicians in the Union at Oxford; listened to sophisticated talk of moral truths, aesthetic freedom, revolution, workers' rights, and war. But for Harry truth lay here – in the tranquillity and timelessness of woods and fields, among the men and women who, like Martin Ford, believed that working on the land could satisfy the mind, fulfil the longings of the soul.

One day he would write about it all. Not with the crude romanticism of a stranger, but as one who'd known the place and people all his life ... Yet how – without betraying them, without disloyalty to what had formed him, given him so much? For he would have to show the hidden, darker side – from which, by virtue of his class, he'd been protected. Ignorance and prejudice; the pain of isolation; cruelty, despair. No beauty ever cancelled out such hard realities. Within the valley, as within himself, were coexistent opposites – which somehow Harry had to reconcile.

Even now, as his father came towards him, Harry sensed the puzzlement that his withdrawal, his reflectiveness, must cause the older man. Yet he couldn't help it – only fend off the intrusion, arm himself with irony against emotion, and with silence in the face of pressures that would try to make him be what he could not. Already he'd resisted the suggestion, made in desperation by his mother, that he go into the Church. But Harry couldn't risk becoming Michael Pennington: he could feel the strength of his own passions, knew what he was searching for.

Ralph Trenaman had lit a cigarette. And Harry

thought, as he accepted one: It's wrong to be so close to someone, care for someone – yet not know them, not care quite enough. Until, of course, too late . . . I should have tried to go with him to Mexico.

Was it some prescience made him think it then? And reject the notion as impossible? It *was* too late. A year, away from all that had become important, far too long: he was committed now to something central to his work, his life. Though it was damnable – that Harry had to choose. That his father would never understand.

'What do you make of her?'

From where he stood, beside the open door, Ralph was watching Alice as she walked across the grass with Mrs Hannaford. They reached the shady corner where his wife and daughter sat; while the housekeeper engaged in conversation, Alice waited silently. She knew her place. And yet, once more, to Trenaman she seemed too striking, too exotic to be here – in such an English garden, among women who by contrast were so pallid and restrained. She made him long for the hotter southern countries of his youth, and for a girl he'd lost . . .

'She's handsome, Harry – don't you think?'

The murmured questions, casual enough, had taken Harry by surprise. His father had appeared preoccupied – but now, this sudden interest in the girl. Still more disturbing was his own reaction: he didn't want to speak of her – especially to Trenaman.

Throughout the tedious hours of luncheon, he'd been all too conscious of her presence in the dining-room. The air of mystery surrounding her, his sense of disappointment – almost loss – when she was gone. He wasn't interested in women; those he knew were useful, ornamental or, like Margaret, assertive. He would never marry – his needs were incompatible with that. But Alice moved him in a deeper way. As a poet, Harry recognized this feeling – powerful, yet for the present undefined. Far too significant to be ignored; too complex, and too private, to be voiced.

146

'If you hear any more of her,' his father said, '– if you learn anything at all, just let me know.'

Already, Harry knew that he would not.

Her name, her story, had seemed unimportant to him then.

But late that afternoon, as Harry walked back home with Margaret from Barton Wood, he saw he had no choice. Alice mattered to him now – not purely as an inspiration, a remote ideal, but as the woman Martin loved. And Harry could no longer claim to be detached, a cool observer of the human scene.

For his perception, finely tuned, had caught the echoes of their music; and, in time, his poetry would trace the cadence, show the meaning of their song.

The girl lies awake, watching the movement of a tree on the far hill. Its branches, black against the eggshell-white of a winter dawn, are tossed by a north-east gale that whips against the corner of the house. The window rattles and the muslin curtain, fine against the glass, is blown aside ... She remembers the window of a ballroom, lit from within by brighter lamps than any she had seen before: she had watched them flicker, watched the shadows of the dancers move across the brightness of the pane. And she had shivered, standing by her mother in that winter garden – seeing not the twisting shadows but the movement of the canvas, like a heavy bird. And from the safety of her father's tent, hearing the sound of wind across the low furze on the hill ...

She holds her child more closely, watches the dancing of the tree.

REGISTER OF BAPTISMS
solemnized in the parish of Ash Ford, County of Devon

1910	September 30	Johanna Grace Ford		
		father Martin Robert Ford	farmer	Ash Barton
		mother Alice Joan Ford		
1914	January 3	William Robert Ford		
		father Martin Robert Ford	farmer	Ash Barton
		mother Alice Joan Ford	deceased	

REGISTER OF BURIALS
in the parish of Ash Ford, county of Devon

1912	June 10	Robert Michael Ford	59 years	Ash Barton
1914	January 5	Alice Joan Ford	21 years	Ash Barton
1914	January 5	William Robert Ford	3 days	Ash Barton

5

He had known that it must end. The sweetness of those summer days, with Alice near; the warmth that had enclosed them, held them in a dream from which neither ever wished to wake. It could not last. Now, Mary knew it all. And as Martin had imagined, nothing at Ash Barton would be the same again.

Yet he was not afraid. That evening, as he checked the sheep, he stood and watched the sun go down behind the shadowed wall of Nymet Woods, the mass of trees impregnable and dark against the shifting colours of the sky. That's how we are, he thought. We change and move and fade, and vanish into nothing, into night. But land remains. It's always there, renewed, and anything that's left of us is part of it. We can't possess it, only honour it – make sure that it continues after we have gone. For mother it's the ownership that matters – status, the appearance of the thing. She wants the farm, but only for herself: she doesn't care what it becomes, or what it means. And she doesn't understand or care what Alice means – to me, to the future of the land.

'You are a fool!'

Incomprehension and contempt. He had anticipated that. An hour ago, he had faced Mary in the parlour. A room they rarely used – but the occasion was a special one. Tonight his mother was expecting Tom. She had come back with Robert from King's Nymet in a mood of triumph: Martin knew that he would shatter it with half a dozen words. Fleetingly, he had remembered Francis's defection, Mary's grief, his own distress at what she'd suffered then. But it was different now – within a few short months so much had changed. His love for Alice had driven out his fear, the self-destructive doubt that had always held him back. Today, it was as if the doing of a thing he'd dreaded somehow generated strength in him – a hardness he had never felt before. Martin was equal to his mother now.

'I shall marry Alice Penfold. You will never alter that.'

From the westward-facing windows evening sunshine slanted on to polished oak, embroidered cushions, glass and silver on the mirrored sideboard, gilded lettering above the keys of the harmonium – unplayed since Francis went away. Against the light a haze of summer dust, fine specks that floated gently in the stillness of the air: a barrier as dense and delicate as mist across the silent room, across the emptiness that lay – would always lie – between Mary and her elder son.

'I won't believe it! Nobody – not even you! – would want to sink so low. My mother might have been Sir Jocelyn's wife – she was a lady, through and through, as good as anyone at Nymet House. Your brother could have married Margaret Trenaman – you might have married her yourself: I'd sooner that than see the parish laughing at you, thinking that you must be mazed!'

'I'm grateful that you care so much – about the parish and what people think! But I would rather that you cared about my life, the woman that I love and mean to share it with.'

'The woman who has trapped you, as everybody knows such women do. That's why those gipsies stayed so long – to tempt you with their wickedness, to trap you. And like a fool you let yourself be caught.'

'Alice isn't capable of such a thing – and you insult us both by saying it. She's pure and good, all that any man could look for in a wife or the mother of his child. We have intended marriage from the start: you had better not think otherwise!'

'I only think as anyone will think – that Martin Ford's been taken in. And I know that Francis would have had more sense, more self-respect. Whatever else he's done he hasn't let me down, he hasn't made us all ashamed, betrayed his family and his friends. As you will do if you go through with it.'

'I shall do it, all the same. I'd rather be a fool than be like Francis. He doesn't know what feeling is!' . . . Or truth, or loyalty – and *you* don't know what Francis is. I could tell you what he's done to Rosie Ellis, I could tell the world – and then you'd really weep . . . Martin had seen the tears in Mary's eyes when she spoke his brother's name. But for himself, only coldness and disgust. His mother wouldn't ever change – and if Francis should come back . . .

'If it's Francis that you want you'd better tell him so! But it's money that he's after, and his freedom. He will never find them here.'

'He would come home if I asked him to.' Mary wanted to believe it – yet at heart she knew that she could not. 'He *would* come home again, for me . . .'

'In that case, Mother, you'll need to find another man to do the work. If you ask Francis to come home again, then I shall go!'

It was a challenge: Mary understood at once. She was conscious, as she'd never been till now, of Martin's power. It stopped her for a moment, frightened her – that calm intensity. Then she met it with a challenge of her own.

'And if you ask me to have another woman in my house you had better understand: I shall never leave Ash Barton. Neither you nor any wife of yours can drive me out. I won't be beaten down. I haven't struggled all these years to buy the farm so that you can throw it all away – just waste it on a common little gipsy from the hedge!'

Mary saw in Martin's eyes the pain she had intended to inflict. Unerringly, she knew where she could hurt him most, exactly where his weakness lay. Not in his love for Alice Penfold, but in his passion for the valley – for the land. Through that, she could destroy him if she chose.

'Just leave him, Mary. Let the boy alone!'

Robert had been standing silently, apart. Even Martin – to his sudden shame – had almost forgotten he was there, discounted him. He'd tried, at milking-time, to talk to him – but found himself defeated by his father's apathy: the interview with Webber, Martin thought, had worn him out. Yet now he seemed transformed. A firmness in his voice; and even – as he straightened up his body, thin and shapeless though it was – a certain dignity.

'Just leave him,' Robert said again. 'Let him do as he must do – and be as he must be.'

'You mean – to lose the farm? To be a fool?' Mary had risen from her chair, scattering the papers from her lap. 'As you have been, as the Fords have always been? Your father lost this place because he couldn't make it work. Your brothers wouldn't even have the tenancy at Town if the Rector hadn't gone against Sir Jos and let them have it out of spite. And you would not be here if you hadn't married me. Both Tom and I have put our money to the farm – but you've forgotten that!'

'I reckon you've forgotten something else. That it takes the three of us to run this farm – and Martin should have gone with us today. Mr Webber wants to see him, *you've* forgotten that. And when Tom Cheldon comes tonight you'd better ask him where he gets his money from. It might not last – and we'll be in trouble then.'

'Don't listen to him!' Mary turned to Martin, who was

staring at his father. Robert had confirmed his fears, his own mistrust of Tom.

'His head is full of rubbish, crazy dreams. Like the stories that he told you when you were a child – when he should have whipped the nonsense out of all of you. But he was always soft. And what is the result? A son who leaves the farm because he's bored – the valley isn't good enough for him. And another son who means to drag us down by marrying a gipsy girl!

'I'll tell you this. If Eleanor had lived she would have had some pride – she would have been worth ten of either of my sons. But *he* killed Eleanor. Your father let her die –'

'You've said enough!' A look of hatred, pure and keen as steel, in Robert's eyes.

'Enough – for now and evermore!' For a moment Mary thought that he would strike her. But instead he pointed at the papers on the floor, then kicked them with his foot. 'I put my name to all of that today – the same as you. So half this farm is mine.' He was shaking now, the once-impressive frame pathetic, tired.

'I shall make sure Martin gets it when I'm gone. I don't care what you do with yours. Leave it to your precious Francis if you want – it doesn't matter any more. Martin can marry anyone he likes!'

As Robert moved unsteadily towards the door he reached for Martin with his hand. His fingers rough with work, and icy cold. The sweetness of the apple-cider on his hair and breath. A note of desperation in his whisper – Martin felt, with a rush of conscience, what it had cost him to rebel.

'She'll finish me, your mother. Don't let her finish you!'

The sounds of any summer evening. Bees still searching in the yellow roses on the wall; a blackbird singing loudly from the hawthorn hedge; lambs calling to each other in the orchard down below the yard.

When Martin came in from the hill Tom Cheldon's horse was tied up by the gate. Another of his fancies, Martin thought – but I'd guess he means to sell: a bit of breeding there, but a bit uncertain-tempered. Just like Tom.

He would be sitting in the parlour now, with Mary. She, no doubt, had told her brother what had happened, would get him on her side. Was it because he'd always been indulgent with her that she cared for him – or because he was so much like Francis? With his curling hair, so very dark, but touched enough with grey to give him some distinction; and the hands, like Mary's own, a little too refined for the demands of heavy work – not farmer's hands. Yet he ran his place at Rincombe on his own ... Where *did* his money come from? Dealing – cattle, ponies, sheep: so Martin had supposed, until today ... It angered him – his uncle's easy money, and the easy ways, the smile that charmed so many women. And that ready laughter. Martin heard it as he went into the empty kitchen. He didn't want Tom's company – not yet. He would face the two of them tomorrow morning. Not tonight.

Martin never knew what passed between his mother and his Uncle Tom. For hours, it seemed, the murmur of their voices mingled with his thoughts of Alice, with the echoes of his father's words – so unexpected and significant. He slept uneasily; and once – with sudden wakefulness – imagined he heard Mary crying and the banging of the heavy door between the parlour and the stairs. At dawn, when he went out into the yard, Tom Cheldon's horse had gone.

'I've a mind to hang that bloody parson from his own church loft – I'd ring a bloody peal and leave him there to rot!'

His fury, viciously intense, had frightened her. Yet she'd been glad of it at first – believing that it sprang from sympathy, from love. They'd always been so close to one another, she and Tom.

'You'd best accept it, Mary.' He had said that, too – but she had hardly heard it, knew he couldn't possibly have wanted her to acquiesce. Then he'd repeated it. 'There's nought that you can do. If the Penfolds have got hold of Martin then he's done for. So you'd best put up with it! He'll marry her, whatever anybody says.'

Tom's face had been in shadow as he leaned back in his chair. Only the restless tapping of his boot against the fender had betrayed his growing anger as he listened; only Mary's knowledge of her brother – all the intimacy they had shared since they were children – made her understand his mood. They had always been alike; both self-absorbed and quickly roused to fierce resentment, often unprovoked. In Tom the bitterness had hardened to brutality, except where Mary was concerned. With her, he'd been so gentle and protective – until now.

'But there's the farm –' she had persisted, still incredulous that he should tell her to give in. She touched his hand, appealing to him. 'Tom, you mustn't let me down! If Robert does as he intends –'

'You married him!' Tom laughed. He was gripping at her fingers with his own. 'You married Robert Ford – when you could have come to Rincombe and been happy there with me. The two of us – but you had to marry Ford! It doesn't matter that he's always drunk, that he's a rotten father to your sons – you want him all the same. You've made your bed and you can sleep in it. With your husband, Robert Ford – you chose him, after all!'

Mary was trying not to weep – her brother hated that. But his contempt was hurting her, too much . . . 'You shouldn't be so hard,' she whispered. 'If Sir Jocelyn hadn't wanted me to marry, and to have Ash Barton –'

'Don't you speak to me of Jocelyn Pennington!' Tom pushed her from him. In the lamplight she could see his face – the thin line of his mouth, his eyes as black and cold as the waters of the Aish in wintertime. 'One day you'll know the truth about that man.'

Too shocked to speak, she stared at him. And saw at last – for just an instant – all the love he had been holding back, that she had longed for when he came. The feeling they had known about since childhood, when they guessed that they were different from the other Cheldons – that they'd always be . . . Perhaps their mother, Sarah, had tried to circumvent it. Perhaps it was the reason she had ruled her sons, had held them together with a bond that had continued even after death . . .

When Mary looked at Tom she saw the passion he had tried, throughout their lives, to keep hidden from the world – by his pursuit of many women, by his cruelty and laughter, by the isolation of his life up on the Moor. She recognized, too clearly now, his hatred of the men who came between the two of them: her husband and her sons. And of course – though she could hardly bear to think of it – Sir Jocelyn Pennington.

'What can you mean – the truth? . . .'

'Forget that, Mary! Just forget I ever said such things. You *must* forget!' He was commanding her – and Mary knew she would give in. As she had always done, with Tom. For his sake she would even have forgotten all the duty, all the gratitude, that she had felt for old Sir Jos. Her brother was too real – her love for him too strong – for her to put a dead man first. Even the man she'd always thought of as a father couldn't make her give up Tom.

'Forget them all – you could, it's not too late!' His voice was softer, more persuasive. 'You could leave the valley, come back home with me. Let them have Ash Barton and to hell with all of them! We could be alone at Rincombe, just the two of us – together as we always wanted. As it should have been . . .'

She longed for it, was tempted – but she was afraid. 'Not that – I cannot do it, Tom!' She wept.

He had reached the parlour door, was shutting it, when Mary called him back. Tom held her in his arms till early light. When he had gone she sat beside the window, watched the dawn, and Martin striding down towards the wood.

Upstairs, as she washed away the tears and changed her clothes, preparing for the day, Mary came to a decision. She would fight for what was left. Alone – and there would be no weeping, no more looking back. She would let things lie a day or two. Then she would have it out – at last – with Michael Pennington.

She crossed the room to the bed she shared with Robert. He was sleeping still, as calmly as a child. Mary wished that he were dead.

6

The sea was a clear uncompromising blue. From where he lay, on a ledge a hundred feet above the shore, he could see the wetness shining as the surf drained off the granite; he could smell the salty rankness of the weed piled high against the stones, and hear the suck of water as it rose and fell and searched – impersonal, yet soothing in its certainty. But a summer tide, he'd learned, was no less treacherous than winter ones. An hour ago he had been swimming there, above a narrow strip of white shell-sand – and he'd felt the tug of currents which, had he been less fit and wary, would have pulled him right across the cove to where the foam and spray rose constantly from blackened spikes of rock.

Now, as the sun's heat burned into his skin, Francis felt renewed. It had been worth the risk – to shed the dirt and sweat of underground, to leave behind the close-packed cottages and find again the light and space he needed. He remembered bathing in the Aish on warm June evenings after making hay – the same sensation of release from hours of weariness; and the same suspension of existence as he gently drifted, feeling the smooth quick fish between his fingers, watching the small white stars of water crowfoot sway against the movement of the stream. Where, in the half-light, Rose had swum beside him long ago, before he'd even thought of making love to her. Or leaving her . . .

How far away – unreal – that seemed. How innocent.

They had been children, playing at a secret life without a thought of consequence. Their making love had somehow been, for Francis, part of all that they had shared before – when Rose had been a strange elusive creature who would suddenly appear and sit beside him on the river bank; or he would hear her laughter, turn and find her watching him . . . And once, as he was riding to an early meet, she'd waited in the wood – had kept him standing while she twisted flowers into his horse's mane and tail, made Francis swear that he would keep them there all day. He'd done it, in spite of Margaret's scorn. Rose never teased or challenged him, like the other Ash Ford girls; she hadn't wept or tried to make him marry her – and he'd never told her that he loved her. It didn't do, his Uncle Tom had often said, to let a woman think you cared. Yet Rose had seemed to love him, in a quiet unquestioning way that made him feel uneasy – guilty – now . . .

Crushed in the pocket of the work-shirt he was using as a pillow, Martin's letter was the only tangible reminder of his weakness – of the life he'd left behind. It had shocked him, shaken all his hard-won confidence, to see himself as those forthright words described: a reckless headstrong youth who had seduced a village girl and let his family down. It was true – as he was forced to recognize. Yet it angered him that even from a distance Martin had the right to moralize, the power to undermine him still. To make Francis feel once more the pain of his rejection – be again the young resentful boy who had come alone to Cornwall in the spring.

The implications of the letter had been clear. If Francis interfered in any way with Martin's plans he would put at risk his prospects with the Trenamans. Not only Ralph but Margaret would learn how he had treated Rose – already Harry knew, and a single word from Martin could bring down on Francis all the condemnation he deserved. And if Ellis should return – as he was bound to do – there would be a further reckoning.

At first it was the thought of Ellis that disturbed him most. He couldn't quite accept that Martin would betray him to Ralph Trenaman. But Ellis was a different case. Francis had been certain, ever since he saw the trapper's gear – the wire and pegs in a tangled heap against the cottage wall – that he and Rose had been found out. The knowledge sickened him – as if the sweetness had been tainted, innocence destroyed. For a time it had been a kind of game, with Rose, to outwit Ellis: but from that moment it became too real, too dangerous. Francis had wondered even then if Charlie Penfold's warning had referred to Ellis – the trapper's vicious temper was well known in Nymet and Ash Ford. Yet why, if he'd been spying on them, had he disappeared without a word to Rose? Why hadn't he come back – and what would happen when he learned that he'd been publicly disgraced, that his only daughter had a child? . . .

In the stillness, in the moment's silence that preceded yet again the breaking of a wave, Francis knew he should go home. He was afraid for Rose.

But if he went back to Ash Barton – for a few days, even – he would not escape the consequence of what he'd done. He would lose all that he had gained. His freedom, and the chance to make something of his life. He would lose Margaret . . . His brother didn't want him back: that was the truth of it. When Martin was determined on a thing he wouldn't yield. And if Francis could at last acknowledge that beneath his own fierce pride there lay a longing to be reconciled, it was too late. Martin saw him as a threat – to his marriage and the future of the farm.

I shall marry Alice Penfold . . . That was the deepest hurt of all. A simple statement of intention which, for Francis, was the hardest thing to bear. It outraged his sense of justice that his brother – who had always given in to Mary Ford – should go against her openly and get away with it. Should choose, in defiance of convention, Alice

Penfold for his wife – when for years it seemed he'd set his heart on Margaret, and her money, to secure the farm . . . How could this be the quiet prudent brother he had always known – had imagined he had known? The sudden change in Martin was, in Francis' eyes, a denial of the closeness they had shared, a destruction of their brotherhood. A betrayal, no less shocking and conclusive than his own abandonment of Rose.

And beneath the pain of it, the cause. It was Alice, Francis knew.

He hadn't wanted to remember her. But images, deep-hidden for so many months, were as insistent as the flowing of the surge against the rock, clear as the coloured sea-thrift by his hand . . . A painted wagon in the autumn lane, where bars of light and shadow marked the brightness of the grass; an old man sleeping by the bank – the same old man whose blood had stained his coat when Francis held him in his arms, in the darkness of the Square. A girl at the doorway of the *vardo*; sunlight on her hair, her face half covered by her hands. Her stillness – then the upward movement of her fingers, long and brown, in an impatient gesture – what had she been thinking, feeling, then? She was afraid of him, in the instant when she saw him first: he'd not forgotten that. Nor the violence of her curse, his unexpected shame, the bitterness he'd felt for weeks . . . But far more powerful and more urgent, the longing Alice had compelled. His longing for her warmth and gentleness, the depth of passion Francis knew he needed in a woman and must go on searching for – might never find again. She would be Martin's wife. His brother's wife –

It was as if he had been hurled by a malicious tide against the pinnacles of rock. The coloured images were gone. He shivered and put on his shirt, took the letter from his pocket, read it yet again.

There was nothing, in those cold uncompromising lines, to give him hope.

For some minutes Francis watched, with a detachment new to him, the steady progress of a fishing-boat which had appeared beyond the entrance to the bay. Against the broad expanse of water it looked far too small and frail to have significance, identity – and yet it moved as if with secret purpose out into the open sea. It would be there all night, alone in the Atlantic darkness, gathering its catch. While someone waited patiently at home – as Margaret would wait . . .

He folded up the letter. Then with fingers scarred and roughened by their contact with the metal of the mines, tore through the hard black writing that he knew so well. The pieces fluttered out into the summer air. He watched them falling, white as gulls that cried and wheeled about the ledge. From where he stood the cliff rose almost vertically. But no more dangerously, Francis guessed, than the disused quarries up at Forda Mill: with Martin watching, he had scaled them often. He was not afraid of heights.

Below him, water glittered, calm and blue. He climbed.

'If Mr Webber wants to see me, Mother, I should go!'

'But I can't imagine why! And it's not as if you have the time – I should have thought that Webber would have realized. There's shearing, and the harvest coming on –'

'Of course he knows all that – he's been Lord Portsmouth's agent all these years, he's bound to know what's going on. And that's exactly why I ought to see him if he asks. Whatever reason Webber has he means it, that's for sure. I know you've never liked him – hardly anybody does – but he's not a man that any farmer in this valley can afford to cross!'

Martin found the agent at his stuffy little office in King's Nymet, in the narrow passageway behind the Stag. Once a coaching inn on the old London road, this was the farmers' rather than the labourers' public house, well known as a place for local business – property or stock, or even gambling for land. For the agent of a big estate it was ideal: he could be as convivial or as private as he wished. A small neat man, his friendliness had fooled a lot of people into thinking they might buy his favours easily. In fact, Webber could be bought – but only when and where he chose. This morning he was brisk and shrewd, wearing – disconcertingly – a bright blue cornflower in his buttonhole.

'So you're the man who'll do the job, that's it? Well, you've got a tidy farm – the land is mixed, of course, but there's a future in it if you're not afraid of work. Take my advice and go for corn, young man. They'll be wanting that if there's a war. The dairying's important – and you've always had a name for decent sheep – but go for corn, that's what the country needs.'

Martin resented being told – yet he knew the agent must be right. He had his contacts in the markets, and the Portsmouth farms had always been ahead. It must be hard for him to see the finish of a big estate . . . But it was nonsense, surely, saying there might be a war – and yet just lately there had been a lot of talk, a scare or two along the coast; he'd heard them speaking of it in the Pennington . . .

'You're lucky, Mr Ford, I'll say that much – between ourselves. The other tenants will have to wait a year or so before we sell again. But I've always known the Cheldons, I've a great respect for Richard – and I know your Uncle Tom, of course.' Webber leaned back in his chair, paused as if making up his mind. 'The fact is, Mr Ford, we like to keep things in the valley if we can.'

So that's it, Martin thought. So that's how Richard Cheldon got to buy up Nymet Barton when Sir Jocelyn died. And it's Uncle Tom we have to thank for getting ours – I suppose he has his uses after all. And yet – why should the Cheldons have the edge when there were

164

richer men like Trenaman around? Why, if the Earl of Portsmouth needed money urgently as everybody said, should his agent choose to sell Ash Barton to the Fords? His inference seemed obvious: we don't want strangers buying up the farms. But Martin guessed – from Webber's all too easy manner and his watchful gaze – that there must be something more.

He answered carefully: 'I think, sir, that my parents have always hoped to buy. My mother, in particular –'

'Quite so. Your mother made her feelings on the matter very plain. But I'll be honest with you, Mr Ford' – the agent's prejudice, at least, was unequivocal – 'a woman cannot run a farm, that's my belief. And should not try to do so, where there is a man. However – I was shocked to see your father when he came in here. I found him sadly changed. Of course I hope I'm wrong, that he'll go on many years . . .' The voice was sympathetic but the eyes were hard. 'Now, as far as we're concerned the sale goes through. But I must be fair to my employers: we shall need to know how things are likely to be run, that payment will be regular – in short, that there will be some continuity. Tom Cheldon will be putting up some money but he doesn't mean to farm here, as I understand. And your uncle has no children – or none he cares to take into account.'

The agent smiled in a knowing way, as man to man. It angered Martin – that he seemed to have a hand in everything, knew so much about his tenants' private lives. He was determined, more than ever, that Webber should not read his mind. He waited.

'So I take it that your parents mean to let you have responsibility. You are not afraid of that?'

'I'm not, sir. No. I shall be glad of it!'

'But you have a brother, Mr Ford . . . Does he not intend to farm?'

He knows, thought Martin instantly. He doesn't need to ask. So what is Webber driving at – and what on earth has Francis got to do with it?

'My brother's gone from home, sir. He's in Cornwall now – at Camborne. He's not interested in farming, he intends to go abroad to be a mining engineer –'

'With Captain Trenaman . . . Of course!' The agent spread his fingers out upon the ink-stained surface of his desk. He seemed, in the silence, to be weighing Martin up. But when he spoke again his tone was casual, his glance expressionless.

'Your families, I understand, were always close. As neighbours, natural enough. But there were rumours, not so long ago, about yourself and young Miss Trenaman . . .'

'They are untrue,' said Martin heatedly. 'It's idle gossip, nothing more!'

'Come, come, don't take offence. A well set-up young man like you is bound to have his plans. In your place, I should think of marriage – nothing better where a farm's concerned –'

'Mr Webber,' Martin said, 'I should be grateful if you'd tell me why you asked me here. I can't believe you wanted to discuss the village gossip or my personal affairs – and I would not have come if I'd expected that. My father said it was important' – he had risen to his feet, his anger overriding caution – 'but it seems to me that we're just wasting time. I've work to do at home –'

The agent stared. Then laughed uneasily, placatingly. 'I can see you're another like your father, Mr Ford – a plain straight-speaking sort of man. But we need not disagree. The matter is important, as you say. It is also somewhat – delicate. And if you were by any chance committed to Miss Trenaman . . .'

'I can assure you that I'm not!'

'In that case . . .' Webber too had risen, scraping back his chair. He went over to the window and, although the morning was already hot and airless, pulled the sash down hard. As he drew the ragged net across the glass some heavy dozing flies fell from it. Martin pitied them as Webber quickly crushed them with his foot.

166

'You are aware, of course, of your neighbour's interest in acquiring – shall we say, some Nymet properties and in particular the land adjacent to his own?'

Don't beat about the bush, thought Martin. But aloud he said, 'I know exactly what you mean.'

'Well, Mr Ford, I think that this will be of some concern to you – as the farmer and the future owner of that land.' He pointed to a dusty map that hung above his desk. 'This shows the rights that go with every farm on the estate. The rights of access, water rights, the hunting, shooting, fishing – all of that will be familiar to you. But what you may not know about are mineral rights – exactly what and where they are. And more especially – in your case – *whose* they are.'

He paused, then pressed a finger to the map. 'Look here – and here. And here –'

'There's nothing marked,' said Martin. 'That's the Nymet valley up as far as Narracott . . . Ash Barton . . . But the mineral rights aren't marked . . .'

'Precisely,' Webber said.

'But why? Why aren't they marked?'

'Because the Barton rights, and those of other valley farms, were never taken up by the estate.'

'And so –'

'The mineral rights, and other rights of course, go with your land. You will find that in the deeds – although until the loan has been repaid the documents remain with us. But you may have my word for it: those rights are yours.'

'But why?' repeated Martin. 'Why should ours be different from the other Portsmouth properties?'

'Because all this' – the agent showed him on the map – 'all this belonged to old Sir Jocelyn Pennington.'

At one time, Webber told him, there was talk of mining in the valley – in the forties, quite a fashionable thing. But the Squire had been against it: he had loved his land. He had even quarrelled with his brother over it. The Rector saw it as a chance to make a fortune and restore the family to its rightful place. But Jocelyn never would agree. By the time he died the boom was well and truly finished; the Exmoor mines were winding down, the Poltimores and Portsmouths had their companies abroad – and no one bothered with the valley rights.

'Sir Jocelyn was in some respects a foolish man. A gambler by nature – wouldn't listen to advice. But he was a farmer through and through. Put all his money into drainage schemes and breeding in the early days – tried new machines, the latest kinds of crop. And then got caught by the Depression, mortgaged everything and died without a penny to his name . . .

'A common story . . .' Webber sighed, and his regret seemed genuine. 'We won't see squires like old Sir Jos again, young man. He had the blood, of course, the line went back and back – but then his daughter married Captain Trenaman!'

He hates him, Martin realized. This man would sooner cheat Lord Portsmouth, sooner help the Cheldons and the Fords than let the Cornishman get hold of any land.

'She met him through the Poltimores. He'd worked his way in Mexico and ended up in charge of all their mines – then came back here and bought up Nymet House. But that's just gossip, isn't it, young man? We must be businesslike – what questions do you have?'

His irony – quite unmistakable – warned Martin that he should not cross the agent now. He was torn between disgust at Webber's deviousness and the necessity to keep him on his side. But he saw he had no choice: the agent's knowledge was too intimate, his influence too powerful to be ignored.

'There's one thing, sir,' he said. 'Does anyone – apart from ourselves – know that the rights go with the farm?'

'Your Uncle Tom. He knows a lot about the mines. There are workings up at Rincombe, so I'm told. If there's anything afoot – a scheme to open up the Heasley mines, or anything like that – he'll know. And he's bound to guess that it could happen here.'

'And the Reverend Pennington?' The Rector's passion for geology had often seemed to Martin something of an eccentricity – yet now it made more sense.

'You can discount him,' Webber said with certainty. 'He's far too old to care about all that. However' – he looked at Martin keenly – 'there are others, as you must have realized.

'There are some people – I shall name no names – who know a good deal more about these things than you or I. They are speculators, Mr Ford – who stand to make more profit in their lives than any farmer in this valley ever will. If there should be a war, your property may be of interest to such men. With an increased demand for metals anything is possible. I may be wrong – but at the least, you will know the rights are yours.'

The interview was finished. Webber straightened up the papers on his desk, pulled out his watch. Martin felt that gratitude was inappropriate: when the agent shook his hand he said, 'I'll consider what you've told me, sir.' That committed him to nothing, after all.

But as he left Webber took him by the arm. 'The times are changing, Mr Ford. And one day men like Captain Trenaman will own the lot of us. I reckon things will be the worse for it – they won't believe in proper husbandry, they won't care nought about the land. Maybe you'll go along with it – maybe you won't. But I'll ask you just one thing. If those rights ever prove to have a market value, don't forget who told you of it first! Good-day to you. And good luck with Ash Barton.'

'Good-day, sir,' Martin said. And as he walked away – So that, he thought, is how the system works!

He evaded Mary's questioning. It was clear to Martin that the agent hadn't wanted her to learn about the rights. His mother's hatred of Ralph Trenaman was as intense as Webber's – yet she still loved Francis, still believed he might return to make the peace. And she would use him then to fight the marriage, to destroy the vision Martin had of happiness with Alice. In the light of Robert's unexpected declaration she would try to drive them out – like Martin, she would never contemplate division of the farm. Possession of Ash Barton, to be gained at Michaelmas, would mean exactly that: whichever brother worked the land would get it all.

At last, by post from Camborne, came the answer Martin had been waiting for.

I shall not be coming home. How can I after what you've done?

7

Early August. Sunday in Ash Ford. Since first light, when a sudden storm broke through the heat, the Aish has risen by a foot an hour. Above the village corn lies flattened in the Barton fields, the heavy swathes like surf half broken on a winter shore, their brightness muddied by the spate of water flowing off the dried-out land.

From the chapel, with its door symbolically wide open, the sound of Preacher Passmore's voice – dramatic, resonant above the steady murmur of a prayer. Then raised to a judgmental climax, and a pause before the ragged chords of the harmonium, the singing of a hymn. The echoes of the chorus reach Rose Ellis where she sits, her infant in her arms, on the steps that lead up to the lychgate and the church. She listens; then without a backward look walks slowly down towards the Aish.

A group of boys – flat caps and ill-cut jackets – lean against the curving parapet of old Sir Jocelyn's bridge. (The Squire, it's said, rode over it a dozen times when it was newly built, in order to convince his people it was safer than the fragile wooden bridge downstream.) There is laughter as the girl approaches. And, as she moves between the lads, their comments – of a calculated cruel obscenity she cannot fail to understand. They watch Rose carefully until they see her take the Nymet path along the river bank. Then they return, with dedicated idleness, to their game of throwing stones into the flood.

*

The rain had cleared the air. By afternoon the sun was warm, the garden dry enough for Michael Pennington to take tea out of doors. As was usual on a Sunday Mrs Hannaford and Alice joined him; afterwards, when he sat half-dozing in the shadow of the copper beech, the Rector felt content.

He had finished, only yesterday, another chapter of his History – and he was conscious now, as so rarely in his life, of something permanent achieved. The writing had absorbed – obsessed him, rather – for a year; he'd begun it, he recalled, in desultory fashion in the weeks before Grace Penfold paid her visit to the Rectory, when he'd seen Alice first. Since then the work had taken on far more significance than he'd imagined possible. As if his study of the Penningtons threw into fresh perspective so much more than those events and characters long gone: as if in re-creating them he held a mirror to his own and Jocelyn's past and found a vindication – almost – of the life that he had lived. This summer, he was certain, was his last – but that no longer troubled him. For this year's harvest-time could hold no terrors: he would have cleared his conscience of its debt. He would keep his word to Grace.

We are becoming like a family, he mused, myself and Martha, and the girl ... She was sewing at a wicker table in the shade, the housekeeper occasionally helping her. With Alice at the Rectory the emptiness surrounding Michael Pennington was filled; he was at peace. But she – in just those few short months – had changed. He'd noticed that. She had lost her air of apprehension, and the watchfulness that made her seem at first like a creature brought in from the wild, its only object being to escape. He had wondered sometimes how the girl could leave behind, at such risk to herself, her people and their close-knit world. But when he saw her with her lover – Martin's visits were no secret now – the Rector understood. Their happiness was of a kind that he had never seen before, would never know. A quality of heightened joy that even he could tell was infinitely rare, a power of feeling that was almost palpable. And yet to him, in his old age, they had the frailty and the innocence of windflowers growing in a darkened wood. He watched them with misgiving – prayed, with a sincerity he found surprising in himself, that they might endure the storm.

Alice saw her cross the grass. Her movement quick and purposeful, her figure neat in Sunday clothes. The Rector, suddenly alert, had scarcely risen from his chair and murmured – 'Mrs Ford!' – than the woman was beside him, gazing at the girl.

It was the moment Alice knew must come. It would be just as it had been in church that autumn day – the unconcealed hostility, the concentrated force of centuries of prejudice within a single glance. Yet this was more – far more – than even the conventional response that Alice in her gipsy childhood learned to fear. For Mary's anger now held in it all the pride and the possessiveness of those who farm the land: those men and women whose identity is inextricably – yet passionately – part of earth and rock.

The Rector waited. Mary's silence, in the summer garden, was more potent than a curse. The old man felt it, sensed that for Alice this was the beginning of the end. While she – though standing in the sunlight – shivered as if cold.

At length the Rector said, 'This is Miss Penfold, Mrs Ford.'

She answered: 'There is nothing – nothing – that I wish to say to her.'

He knew, with an unexpected access of determination, what he ought to do. 'Let us go into my study, Mrs Ford.' He turned to Alice. 'Mrs Hannaford will stay with you, my dear. Wait here until I come to you.'

His firmness, and the affection in his voice, gave Alice

courage – and astonished Mary Ford. She had always thought the Reverend Pennington was strange and unpredictable, cut off from the realities of life; and she had seen him as a gentleman – above all else, as the brother of Sir Jos. But he did not treat this girl as an inferior, a servant whose position in his household was due solely to his eccentricity – some charitable whim: she was at ease with him, had clearly won him over with her gipsy ways just as she had enchanted Martin. There could be no doubt of it. As Mary followed Michael Pennington into the house she felt her resolution strengthened – all her hatred reinforced.

'I shall oppose the banns!' She had refused the chair the Rector offered, scarcely waited till the study door was shut before she made her declaration. 'I shall speak out against them,' she repeated. 'Martin cannot marry her – she's trapped him into it –'

'I hoped,' the Rector said, 'to talk to you this morning. I am sure that Martin must have told you so. I waited in the vestry with Miss Penfold – but you did not come.'

'I wished to speak to you alone. I will not discuss the matter with the girl. She has deceived my son, she's lied to you. You should refuse to marry them. You *must* refuse!'

'You are mistaken, Mrs Ford. I have neither wish nor reason to refuse. The girl, as you have seen, is perfectly respectable – I believe her to be good. I should not have her in my home if she were not. If you have proof against her then oppose the banns. But I must warn you: I have written to the Rector up at Lydiard where her birth was registered. He has replied to tell me that her father sometimes went to church there – and indeed is buried there. He was – so far as any gipsy is – an honest man. You will find nothing to prevent her marrying your son. I am quite sure of it.'

'And I am sure that you – the Rector of this parish – have a duty to prevent all wickedness and immorality. If you do not you will become a laughing-stock! The people of this village, of the valley, they will be against you. No one wants the gipsies here. The Fords and Cheldons – all of us will be disgraced if Martin marries her. And if you let it happen I shall never set foot in your church again!'

For a moment Michael Pennington was shaken by the woman's vehemence, the overt malice in her voice and look. He recognized the truth in what she said: the hardness of the valley people could destroy the lives of those condemned by circumstance. He had himself stood by and let it happen to Euphemia – and it would happen to that other girl, the trapper's child, whom he had seen that morning sitting on the churchyard step. There was no reason in it – just the blindness of incomprehension, of indifference to pain. The Rector knew he would not alter it in Mary Ford.

'Your threats don't trouble me,' he answered quietly. 'I shall do as I think right. They have chosen to be married – there can be no wickedness nor immorality in that. But Martin is your son!' He appealed to her at last: 'Does Martin's happiness – his life! – not matter to you –'

'No. He can no longer be my son.' Her gaze was steady, voice emotionless and clear – yet every word was charged. 'My other son, the son I loved, has gone. But Martin – even if he stays – will mean nothing to me now. I would rather see him dead than married to that girl.'

Mary's calmness carried more conviction even than her anger. Michael Pennington was certain she was dangerous. He glanced out of the window. Alice and the housekeeper still sat beneath the tree, the pony gently browsed beside the paddock rail. A pheasant called, deep in the shadow of the little wood. The cry, peremptory and harsh, aroused the Rector's consciousness that he – like the Penningtons whose spirit he revered – must fight for all that he believed in now. For all he had dismissed as dead and meaningless: religion, honour, even love. Throughout his life he'd been a timid man, afraid of feeling, of commitment – now, close to the end, he would cast away his fear.

'You are very like your mother, Mrs Ford.' She stared, caught off her guard. 'So very like her, both of you,' he murmured, almost dreamily, 'yourself – and of course, your brother Tom . . .'

'What difference does it make? And what has Tom to do with this – with Martin?' Mary had moved closer to the Rector, was standing at his side. She saw that he was gripping at the ornate carving of his chair with hands that shook, in spite of all his effort at control. Yet he was smiling, an expression in his heavy-lidded eyes that disconcerted her – alarmed her with its sudden strange intensity.

'You see,' he went on more emphatically, 'I knew them all when they were young. The Cheldons and the Fords. And long before that even, I knew Sarah Blake – when I used to ride with Jocelyn up to Forda. She was a woman who could bear no opposition to her will. And I see you are the same.'

'What can you mean?' Mary almost whispered it. The old man's words had filled her with an unexpected fear: there was something he was keeping back – as if intending to torment her with uncertainty. She felt a longing to escape – but for Tom's sake, if not for her own, she must hear the Rector out.

'I remember it so well. How all the young men of the valley were in love with Sarah – with her long black hair, her eyes so blue, so bright and laughing . . . Even I could see that she was beautiful – the kind of girl who could destroy a man, so easily. Sarah knew she had that power –'

'But Sir Jocelyn always loved her. My mother said he would have married her –'

'I thank God that he did not! She would have made him wretched. As she did her husband, Francis. There

176

was only one your mother ever cared about – and that was Tom.' The Rector paused.

Mary did not dare to look at him. She was certain he would never guess – could not imagine – the kind of love she felt for Tom. Yet she must no longer underestimate the Rector. He was not a fool. What was it he withheld from her – and why?

'Have you not wondered, Mrs Ford, about your brother Tom? How he got his farm at Rincombe – why he left the valley whilst your brothers stayed? Your mother knew it all. But she kept it secret – Tom was always able to persuade her, you remember that . . .'

'What does it matter now? I didn't come to talk of her – or Tom. Whatever Tom has done it's nought to do with Martin or his marriage, nought to do with any of us now. My mother's dead and gone, the past is over with – and if you won't speak of what's important then I'll go!'

The force of Mary's anger and uncertainty, at last beyond restraint, showed Michael Pennington he had the upper hand. But he must keep her there – make sure of it. He stood, with all the dignity accruing to a man who spends a lifetime in the service of his God.

'And if you refuse to listen to the truth you will regret it, Mary Ford! Your son and Alice are important to us both – their lives are shaped by what we choose. But first that choice is shaped by what we are, by what has happened to ourselves. You say the past is done with – but it matters to us now!

'I believe a pattern is imposed upon the present – and the future – by the past. Sometimes it is repeated in a way we recognize, more often it is hidden by events – its meaning lost. And yet the threads that bind us all together are so strong, we cannot break them even when we try to leave the past behind. What happened long ago to Tom – here in this valley, in this village – has involved us all. My brother Jocelyn, you and I and

Sarah Blake. And even poor John Reed who blows the organ in my church – yes, even he was part of it!'

'What was it – tell me what it was!' Mary had to listen to him now. This was not the Rector she had known – his sermons filled with obscure scholarship, his manner vague, detached. He was speaking with conviction and authority.

'There was another gipsy girl. Euphemia. She was a Penfold – Alice is her niece. She came here to the valley more than thirty years ago, about the time that you were married – your husband's father farmed the Barton then. She was in service up at Nymet House, but whether Jocelyn took her in or whether her own people sent her there I do not know. But I do know that Euphemia had a child – and the father was your brother Tom.'

The Rector glanced at Mary. No response, only the fierce compression of her hands, their knuckles hard within the fabric of her summer gloves.

'Your mother had gone back to Forda Mill, and Richard was at Nymet Barton, Tom was working with him there. Though Tom was feckless even then – he always needed money, never paid it back. A charmer, as your mother was. When Sarah knew about the girl she turned to Jocelyn, knowing he would help her when she needed it. And for a time Euphemia went on living here – in a cottage on my brother's land, the one below Ash Barton, in the wood. She had her child there, they were safe enough – until the village people found her out. And then . . .' the Rector's voice was low, as he remembered, 'then Euphemia died.' He sank back in his chair; the effort had exhausted him.

'You say – she died?' Mary was suddenly alert. 'There was a girl, we heard of it – they found her in the Aish. It was the year before Sir Jocelyn let us have the tenancy, September-time. She was drowned below the bridge, the old bridge just below the trapper's house. Was that the girl who Tom –' Her eyes, a clear hard blue, were fixed on Michael Pennington. For a fleeting instant he could see her pain, till then so deeply hidden – like the powerful movement, almost imperceptible, that brings the changing of a tide.

'The girl your brother Tom betrayed.'

'But they are all the same, those women. She must have caught my brother just as Alice Penfold caught my son!' It was said with utmost bitterness.

'Believe that if you will. When I baptized her child she said her lover had not been to her for weeks – I did not know then who he was. She thought he had abandoned her, I believe it preyed upon her mind. Your brother left her ill, alone and destitute. At last she went into the villages in search of work – she didn't want to beg, only to make provision for her child. But she found nothing in King's Nymet, nothing in Ash Ford.

'Euphemia came to me again at harvest-time. It was dark and very late. It seems she'd walked as far as Narracott and right down to the junction, thinking she might get as far as Barnstaple, find something there. But they wouldn't let her on the train. When she reached Ash Ford again, some village people followed her – tormented her. That night the moon was full. They went down through the wood and played rough music at her cottage door. John Reed, the culpritcher, had stirred them up against her – he was a Bible man in those days, went around the valley preaching of the vengeance of the Lord. And Peter Braund, that was the blacksmith then, he was another one. She was weeping, I could see that she was terrified of going back, but all the same' – the words were scarcely audible – 'I refused to let her stay. And, God forgive me, that was not the end of it. They hadn't done with her . . .'

'But Tom was not to blame for that. He'd nought to do with it –' The Rector didn't seem to hear.

'They hadn't done with her. There were farmers in the Pennington that night – the Snells, your brother

Tom, the Luxtons, all the Fords except for Robert. When they heard the music, all the clatter in the lane, they went outside and planned to hunt the stag. It used to be a sport, to find a guilty man and hunt him down through all the parishes. But they thought Ellis was the father of her child; perhaps Tom told them so – or maybe Philip Snell, he had a grudge against the man. At dawn they gathered at the trapper's cottage with their horses and the hounds as if it were a proper meet – and they were drinking, passing round the cup, for all that some of them were chapel men. They started out along the valley, Ellis was already at his traps. But very soon they lost him – he knew every corner of the woods – and so they rode right on through Narracombe and over High Ash Hill. At last they came back down the Aish – and found Euphemia.

'Your brother was ahead of hounds – he always did ride hard. And it was misty at the river, which was running high, with water right across the lane on both sides of the bridge. Maybe the girl had tried to cross but missed the way; maybe she heard the hunting-horn and was afraid to meet the hounds. Perhaps she wanted to destroy herself. Or it's even possible that Tom –' he saw the look of dread in Mary's eyes. 'But no one knew the truth of it. If anybody knows what happened, it is Tom.'

Silence in the Rector's study. Only the motion of a finger on the carriage-clock upon the marble mantelpiece, the flicker of a ray of sunlight on the polished surface of the desk.

'They brought the bodies here. Then Jocelyn came; we found out what we could but Tom had vanished up to Forda – your mother was distraught. For her sake Jocelyn kept things quiet and helped your brother get his place up on the Moor. The Penfolds threatened him but nothing came of it. And Jocelyn was the Squire, he didn't want a scandal in the valley, his tenants were involved – Euphemia was just a gipsy girl . . .'

Mary's hands were clasped in front of her, her head was bowed. The Rector could not see her face. At last she said: 'Why should we trouble with her now?'

'We caused her death. We are responsible – I have thought it since I learned what happened in the village. John Reed wrote all that down, he couldn't speak of it – he is convinced his accident was sent to punish him, a judgment of the Lord. Perhaps he's right. The girl is buried here, but only John remembers it . . .'

Still Mary gazed in front of her. He made his last appeal – yet he was certain he had failed. 'We have the chance to change the pattern, Mrs Ford. To let your son find happiness with Alice – to let them have a future, not the burden of the past!'

'And if I will not?'

'I shall let the past be known. As far as lies within my power I shall put right the wrong we did Euphemia. The Penfolds suffered an injustice so that Tom could be protected – I will tell the truth if need be to the present magistrate, to Captain Trenaman. He is a fairer man, for all his faults, than ever Jocelyn was.'

'You cannot do it! Not betray the people here, my brother and your own – bring shame upon the Penningtons –'

'I am the last.' He said it wearily, and yet with pride. 'I would rather that my name was finished than dishonoured any more. But I will let the past – both yours and mine – lie buried, if those two young people are allowed to live their lives.'

She saw that Michael Pennington was old. His voice, for all its recent passion, weak and thin; his body trembling with fatigue. He would not last the year out, Mary thought. For the present she must acquiesce – but not for Martin's sake. She would do it, if she must, for Tom.

Her answer sounded like a challenge. 'Let them marry, then. And let them take the consequence!'

*

Alone, the Rector poured himself a brandy; the pain had been severe of late. He needed to renew his strength, there was still some writing to be done. Another chapter of his History – and it would be the last.

Down in the garden, Mrs Hannaford and Alice gathered up their things. The air was growing cool. It would soon be time for evensong.

8

The village was divided. There were those who supported Preacher Passmore, the chapel crowd whose vocal righteousness made clear the moral certitudes of two hundred years of Nonconformity. Mary Ford had always been religious: now the fanaticism Trenaman had feared took hold with a singleminded power that shocked the gentler people of the parish. For there were a few, the culpritcher among them and – surprisingly, to those who knew her regular severity with youthful apple-stealers – Martha Hannaford. She was entirely loyal to the Rector and expressed her own opinion without restraint.

It was quickly known that Mrs Ford had quarrelled with the Reverend Pennington. Roger Braund had seen her leave by the side-gate of the churchyard. From the vantage-point of his bench outside the workshop (his forge, of course, was always idle on a Sunday) he had watched her go into the empty chapel where she must have stayed for more than half an hour – by the time she left the Rector's evening congregation were in church. It was rumoured on successive Sundays that she would forbid the banns: but those who hoped to hear her do so were frustrated. Mary never went to Ash Ford church again. As she had predicted, all the Cheldons were against the marriage – even the two old men at Forda Mill were disappointed in their favourite. But Martin went to call on them with Alice: he was certain, as he told her afterwards, that his uncles had been charmed by her –

they would relent. The Fords at Town Farm were embarrassed by it all: as tenants of the Rector they could not openly rebel. But Robert's aged father was incensed. He'd known old Parson half a century, had always had a great respect – but he was sure the man was mazed to let a gipsy woman marry in the house of God!

Joe Pike, in his evening forays to the Pennington, spoke out in Martin Ford's defence. She were a proper maid, were Alice Penfold, and she'd make the boy a proper wife. Joe almost came to blows with Roger Braund when he refused to shoe Ash Barton horses: 'I shall do 'un for the sake of Mistress Ford,' the blacksmith said at length, 'but if I get ahold of Martin I shall speak my mind!'

At home, both Martin and his father were surprised by Mary's self-control. While she made no secret of her breach with Michael Pennington – indeed, spoke of him only with contempt – she neither wept nor threatened. Even when a note arrived from Nymet House, she said no more than 'I am done with Laura Trenaman!' Mary threw the letter in the stove, unread. When Martin mentioned Alice or arrangements for the wedding Mary's silence – her refusal even to acknowledge that a change was imminent – had a more profound effect than words. Though Robert took it as a welcome respite Martin was alarmed. He did not trust his mother, knew this was at best a temporary truce. If she could not get her way by direct intervention Mary would resort to guile.

Martin could not bear to tell his fears to Alice – could not mar her present happiness. It seemed to her that no one would prevent them now: she was still afraid of Mary, nothing altered that – but the Rector had prevailed and she believed in him implicitly. For the first time since her coming to Ash Ford she felt secure. Whenever Jessie Pike described (with all the wisdom of direct experience) a fresh example of the village women's prejudice, the girl refused to listen or be warned. If she had any doubts they were dispelled by Mrs Hannaford: 'You won't let Martin down, not after all you've learned from me. And Mary Ford will find that out. But if you need me – any time at all – I shall be here.' She was relieved that Alice, after months of trepidation, showed such confidence. 'I shall have Martin – he is all I need. If only my mother could have known . . .'

Grace would not come to her. She had accepted that. But sometimes Alice longed to see her, find a message from her – there was none. When Martin told her that there might be gipsy men among the casual labourers at harvest-time she waited eagerly – perhaps she would see Charlie with them, or the Smiths . . . They didn't come. She thought of Isaac then, how he had impressed her with the need to speak to Captain Trenaman: it troubled her that she had failed. Yet she no longer felt such urgency to find out more about her father. Alice knew she was forgetting Will, the pain of losing him had eased. And the Captain was away from home, so Harry said. When he returned – the girl was sure of it – she would discover what he knew. She would go to Nymet House, and meet the women there, as Martin's wife.

As the summer turned to autumn, Alice made her preparations. She could face the future, now, with joyful certainty.

'Fine lace from Honiton! New gloves from Torrington! And ribbons, ribbons for the maids!' Loud cries of cheap-jacks, raucous music from the coloured round-abouts; a steady beat of engines and their sudden hissing steam; the crack of rifle-fire and shouts of disappointment from the watching crowd . . .

It was Joe who said they ought to go to Barum Fair. A fine September day, the corn was in, the geese already grazing in the stubble-fields. Along the river-meadows flocks of gulls had gathered, flying far inland in search of detritus from last month's heavy floods; above the widening valley oak and elm, already touched with autumn colour, rose in ranks against the sky; between the hills the train moved steadily, its smoke and carriages at times reflected in the waters of the Taw. As Alice watched them she remembered how, in spring, she came to Martin – knowing only that she loved him, knowing nothing of her future life. He was beside her now, with Harry sitting opposite. The train was crowded with so many farming families from villages along the line, with townsfolk from as far away as Exeter. Yet when they came to Barnstaple she would recall that other life – which she had left, that April day, so far behind . . .

At first she felt self-conscious in her well-made clothes, with her hair done up in braids, her hands so smooth and clean. These were the people she'd grown up amongst – she was always, until this year, one of the many gipsies at the Fair. One of those who sold the country people fairings – jewellery cheaply bought, its brightness polished by the little children as they sat outside the van, the gold and silver which in time would fade and tarnish; or the fabric pieces picked up one week from the back door of a mill and sold next week as perfect to the women of the farms. And she recognized the men, their jocular persuasiveness when striking up a bargain, the wary sharpness of their eyes. They stared at Alice and she knew their thoughts – a gipsy *chi* in *gorgie* finery would sell herself to any man.

But no one spoke to her. And when at last she summoned courage to approach a group beside a tattered tent, they would not listen to her urgent questioning – the children laughed and spat at her, the women turned away. Martin saw that she was close to tears.

They left the Fair when it was dark, the press of people even greater and the drunken shouting, laughter, fighting more alarming as the gas lamps flared. They paused, the three of them, beside a stall. And it was

186

there that Martin saw him – staring at them as they moved into a patch of light. He was lean and silver-haired, with dogs at heel; his garments neater and more prosperous-looking – yet his eyes, their hostile keen expression, were the same.

The girl moved on but Harry, turning for a word with Martin, saw his sudden watchfulness. The man, with a movement quick and yet deliberate, had slipped away. 'Who was that?' Harry asked. There was something curiously familiar about the figure – something that he couldn't place.

Martin was silent for a moment, staring . . . Then he looked at Harry, made sure Alice couldn't hear.

'It was Ellis!' Martin said.

She was married from the Rectory. It pleased the Reverend Pennington, when he saw her come into the church, that she was carrying the last sweet-scented roses from his garden – quite as if she were a daughter of his own. Their colours, gold and crimson, gave a touch of brightness to her plain grey gown. (White would have been unlucky, Alice had insisted: for a gipsy, she was certain it meant death, but Martha Hannaford had failed to understand.) To the surprise of those who – out of curiosity and habit – had assembled by the lych-gate to observe the bride and groom come from the church, Alice left her husband's side and ran along the path. When she returned she was without her flowers. She had placed them, with some others put there by the culprit-cher, upon Euphemia Penfold's grave.

'. . . I must say,' Margaret wrote to Francis, 'your brother's wedding seems to have been strange!' (As usual her letter, with its frequent underlinings and the writing so enthusiastic and unformed, was difficult to read.)

Harry gave the bride away – he was reluctant when M.

asked him first – quite understandably. But then he did agree and now says he is glad of it, that she's a most underlined delightful girl and he thinks Martin is a <u>lucky man</u>! I cannot say that I agree with him – though I am <u>very fond</u> of M. and wish him well. Your mother didn't go, of course. Your father evidently did but sat right at the back and didn't speak to any of them afterwards. Not that there were many people there – just Mrs Hannaford and old John Reed, Joe and his wife – which when you think of it is very sad. There are so many of the Fords and all your Cheldon relatives: if M. had married Charlotte Snell or some other farmer's daughter they would all have come. But I suppose that a <u>dynastic</u> marriage of that sort just didn't have the same appeal – C. S. is a cousin of the Cheldons after all (but very rich!). I must say if, or rather <u>when</u> I marry I shall make sure Father lets me have a proper 'do' – your brother didn't even have a wedding-breakfast, just some bits and pieces at the Rectory. I gather Uncle Michael didn't seem too well.

We shall be down at Teignmouth very soon – and after that my relatives on Dartmoor have some hunting planned (I do think you must miss it terribly!) But then I'll come with Mother down to Plymouth – we intend to make sure you and Father get a proper send-off, though it will be sad. I suppose I'll cry and make myself look stupid as I always do when I say goodbye to anyone – but most of all to you!

I <u>hate</u> to think how different everything will be – with you and father gone, and Harry finishing his time at Oxford. Martin married. Suddenly it seems as if we've lost each other, that our lives have changed – and all within a year . . .

She's right, thought Francis, as he sat among the half-packed baggage in his rented room. It is a year. Since I decided I would go, since Rose . . . Since Martin ended everything. It's over now. And we never found the gun.

Grace Penfold heard the bells. They rang as clearly and

as sweetly through the valley as the sound of water in a moorland stream. From the top of High Ash Hill she listened. She could see the village roofs, their drifting smoke, and down among the trees the grey tower of the church; below, the twisting road and high-arched bridge; the Aish – its flow untroubled, bright. And on the steeply-rising hillside opposite, the dark of Jason's Wood.

A year ago she had not known what waited there. Yet Grace had seen it, felt it all so long before. The bells that rang today for Alice echoed through the shadows then – and nothing could be changed. The past had played its hand, the bargain had been sealed: the unseen reckoning would come.

Grace knew she must accept. For her, the grief of losing Alice was a part of something greater – part of all the burden she had learned to bear, and yet far more than that. Her love had let the girl herself decide, had let her go: she saw that Alice loved her in return – far more because the choice had been her own. It was a bitter thing for Grace, to leave her daughter with a woman who was hard, whose hatred could destroy. Yet she knew that Martin needed Alice – and without him she would never be complete. For him the girl had left her way of life, her peace, behind.

This time the woman could not see what lay ahead. As she walked away from High Ash Hill she looked down at the Barton. Alice would be there. The valley held her now – and it would never let her go.

*He saw forgotten villages and the remains of farms. The empty
cottages of peasants whom the marching soldiers passed in flight
along the muddy road – some had their belongings with them,
pushed on makeshift carts or tied in bundles on their backs. But
many had left everything behind. He saw crops rotting in the
fields, an orchard full of apple-blossom, where a house-cow
wandered, calf at heel; a few abandoned hens beside a farmhouse
door, a half-set kitchen table with a jug still full of wine. The
fragments of a life he recognized, had thought secure. And later in
the trenches he will think of Rose, imagine the sweetness of her
smile, her warmth and tears, the child whom he may never know.
He will remember all the innocence of making love; he will regret
that he ever left the valley, ever left his home. When he sees the
deep blue haze of violets – sudden as a revelation – on the shell-
worn hill, or hears a blackbird singing in the naked branches of a
silver birch – he will long to be in Barton Wood again, in spring.*

ROLL OF HONOUR
In memory of those men of this parish who gave their lives
for King and Country 1914–1918

Braund, Roger Philip   Ash Ford   35 yrs   Sergt   Devon Yeomanry
Cheldon, David John   Ash Leigh   18 yrs   Pte   6th Devon Regt
Cheldon, Richard   Ash Leigh   22 yrs   L.Cpl   2nd Devon Regt
Ford, David Michael   Town   20 yrs   Pte   2nd Devon Regt
Luxton, John   Eastacott   29 yrs   L.Cpl   Dorset Yeomanry
Parrish, Geoffrey James   Ash Ford   24 yrs   Gunner   Royal Artillery
Pike, William Joseph   Ash Ford   19 yrs   Pte   1st Devon Regt
Snell, John Robert   Narracott   30 yrs   Cpl   4th Somerset Rifles
Snell, Peter   Forda Bridge   19 yrs   Pte   Dorset Infantry
Webber, James George   Ash Ford   21 yrs   Cpl   6th Devon Regt

9

In the winter – just as Mary Ford had hoped – the Rector died.

At first there was an upsurge of nostalgic sentiment, short-lived and spurious. Few people in the valley ever cared about him as a parson, even fewer understood him as a man. But he had been an institution to them all – the last remaining relic of Sir Jocelyn's day, the last male Pennington. A brief obituary was published in *The Times*, which mentioned that he had been working on the final volume of his family History: there was little more to show for a career that spanned the whole reign of Victoria.

But Alice wept. Her grief was genuine – as the old man's unexpected warmth had been. He was a link, however tenuous, with Grace – his death and Martha Hannaford's departure could only make her feel bereft. There would be a stranger speaking from the pulpit; strangers in the only place the girl had thought of as a home. The incumbent of King's Nymet took on all the parish duties and the Rectory must soon be sold (the Church, as usual, badly needed funds). In time – when war brought still more change – the house would be a hospital, a small hotel, a school . . . But Alice would see none of that. For her, the echoing half-empty rooms, the tangled garden with its tall enclosing trees, would be the place where she had ceased to be a gipsy – where, through Michael Pennington, she glimpsed a gentler and more graceful way of life, long past . . .

She went there for the last time on a February morning. Ice along the margins of the lane, across the puddles by the bridge; a stiff north wind that blew between the leafless hedges and the roughened fields, their colour faded, summer richness gone. Beside her Martin walked in silence. There were times – more often since their marriage, Alice felt – when he seemed distant and cut off from her, absorbed in some deep process of deliberation that he could not share. And yet quite suddenly – as now – he would point out an alteration in the land, a movement of the stock, a subtle change that was significant. Or he would touch her fingers with his own and she would know that even in his silence lay a need that was acknowledged, closeness that could never be destroyed. Inside Ash Barton Mary's constant vigilance oppressed them both: she seemed to note each word that passed between them, every gesture that they made. As if she must be watching, waiting, planning – Alice could not guess for what. She felt much safer out of doors. She often walked the hill with Martin when he checked the sheep, or she would fetch the cows for Joe. And as she grew accustomed to the rhythm of each day she found in it a reassurance, a simplicity that gave her strength. A strength that she would need: before next autumn there would be a child.

Alice would miss Martha Hannaford ... But it was strange – the housekeeper had aged quite visibly, was somewhat vague and ineffectual as Michael Pennington himself had been. She appeared to have lost spirit since his death – as if her briskness and efficiency had only been for him. 'You'll come and stay with me, my dear,' she murmured. She would settle in a quiet house at Sidmouth and would manage on the sum that she had set aside, together with the small annuity that her employer left her in his will.

Before they said goodbye the housekeeper took Martin to the study. All the Rector's things had gone – his desk and books, the portrait of his mother, clock and candle-sticks from off the mantelpiece. The room was chill, seemed hollow: Martin was relieved that Alice had stayed down with Mrs Pike.

There was something, Martha Hannaford explained, that Reverend Pennington had left for him – 'He told me where to find it, just before he died. And he was most particular. Don't let him have it until everything is settled, that's exactly what he said, don't give it to him till you leave – and he is not to question you. He didn't want me troubled, I suppose, about the things that happened. I was with him for so long . . . and he was always so considerate . . .'

From the cupboard where the Rector kept his brandy she took an envelope addressed to Martin, and a leather-covered book on which, he saw at once, there was a gilded crest – the emblem of the Penningtons.

'He said,' continued Martha, 'something else – that he was anxious for John Reed. I don't know what he meant, but he said it several times and I could see that he was troubled. Reed came here when the Rector passed away and I am sure he wished to tell me something. But he wouldn't write it down – I couldn't seem to make him understand . . .'

The housekeeper was tearful. 'I shall go and see him,' Martin promised, 'very soon.'

They walked back home along the river. Alice didn't question Martin – he could tell that visiting the Rectory had saddened her. By the time they reached the trapper's cottage she was shivering. He took her hand. 'The house was very cold,' was all she said.

There was smoke from the cottage chimney and the windows had been cleaned. A girl was at the doorway. She went in quickly as they passed.

Perhaps I should have told her I saw Ellis, Martin thought.

*

The evil in your valley killed Euphemia.

Grace Penfold had been right. Martin often wondered what she meant – and now he knew. It was all there – in the Rector's private journal, written down in the Rector's neat well-educated hand. All that he had learned from old John Reed, Sir Jocelyn Pennington and Tom: all that he had spoken of to Mary Ford.

'I am entrusting this to you,' he wrote in the accompanying letter, 'since I fear your mother may attempt to use the information but will never tell the whole of it. You ought to know the truth.' Martin took his point. If Mary wished she could cause Alice great distress: for that, she need not implicate her brother Tom.

But there was another reason. 'Captain Trenaman has asked at Lydiard about Alice and her father Will. He evidently came across the father several times – when drunk or violent he often made complaints and accusations in connection with the Penningtons. The Captain was himself in court at Exeter and heard the man. There is some mystery about his death, my friend at Lydiard mentions it. Alice would not speak of it to me – but as her husband you may wish to find out more from Captain Trenaman. He does not know of Tom's connection with Euphemia, I told him nothing – but the time may come when he should hear of it. The decision must be yours.'

Martin knew at once what he would do. He owed so much to Alice and to Grace. How could his mother say the marriage brought her shame – and yet feel no shame for all that Tom had done! Will Penfold's death was surely part of it, the Rector had implied. But why? Could there be more?

A folded document, a second note attached to it, was also in the envelope. This must be to do with Alice, Martin had supposed. But the writing looked so hasty, weaker ... and the note was dated just before the Rector's death. It was short – but its brevity concealed much agony of mind.

'This came to me with other papers needed for my book – I wish that I had never written it. I ought to burn this, yet someone has to show the truth at last. They are his children – both of them. I am certain of it now. The past is terrible –'

The document spoke for itself: 'In confirmation of my free authority to purchase property at *Rincombe* in the interest of *Thomas Cheldon*, as my natural son. And this to be the sole inheritance he shall derive from me. All other claim that he may make of my estate is null and void. *Joc. Pennington.*' It bore the name and stamp of a firm of London lawyers, and Sir Jocelyn's seal; across the top was written in a different hand: '*Retain until instructed*' and, beside a second date, '*Deceased*'.

For a long time Martin sat alone. When he heard Alice coming up the stairs he waited for her gentle knock but did not answer. After she had gone again he stood beside the window of their room and stared across the valley – just as he had done when looking for the flicker of a gipsy fire, the steady smoke above the wood. But he saw nothing. Only the increasing darkness of a winter afternoon.

At last he went across the room and from the bottom of a chest of drawers took out a photograph. His brother Francis, confident and careless, seated on a horse below the steps of Nymet House. In Martin's mind, a second photograph – seen long ago when he had gone with Harry Trenaman for Latin lessons at the Rectory. A faded picture in a silver frame upon the study mantelpiece: Sir Jocelyn Pennington on horseback, with his hounds and kennel-man beside him – handsome even in his middle years, like Tom . . .

The fragments, placed together, suddenly made sense. The secrecy surrounding Tom's betrayal of Euphemia; the ties – so dangerously close yet unresolved – between Sir Jocelyn Pennington and Sarah Blake. The persecution of the Penfolds, and Will's grievances – his death, perhaps . . . But how could Martin speak of it to Trenaman, to

Alice? He could not tell them anything of this! That Mary, though she might not know it, was the daughter of Sir Jos – no wonder she had cared so much for him. That Tom, the son who but for circumstance might well have been his heir, had clearly known it and had used his knowledge, without scruple, to make himself secure. This was the truth that Michael Pennington had had to face: he'd found it terrible to bear. But it was terrible to Martin now – he hated it.

Always, he had been so proud to be part Cheldon and part Ford – good solid yeoman stock that had its roots so firmly in the valley soil. He had believed that what he offered Alice, as his wife, was so straightforward, upright – pure. Yet now all that was gone. He had no wish to share the same blood as the Penningtons: the landed squires, related to the aristocracy who had oppressed and patronized for generations, whose security was based on money – not on closeness to the earth. His pride was shattered. Even truth was just another trap.

But most of all, what haunted Martin was his memory of Rincombe. Of his mother and his uncle Tom, the passion they had always shared – which he had never really understood or faced. He comprehended it at last – too well. Their isolation from the other Cheldons; their resentment of the world, of happiness, because they had so little of their own. Was theirs the evil Grace had meant? The cold destructiveness in Mary that had always made him feel afraid; the lack of conscience in her brother, who had caused Euphemia's death. Or had Grace feared the mindless cruelty of country people – people Martin took for granted, thought he knew and trusted . . . Was that evil in himself – a part of him?

He must remember Alice. She was his reality. Her love was clear as light, would never change . . . Yet now he had a vision of his life without her. Of a vacancy where there had been reality and warmth, an echo where he once had heard her voice. And only grief where there had been such joy. Each way he turned were shadows or reflections – Martin could not see her face or find himself. The farm where he was born, the land for which he worked, were meaningless – the valley earth too frail to bear his weight . . . He saw the future as Grace Penfold saw it, warned him –

Martin looked across the valley, as if seeking for some sign – some hope, some brightness from a hidden flame. But there was none. The darkness was complete.

Johanna's birth restored his pride. As always, the increasing light and length of days – the spring renewal and the summer's growth – brought reason to his mind, drove out the blackness Martin felt at the beginning of the year. To see Alice with their child was a fulfilment far exceeding expectation. An achievement richer than the harvest – a defiant confirmation that, against all odds, they were together at Ash Barton.

In the aftermath of triumph, Martin made a conscious effort to dismiss the past. He couldn't let it spoil the present – must not risk allowing it to come between himself and Alice. If he told her everything about Euphemia she would be wretched: even if she did not love him less because of all that Tom had done she might lose heart – begin to question whether she should stay. Already, he had seen the growing tension in the house. Between the women there would never be co-operation, peace. At first he had begun to feel that Mary's violent hostility was over, superseded by consistent – though restrained – dislike. But since the death of Michael Pennington the woman had in subtle ways increased her pressure on the girl. She showed no sympathy for Alice in her pregnancy, made no concession if the girl showed signs of weakness or fatigue: as a gipsy – Mary made it clear – she could not expect support or tolerance of any kind. Though Mary was too clever to show overt cruelty she knew her power – and would use it when she chose.

Alice recognized the danger. But, as Mary quickly saw, she was ill-equipped to cope. She had been used in childhood to the confrontations – quick and fierce and physical – between the women of the camp. She would not have been afraid of that. So often, after fights, she would see those women arm-in-arm, singing and laughing at the men. And always, in the face of common enemies or at a time of need, they set aside their quarrels – would be joined together in a common loyalty. It wasn't courage Alice lacked. But she was young: against the older woman's hidden weapons she had no defence.

From the first she was anxious for Johanna. She would not leave her in the house with Mary but was often seen, the baby close-wrapped in her shawl, out on the hill behind the house or sitting on the river bank. 'She's still a gipsy!' Mary said to Robert. 'She can never hide it – and Johanna will grow up the same!'

When Alice saw the trapper's cottage garden bright with flowers, or when she heard Rose Ellis singing to her child, she longed to find a place where she could be with Martin. She had always hated winter – being cooped up in the van, surrounded by the dirt and clamour of the camp. But Ash Barton would be worse: with Johanna to be cared for there would be no peace from Mary's constant needling, no escape . . . But when she spoke of it to Martin, and reminded him about the empty cottage down in Barton Wood, his anger – for the first time since their marriage – frightened her. There could be no question of it – that was the last place in the valley he would ever choose to live!

Then he saw that she was hurt. 'We *must* stay at the farm,' he said, '– we shall lose it if we leave. I know my mother would get Francis home. We have to stay! Perhaps she'll go when Father dies –'

'You mustn't speak of that,' cried Alice. She was becoming fond of Robert. Though he said so little he was gentle with her; when he thought that Mary wasn't looking, even kind. 'We gipsies say that it's unlucky – if you speak of death, you make a death! Don't ever say such things –'

Martin laughed and kissed her. Then he took Johanna in his arms and said: 'We shall be all together, on our own, one day. Ash Barton *will* be ours!'

He did not go to see the culpritcher. Sometimes at church he glimpsed the old man in his usual place behind the organ. Martin never stopped to speak to him, though he remembered what the housekeeper had said. Whatever John Reed knew, whatever he had hoped to tell to Martha Hannaford, would be connected with Tom Cheldon – with Euphemia's death. Martin was convinced of that.

And – cowardly or not – he was resolved to leave the past alone. It was better buried, Grace had told them so. He could not jeopardize the future, all his peace of mind with Alice and Johanna, even if it meant injustice or evasion of the truth. It was easy to avoid John Reed: Martin hardly went into the village, since his marriage he had given up his evenings at the Pennington. His family and farm were more important to him now. For their sake and his own, he would not speak to Captain Trenaman about the Penfolds unless Mary forced his hand: so far she had not tried to use her knowledge in her battle against Alice.

But even if she did, Martin would fight his mother to the last. Mary would never drive them out.

10

Western Morning News   *29 December 1910*

It is with regret that we report the unexpected death last month, while travelling abroad in Mexico, of Mr Ralph Pascoe Trenaman of King's Nymet. Although not a native of this county Mr Trenaman was well known as a magistrate, landowner and businessman, and much esteemed as a member of his local community, having been resident at Nymet House since his marriage to the Hon. Laura, daughter of the late Sir Jocelyn Pennington. His loss, at the comparatively early age of 63, comes as a tragic piece of news at this festive season to his wife and four children; the eldest of his sons, Mr Harry Trenaman, recently graduated from Exeter College, Oxford.

It is understood that Mr Trenaman was accompanied on his journey by Mr Francis Ford, of Ash Ford, who was with him at the end and has communicated details of his decease to the family. The funeral took place at Pachuca, Mexico, where Mr Trenaman lies buried in the Methodist Cemetery, amongst many others of his fellow Cornishmen. A Memorial Service is to be held at King's Nymet in the New Year.

In later years, when Francis found that he could view things more objectively, he came to the conclusion that Ralph Trenaman had not intended to return. It wasn't anything specific – more a series of impressions which would only finally cohere when he himself had come to terms with what it meant to leave the valley: why – in spite of everything – it would always draw him back.

In Mexico he saw Ralph change. Within a space of weeks the respectable veneer, the image of the landed country squire and English gentleman had gone. As if those comfortable layers had been stripped away to leave, not a hollow heartless core but a renewed and passionate intelligence – too long held down by the demands of social expectation, the restraints of class. Even on the boat, when Trenaman described the people and the places he had seen when young, he had begun to alter, growing daily more communicative, more alive . . . Later Francis would perceive the irony.

But it was quickly clear that Trenaman – perhaps deliberately – had minimized the dangers they would find. Once there, he calmly shrugged them off with a gesture almost Latin in its nonchalance. He'd seen this coming years ago, he said. The violence, the signs of revolution – even in Pachuca – had been there. 'We Europeans have exploited Mexico for centuries. Who can blame the people if they try to claim their country, their resources, for themselves at last? We saw it – but we didn't listen to the warnings. Now it's all begun – the strikes and confrontations, the brutality of soldiers and police – we have no right to be surprised.' He had looked around the little courtyard where they sat, surrounded by the richness of the evening light, the heavy scent of flowers – roses and camellias, geraniums, pale lilies with enormous stamens, dusty gold. 'In England we don't understand. We've been peaceful for too long, avoided all they've had in other countries – Germany and Italy and France. But we shall see it. One day it will come to us, involve us all . . .'

He was like this when we went to Heasley, Francis had recalled. But I didn't really know him: I only saw him as a businessman, a profiteer. And it was money, independence that I wanted then. Yet now there's more to it than that . . .

His year with Trenaman had proved to be an education, an enlightenment. Francis was drawn by this country of extremes – its beauty startled and entranced him; its poverty – like nothing he'd imagined – had appalled. He could see why many of the Cornish people, having reared their families and made their fortunes, at last were going home: and he could understand why others, drawn there by the freedom it had offered, held there by their love for Mexico, remained. The challenge and developing technology of mining, with its many hidden secrets, fascinated Francis still – and if he couldn't stay here in Pachuca there was the rest of South America, or California. All that awaited him.

He was forgetting home. The quarrels with his brother now seemed trivial, and even Rose had faded to an insubstantial shadow . . . He wanted it that way: his life had just begun. Francis felt that he would do as Trenaman, when young, had done – but he would never make the same mistake. He would never let commitment – in particular, commitment to a woman – hold him back.

Yet always, in a corner of his mind, the image of a narrow valley with its scattered farms, the cottages where men and women laboured, generation after generation, on their patch of land. They were no different – those he left behind – from farmers, peasants, anywhere. One day he would discover that – when war and its destruction made him long for peace, for quiet woods, for a security he'd lost.

By then he would be used, though never reconciled, to death. To its choosing of a moment, random-seeming and yet arbitrary; its emptying of lives that had seemed full of hope. When he remembered Ralph – one minute confident, alert, the next a rapidly depleting vessel – Francis had to tell himself: That was his choice – he wanted to be there.

And he remembered something else which, more than anything perhaps, explained the Captain's choice. A woman standing with the mourners (there were many more than might have been expected) at his funeral. She was a little way apart. Her features, delicate and yet suggestive of an independent mind, were dark – as dark as Alice Penfold's, Francis thought. She did not weep. Yet when the moment came for her to pass the grave she clearly felt emotion: it was in her pose – the head bent sorrowfully down, the movement of her black-gloved hand across her eyes. Was this – was she – the reason Trenaman came back to Mexico? And might he have remained, in spite of revolution or the claims of family and friends, for her?

Martin went at once to Nymet House. He found Laura Trenaman composed, tight-lipped: as the agent Webber said, she had the breeding – now, in her reticence from open grief, it showed. She had despatched the younger children to relations, all the practical arrangements were in hand. Francis would remain in Mexico to sort out Ralph's remaining business – Martin was surprised at that. But Laura trusted Francis, he was proving very capable, her husband had thought very well of him – The self-control had slipped a little at that moment: it was soon regained.

But it was all – in Margaret's words – so wretchedly, so cruelly unfair! She fought the knowledge of her father's death, expressing fervently the bitterness and anger Martin had foreseen: she had always been emotional, at times extravagantly so, yet seemed unaware of others' needs. Why couldn't Francis have come home at once to comfort her? She would write and tell him that he should have done! In such a mood she reminded Martin of his mother – he was glad he had not married Margaret. He checked the thought as inappropriate, and let her weep.

Harry blamed himself. He looked and sounded ill. He felt the blow as something physical; and with all the sensitivity of his creative mind, he agonized. His tears shocked Martin. But the damning certitude of Harry's self-reproach alarmed him even more. It was his fault, his own blind lack of courage – he had failed his father . . . Worst of all, deep down he'd known it, Harry said: 'I should have gone with him. But I didn't care – I didn't care enough!'

That evening at the Barton, Mary had repeated it. 'He should have gone with him to Mexico. His own son should have gone – not mine! If Trenaman had taken Harry he might not have died!'

She didn't need to say it served him right. His taking Francis from her had been unforgivable – death could never alter that.

'Ralph Trenaman was just a trouble-maker – I suppose they'll all forget that now he's gone. I won't forget: he had a lot to answer for!' Mary looked at Alice as she said it.

Martin knew exactly what his mother meant. And when he went upstairs to Alice later he could see that she had understood, was thinking of it still. Their marriage would have been impossible had Francis stayed at home.

As they lay together in their room, the curtains tightly drawn against the winter rain, Alice spoke – at last – of Will. How she had grieved, as Harry grieved, because she wasn't with her father when he died. 'He is feeling that he killed him – I felt that,' she said. Because Will had wanted her to stay in Bridgwater that night – and she had not.

'There was a dance,' she said. 'We heard the music coming from the hall, it was in the middle of the town. And my father wanted me to go to it with him – we often danced but Mother usually went back with the little ones to find the van. The Fair was almost over, just like Barum Fair it was, with people singing, torches blazing – always, every year, we went. But it rained that night. My brother Charlie made my father mad – they often quarrelled, often fought, the two of them. And Isaac took my father's part – the last we saw of them they both were singing, drinking in a pub down on the quay. I didn't want to dance, my feet were wet and I took Charlie home, he was too drunk to find the way.' She smiled at Martin in the darkness, took his hand. 'You see? That's why I never mind your father drinking – I got used to it, and it doesn't matter – he is always kind.

'We waited all day at the camp. They didn't come. The other vans had gone, and still my father didn't come. So Mother went into the town to look for him. She found the hospital, but she was just too late . . .' She told him then what Isaac said to her about Euphemia, how Will had meant to speak about her death to Trenaman. How he was certain it was someone from Ash Ford who got him in the end – 'That's what he said to Isaac . . . But I didn't keep my promise to tell Captain Trenaman, I only saw him once before he went –'

And it's too late, thought Martin. We shall never know what Trenaman found out – he cannot help us now. I should have gone to see John Reed . . .

'That autumn when I came here first, I wanted to go back – before we left the Moor. It would have been a year – you must always put some flowers for someone you have loved, each year, the day they died – my mother understood. She wouldn't let me go, she was afraid I'd find out something terrible . . . Then later when I might have gone, I didn't. I could not, because –'

'Because of me?' . . . 'Because of you!'

Martin held her in his arms and listened to the rain, the gusts of wind that blew the sudden hail against the corner of the house. The room was still; Johanna slept.

'But it wasn't you that killed him,' Martin said at last. 'Whatever else – whoever else – it wasn't you, my love!'

'I can't remember,' Robert said. He was in the barn with Martin, shifting hay. Already there were early

206

lambs, and it was bitter cold. They would have to bring them in.

His father had seemed stronger, happier since Alice came. As if she had renewed his failing courage, brought him hope. Or perhaps it was Johanna – Robert's consolation for the loss of Eleanor, so many years ago. He was more inclined to talk, to take an interest in the farm. He might even, Martin thought, remember Will . . .

'There always was a lot of Penfolds – but I don't remember him.'

'But he remembered you. He told his wife that he was grateful to you – and he knew your name, he knew Ash Barton –' It seemed useless. Robert's memory, like so much else about him, had declined. Maybe Webber had been right . . .

'Tall, like Alice, and red-haired. Quick-tempered –' There was no response. Then Martin took a calculated risk. 'And he might have been with Uncle Tom a time or two – perhaps at Bampton, at the pony sales, the Fair –'

'He wasn't,' Robert said. 'It was at market, not the Fair. South Molton, in the George on market day. He was asking for Tom Cheldon, that was it!'

'But *when* was it?'

'Four years ago, or maybe five. Or six . . . But all the farmers were in there as usual on a Thursday, and your Uncle Tom, he was with Philip Snell. They had their heads together, that surprised me, I remember that. The gipsy fellow came in after them and asked the landlord who they were. Tom didn't like it, not one bit. There was an argument, a bit of a to-do, the gipsy wouldn't leave, Tom knocked him down. The landlord, he was talking of police but I said Tom caused all the trouble, which he did. Perhaps the gipsy found out who I was, I wouldn't rightly know – but Tom was none too pleased, I tell you that!' Robert laughed. 'I tell you, he was hopping mad – in fact, I don't know which was worse for temper, the gipsy or your Uncle Tom!'

Then with a sudden swing of mood he stared at Martin. 'Don't say nought of this to Mary – she won't hear a thing against your Uncle Tom! You know how Mother always is –' Robert's tone was anxious, almost pleading. 'I'd forgotten it –'

'That's right,' said Martin wearily. 'Just let it be. It doesn't matter any more!' It was the confirmation he'd expected – but he'd asked for it for Alice . . . He would rather not have known.

At last he went to find John Reed.

When Martin reached the cottage by the church he saw the window-blind was down. The garden looked neglected and the back door – in the daytime, even in the coldest weather, always left ajar – was locked. He knocked and waited; then impatiently tapped on the glass and tried the other door. That too was locked.

The Pikes' house was the end one of the row. They hadn't seen the culpritcher for several days. But he'd been acting very strange-like, Jessie said, ever since old Rector died. Sometimes he went out on the road again just as he used to do – with his pockets full of papers which he gave to folk or left at cottage doors. And one time, backalong, he went right up to Narracott – no jacket on nor hat and it were pouring rain – the Snells had brought him home. Then he was pretty ill, no wonder, shut hisself away – excepting that he always went to church and never missed for all that he was getting like a shadow . . .

It was lambing-time. As usual Martin didn't leave the farm for weeks. Neither he nor Alice went to church till Easter. The weather was still cold. They wrapped Johanna in her shawl and took her with them – Alice was reluctant, even though she knew that Mary was at chapel, to let her stay behind.

Church was crowded, bright with primroses and willow-palm. Alice thought, as always, of the Reverend

Pennington. She missed him – yet with Martin at her side she was content. Though people stared she sensed that they were merely curious, not hostile; they were beginning to accept her ... But she couldn't see John Reed. There was a stranger in his usual place behind the organ. Martin, too, had noticed it.

They took the side path through the churchyard afterwards. They passed Euphemia's grave. The primroses from Jason's Wood were almost out – there were no other flowers. The cottage steps were slippery and thick with leaves, the yard unswept. But this time, Martin saw at once, the back door wasn't shut – that gave him hope. No one answered when they knocked. Inside they saw that everything was thick with dust and spiders' webs – the heaps of books and papers, bedding in the corner by the empty fireplace, pots and china on the dresser shelves. The little attic room was dark and empty, the tall clock at the bottom of the stairs had stopped.

The culpritcher had gone.

11

That summer was the hottest, driest, anyone had ever known. Even Robert's father, who was very old, had never seen nought like it. The blacksmith, sweating as he shod the restive horses at his forge, was certain that the heat was worse nor South America where Francis Ford was to! In June the village boys caught trout in buckets at the bridge; by August they could walk right up the river-bed as far as Forda Mill, along the hot bleached stones. In the few remaining pools the fish lay panting while the herons, quick and predatory, watched.

They had little water in Ash Ford. Some of the larger cottages had wells, but many people used the village pump – soon that was running dry. There were several short sharp storms, September-time; but the drought continued till October – when, within a week, the Aish had overflowed its banks and the wooden footbridge up at Forda had been washed away.

At the Barton both the wells ran dry. Martin carried water up in wagons from the river for the stock until the ford dried out: he then, reluctantly, drove all the sheep and bullocks down beside the Aish. There was little grazing even in the marsh. Though the hay had been quite plentiful and sweet the other fields were burnt – there would be hardly any corn, and hardly any roots for winter feed. By autumn Joe and Martin were exhausted, Mary's temper even more uncertain, Alice anxious for her child. Only Robert seemed at all content: the cider should be good this year, he said.

Down at the trapper's cottage Rosie Ellis took in washing, mainly from the shop and from the Pennington. She seemed to manage pretty well – each day the river bank was white with linen set to dry. When Alice went down to the bridge for water she would stop and speak to Rose: at last – perhaps because she had Johanna now – the barrier between the two of them was gone. Alice never questioned Rose about her past, and the younger girl had lost her fear. Those long hot summer days saw the beginning of a friendship which, in years to come, would draw their children close.

The affection Alice used to feel for Isaac Penfold had become transferred to Martin's father. She would sometimes fill his pipe, a dutiful procedure he had always felt that Mary should have done. Often Robert sat beside the stove and stared, saying nothing for a time; but when Mary left the room he talked to Alice, took Johanna on his knee or showed in other ways that the affection was returned. When Robert came in from his work he would look at Alice keenly, maybe touch her arm and ask her, 'All right, maid?': she was gratefully aware that even this slight show of sympathy was more than anyone, except herself, would get. But Mary's watchful jealousy disturbed her. Robert's small attentions were a risk to both of them. Unwittingly, Alice caused his death.

One March evening, Mary – fired by an energetic sermon on the topic of the demon Drink – returned from chapel to find Robert in his usual chair, asleep. As a rule he took great care to drink only in the barn; but Alice, seeing he was tired, had fetched his cider in. His empty mug was on the kitchen stove. The preacher Passmore had exhorted all his listeners to go back home and save the sinners they had left behind. Mary took it so to heart that without removing coat or hat she went straight out to the barn – where Robert, just that afternoon, had been racking off last autumn's cider. It would be, so he predicted, the best he'd ever made. Purposefully, Mary knocked each barrel open at the bottom bung. Then she went back in and served the evening meal.

Next morning Robert worked as usual in the yard. The milking finished, all the cows let out, he walked over to the barn – to find a sweet gold stream of cider running from beneath the door.

He seized the nearest weapon – a sharp reaping-hook that hung against the wall – and rushed into the kitchen to his wife. She calmly closed the passage door against him, bolted it, and called upstairs to Alice to go out for Martin. He was looking at some ewes in the field behind the house.

Joe Pike described it later in the Pennington. ''Twas terrible to see. All frothing at the mouth he was – like the river when 'tis come to flood, all little bubbles at the edge. And Robert went for Martin with the hook but then he fell down sudden-like and rolled about the yard – 'twas terrible, I hope I'll never see another such. And Mistress Ford were weeping, little maid were standing there all mazed. Only Martin had his wits about 'n, see. Robert, he was too far gone to think of aught except his bliddy cider – 'twas his masterpiece, and all that he had worked at gone into the mire!'

Robert lingered on for several weeks. But suddenly, as if his will were gone at last, subsided in the chair beside the stove and slept. Mary left him when she went to bed one night; in the morning he was dead, with the cat still on his knee.

Francis came home for the funeral. Neat-suited, almost elegant, he seemed to have left the valley far behind – the antiquated serviceable clothes, the heavy bright-nailed boots; the men's Victorian sobriety, the clear complexions of the plump-faced girls. They were no longer Francis' world. The context in which he functioned now was far removed from Martin, or the men and women who attended Robert's funeral. It was the last occasion they would be together as a family; the end of making cider at Ash Barton farm. What remained was drunk by Robert's neighbours in the kitchen afterwards – it wouldn't do to let it go to waste. For years the cider-press stood idle, and – too cumbersome to move – eventually rotted in the corner of the barn.

The difficulties of the drought, the cold wet winter that succeeded it; the shock of Robert's instability and death, weighed heavily on Martin. Though he didn't altogether blame himself as Harry had, his sense of guilt was strong. So often he had longed to have Ash Barton to himself – had thought things would be so much easier with his father gone. Now half the farm was legally his own – Robert's will confirmed it; and by right of occupation, if by nothing else, he was effectively the master here.

Yet Martin was troubled by it all. He could see that Alice wasn't happy. She had genuinely grieved for Robert and, within a month of losing him, miscarried with a second pregnancy. As always Mary had been hard on Alice – this time, the girl's resilience was less. Martin saw it, tried to ease things for her, but with harvest coming on he could spend little time indoors. She found his silence, in the few snatched moments when they were together, more oppressive; he was always tired, impatient with Johanna – that hurt Alice most. It seemed that Robert's death, which should have brought them closer, had divided them.

And there was Francis. He had been in Cornwall since the spring. At first that didn't bother Martin. Harry told him Francis had been several times to Nymet House since Robert's death, but it was clear he had no wish to come back home – he would hardly run the risk of meeting Rose. Even at his father's funeral he had been distant with them all; and Mary later had reacted strongly to his coldness. She had gone into his empty

213

room and wept for hours, so Alice said. Since then Mary hadn't mentioned him.

But he was still in England by September. Martin thought he knew the reason why.

The agent, Webber, had of course attended Robert's funeral. Afterwards, with all the relatives and friends, he had come back to the house. As usual on such occasions the heavy drinking and the conversation lasted several hours. And even though the agent did not quite directly speak of it, Webber's handshake and his glance were meaningful enough: he had remembered – and wished Martin to remember – that they'd talked about the Barton rights. But Martin noticed suddenly that Webber was with Francis. This in itself might not have been significant – except that standing by them, leaning carelessly against the parlour door, was Tom. His laughter – maybe slightly muted out of deference to death – was no less easy than before; his confidence unchanged. He was staring with great interest at Alice. She was quietly helping Mary – but thank God, thought Martin, she knew nothing of Tom Cheldon yet. And she must never know . . .

His anger at the sight of Tom, his shame at all he must conceal from Alice – from the world – were almost blinding. Martin could not bear to see him there beside his brother: they were so alike. With Francis older, more good-looking in his well-cut suit, their resemblance to the Penningtons was striking – how could anyone not notice it! But Tom had not been near the Barton since the day they sealed the purchase of the farm: the day that Martin told his parents he would marry Alice. Tom, that night, had made his sister weep – for reasons Martin now could understand, could only find repulsive. When he saw his uncle run his fingers down the polished side of the harmonium, then rest his calculating gaze on Alice, Martin felt as if his own pure love – the sweetness of that recognition on the hill at Forda – had been violated. Tom was evil. He believed it now.

214

He had forgotten, in the fierce conviction of that moment, all about such practicalities as rights – the implications of a possible co-operation between Francis, Webber and his uncle Tom. But later it came back to him. And the longer Francis stayed in England, the more he went to Nymet House, the more likely it must be.

Long before, in Webber's office, it struck Martin that Ralph Trenaman might tell Francis of the valley farms – his long-term interest in the mineral rights the Penningtons had owned. That danger had receded with the Captain's death. But now it was quite clear that Francis had a stake in Laura Trenaman's affairs. Harry had confirmed it. Only lately he'd explained to Martin that he quite enjoyed the running of his father's small estate – but he couldn't get to grips with all the mining business, his mother was quite satisfied that Francis could do that. Harry had been walking down through Barton Wood with Martin at the time: 'You know,' he said, 'I never thought that I'd be happy stepping into Father's shoes – and yet I am. There's not much time for writing, I'll admit, I've almost given up, but at least I'm not in smoky London working as a hack. And not in Oxford being intellectual, cooped up with all those dull old academics. This is real, the valley – where I'll always want to be. And where I reckon I shall end my days . . .

'And you –' he had taken Martin's arm '– you were right to marry Alice. She's the perfect wife for you, and there's Johanna – you're a lucky man. Francis must be pretty envious. But I wouldn't be surprised –'

It was Michaelmas when Martin knew for sure. He came in late for supper – and could tell at once that his mother was upset. Not just upset, but furiously angry. Alice wasn't in the kitchen. Mary sat alone. On the table – it wasn't even laid – a letter.

'Read that!' Mary said.

'I leave next week for South America. I shall be away a year, or maybe two. This time Bolivia, Peru.

I thought that you and Martin ought to know. I am engaged to Margaret.'

Francis had found Alice changed. He had expected he would see the gipsy girl who cursed him when they met. But all that forcefulness had gone. At church beside his brother, in the parlour at the Barton, Alice looked respectable and neat, conventional as any local girl whom Martin might have chosen as his wife. He remembered her as dusty and distraught, her long rich-coloured hair unbound. In the lane she had been open, purposeful and passionate – he never thought to see her silent, enigmatic, cold. And yet Francis sensed a harnessed energy about her, something unrestrained beneath the quiet surface of the farmer's wife.

He blamed his brother for the change. But Francis was disturbed to realize he minded – that, in spite of everything, she had the power to move him still . . . It angered him to see Alice at Ash Barton, angered him that Martin was secure. It was clear that he was now regarded as the owner of the farm. No one knew or cared, at Robert's funeral, what Francis had achieved. As his resentment deepened so it came to seem quite logical that he should marry Margaret. He didn't want to settle yet: she understood. Any consciousness that he was using her was instantly suppressed – simply, he enjoyed the status and the scope that their engagement gave. She loved him, would be patient till he got established. And especially – this meant a lot to him – he would be loyal to the memory of Trenaman.

That summer, when he came from Cornwall for a week at Nymet House, he rode across the Moor from Heasley to his uncle's farm at Rincombe. That meeting finally decided him. There had been fresh investigations, Tom told Francis, into opening the disused mines: it wouldn't be straightforward but it could be done. New workings, new machines. As Francis rode back home he made his plans. More travelling, more contacts and investment in America, more technical experience. Already he'd made money for himself and Laura Trenaman. With Margaret behind him he would show the valley what the Fords could do!

At Middle Aish, where the Penningtons had put their first great manor, he would build a house. Right on the edge of Barton land. While Martin struggled with the farm, Francis would grow rich on profits from the mines – on Exmoor or abroad. Alice hadn't brought his brother anything: Margaret had her own inheritance . . . And Rose? He would see that she was well provided for, he would not neglect his son. Perhaps, when Margaret was absorbed in domesticity – if, as he expected, she proved cold – he'd find himself well placed. The chance of other women when he travelled; in the valley – Rose.

One day, Francis was convinced, there must be problems at Ash Barton. He could wait. Then he would take the chance, get all his share from Mary. And buy Martin out.

For Mary Ford, Robert's death proved no release. She had wanted him to die. But now that he was gone she felt her isolation. As his wife and mistress of Ash Barton she had known the farm was hers – it was the only compensation for her thirty years of married life. Without him there, she could see the future pushing her aside. Martin, Alice and their child would take possession. And she would grow old . . .

As a girl in a family of boys Mary always knew she was alone. Then, she had done everything to prove she was her brothers' equal – worked beside them in the fields, learned how to shoot, and rode astride. But she meant nothing to her mother: men – her husband, lover, sons – made up the whole of Sarah Cheldon's world. For Mary

217

there had only ever been one man, apart from old Sir Jos. Until she married, Tom was at the centre. Everything.

Now Mary had no place – she was neither a mother nor a wife. She had lost Martin to a gipsy, Francis meant to marry Margaret. Her bitterness, her disillusion, were intense.

One morning – it was a year almost to the day since Robert died – she went out into the yard. She gave instructions to Joe Pike. When Martin came in from the hill he saw the trap and pony ready, Mary in her Sunday clothes. In the sunlight she looked younger, almost pretty Martin thought.

'I am going up to Rincombe,' Mary said. 'To Tom!'

12

They were alone at last. For a whole sweet spring-time month the farm was theirs. They walked together through the fields, beneath the trees – the crimson, gold and bronze of newly opened oak, the fresh pale greens of beech and elm, the stretching fingers of the ash. Johanna, old enough to be entranced by lambs and flowers, ran barefoot through the long bright grass or lay among the bluebells at the water's edge. Through warm still afternoons a herd of pregnant hinds, untroubled by the hunt, grazed gently in the lee of Jason's Wood. By night along the Aish young otters ran among the misty reeds, between the willow roots; their pure clear whistle echoed through the marsh. On High Ash Hill at dawn the cuckoo called.

The passion they had known at the beginning – all the longing of those moments in the church, the joy of Alice's return – was now renewed. In making love they found a depth and certainty that cancelled out the losses and division of the last twelve months. Martin's fears and introspection vanished. There would be another child – a New Year's child. The son he needed for the farm . . .

Their happiness, in Mary's absence, was complete.

She came back harder, more determined than before. Martin's weakness, Mary realized, lay in his strong affection for his wife and child: she would exploit that love. She waited for her opportunity. It came – that harvest-time.

Through the summer Alice went more often to the trapper's cottage, where Johanna played with Rose's child. The boy was always in and out of water, just as Rose herself had always been. She had grown up beside the river, knew its moods – its sudden red-clay spates, its gentle murmuring, the silence of its deepest pools. Sometimes Alice left Johanna at the cottage while she walked on through the wood: she saw no harm in it – she trusted Rose.

Until the day when Mary said, 'There was a girl drowned at the bridge. It happened years ago – she was a gipsy like yourself.' She was watching Alice carefully and saw her shock. Then added: 'You should take more heed – that Rosie Ellis won't! She's irresponsible, immoral – and her father was the same. They said he knew the girl who died . . . They said her child –'

But Alice didn't wait to hear the rest of it. When Martin went to find her she was lying face down on the bed, Johanna fast asleep beside her. It was clear she had been weeping – yet she could not tell him why. At last she cried, 'Euphemia!' – and wept again.

He went downstairs to Mary. 'Mother!' Mary turned her back.

'Mother!' Martin shouted it. 'Just leave my wife alone!' He looked and sounded so like Robert – when he came at Mary with the reaping-hook. But he was younger, stronger –

Martin gripped her shoulder. 'Mother –' Now his voice was dangerously calm. 'Tell me what you said to her – about Euphemia!'

'I told her,' Mary said defiantly, 'I told her that she drowned. And that she shouldn't take Johanna to the bridge. All day she's been down there with Rosie Ellis – but I don't suppose that Alice cares what happens to your child! And maybe you don't care! A gipsy woman never does look after children as a proper mother would – what else can you expect? Johanna might have drowned – Alice might have harmed herself –'

She could have found no stronger argument. Already Martin felt concern for Alice in this pregnancy, had warned her not to do the roughest work or climb the steepest hills. She had lost one child – it might have been their son – But she had laughed and teased him: in her new-found confidence she knew that nothing could go wrong. My mother never troubled, she had said. And with Johanna she forgot that first obsessive carefulness. Alice didn't want her daughter to grow up a lady – children were like puppies, not to be indulged or cosseted. Johanna would be strong and free, as she had been. It was what Martin wanted too. But he was anxious all the same . . .

'She could have harmed herself!' repeated Mary. 'If your wife won't do as she is bid then you should speak to her again – if Alice won't take heed –'

'It's you that won't take heed!' Martin had let go of her but Mary heard the fury in his voice. 'Whatever Alice does you have no right to interfere – no right to tell her things she shouldn't know. Maybe she ought to take more care – but this time you're the one that's done the harm. God only knows what this will do to her!'

His mother might have reason – yet Martin had seen Alice's distress. And he had thought that she would never learn about Euphemia! The damage had been done: but he must see to it that Mary told her nothing else.

'In case you haven't realized – the Rector told me all about Euphemia's death. And Tom! Before the Rector died he warned you what would happen if you tried to interfere. Alice heard about Euphemia from her mother – but she didn't know that she was drowned.

'Maybe you told her that on purpose, Mother – God forgive you if you did! And God help Tom if I tell Alice – anyone! – what he has done. It's not too late – not even after all these years – to make him pay. And if you don't leave my wife alone I'll do just that – as the Rector

221

would have done. I don't give a damn about my uncle, he can rot in hell and it would serve him right! I could set the Penfolds on to him tomorrow –' Martin saw his mother's fear. And he knew that he had won. She would say no more.

'But Alice matters to me, Mother. As you know. Johanna and the baby matter. Leave them be.' He said it quietly. 'Father's gone and I am master here. Just let them be!'

He was exhausted. All day long he had been working in the harvest-field. The sweat and dust still clung to him. His face was sunburnt but his mouth, his finger-tips, were white with tension. All he'd wanted when he came into the house was sleep, and silence. And his peace with Alice. That was gone.

There was no need for Mary to say more. She knew it. Knew that this would come between the two of them. The seed was tilled – and Mary watched it grow.

She saw how Alice made an effort to be strong for Martin's sake. And how she failed. Euphemia's death preyed on her mind, as it had done when Alice came back to the valley. This time she could not exorcize it, could not tend the grave or plant her flowers – could not forget. Mary saw how Martin grew more anxious and more watchful; and when Alice was neglectful of Johanna – more severe.

The river seemed to draw the child. Maybe because it was forbidden her, maybe because she missed the company of Rose's boy. She was getting independent and could find the way down to the cottage by herself. Alice didn't always notice till it was too late: then she dreaded fetching her and meeting Rose – more than ever Alice needed friendship now. But she could not explain . . . One day Rose brought Johanna back. Martin met them at the gate and hardly thanked her. When he came inside his fury frightened Alice and the child. Martin knew the reason for it – seeing Rose's son had only added to the apprehension that he felt. The little boy had fair hair like his mother's, but his eyes – so very dark – were Francis' eyes. And if Alice did not have a son . . .

The winter came. And Mary watched them still: the harm was even greater than she'd hoped. She felt her power. It was just as when she had opened up the barrels – when she stood there in the barn and watched the golden-brown of Robert's cider trickle slowly through the dust.

But Martin still loved Alice. He gave her flowers at Christmas – roses in a box with ribbon; snowdrops from Johanna, who had gone with him to Barnstaple to see the lighted shops and hear the brass band playing carols in the Square. A wild extravagance it seemed to Mary – she had never had that as a girl. They found a tree down in the wood and brought it in for Alice: she was pale and very tired by now, the baby seemed to drain her strength – but Martin knew that he had pleased her. He could see it in the brightness of her eyes. Her laughter, lately so infrequent, had renewed his hope.

She couldn't go to church on Christmas Eve – that troubled her. It snowed a little. Mary stayed behind, she said she would miss chapel just for once. Martin thought it strange. But he went off to Ash Ford alone. The house was quiet, Johanna soon asleep, and Alice resting upstairs in her room.

By the firelight, Mary thought of Tom. Of how when she was young he bound her to him, made her swear she would love no one else; of how, here in the parlour, she refused to leave Ash Barton – his pain had hurt her then. And how last year she went to Rincombe believing that he wanted her. But she had found him cold. He had rejected her. And when in her despair she asked him why, Tom laughed – and said, 'Ask Martin why!' . . . She hadn't understood. Tom laughed again – that bitter laughter – 'Just ask Martin – he's married to a gipsy girl!'

At Robert's funeral she'd seen Tom watching Alice. Mary should have guessed it then. But now he told her. He had truly loved Euphemia. He'd not abandoned her as Mary thought – not just seduced and left the girl: he loved her – Tom admitted it. They might have married if his mother had not come between the two of them – if it hadn't been for Jocelyn Pennington! 'They parted us,' said Tom. 'They promised we should be together here at Rincombe. I told her so when I left her at the cottage. Then I didn't see her – till she died –'

He had not meant to kill Euphemia. 'I saw her near the bridge. She had the baby in her arms, she must have panicked when she heard the hunt. It was misty – but she saw me, knew me. And I shouted when she ran towards me, I tried to warn her of the flood. Maybe she couldn't hear, the water was so loud. I knew that she was terrified – but I heard the other horses and the hounds – I left her there . . . I didn't know that she would fall . . .

'But later when I saw her, when they buried her, I remembered how Euphemia tried to come to me across the bridge. Then I wished that I had died . . . She was the same – her eyes, her hair – she was like Martin's wife!'

Mary had believed him. When Tom looked at her and said, 'If you hadn't married Robert, I should not have loved Euphemia,' she knew it was the truth. And she remembered that he had been young when all that happened. Now he needed her – as he had always done . . . Then she forgot the outside world, the Penfold threat, Ash Barton and her sons. She had forgiven Tom. But she could not forgive the girl. Nor Alice, who was like Euphemia. The one had come between herself and Tom; the other had made Martin love her, she would take the farm . . .

She heard Alice come into the room. *I hate her. She has what I shall never have. He comes with gifts and sets them in her*

*lap: his land, the safety of his name, his strength and certainty.
The certainty of ordered fields, the hedges and the spring-time
woods. His love – clear as the sun's white patches on a golden
field in August, warm as the sheltered garden by the house. His
children – all their future joy.*

Alice sat beside the fire. She had been putting little
packages beneath the tree. Earlier she'd helped Johanna
wrap them. In the parlour there was holly, mistletoe.
She had seen Martin looking cheerful as he went into the
yard. Perhaps she should have gone to bed as he had
told her – but she wanted to wait up for him, to have
him come in from the cold dark night and find her
stronger . . .

'Does Martin know?' asked Mary suddenly.

'Know what?'

'That you are giving presents to that girl.'

'You mean – to Rose? Why not?'

'You know that he won't like it,' Mary said.

'It's Christmas. How can Martin mind! Johanna
wanted to – And it's only little things –'

'Very well. It's up to you. But don't say I didn't warn
you. Martin won't want any more to do with Rose.'

Alice didn't answer. Reason told her Mary must be
right – yet she had hoped he would be gentler for
Johanna's sake, would understand . . .

'In any case, if Rose's father should come back he'll
soon put an end to it. Ellis never liked Rose having friends,
she was frightened of him. Everybody was.'

'Come back?' Alice saw him – blood-stained rabbits in
his hands, the vicious-looking dogs. His eyes . . .

'Joe says that he was seen at Molland, on the big estate
up by the Moor. Jessie has an uncle working there – they
have several keepers, trappers too.' It was true. She had
heard Joe telling Martin. 'So he's getting nearer home.
And maybe Rose will go. Ellis never knew she had that
child. Unless – maybe he heard it and that's why he's
coming back.'

'But – what would he do?' Alice sounded terrified. She hardly knew the reason for her fear. Till she remembered . . . The trapper – he had known Euphemia – Mary told her that before. And he must have been there when she drowned, there in the cottage by the bridge. Where Johanna used to play with Rose's boy. When everything had seemed so peaceful, innocent . . . 'What would he do to her?'

'Who knows!'

Mary guessed that Alice's imagination, overwrought already, must soon provide an answer. And she wouldn't dare to tell her fears to Martin: she would not risk his anger. Without her husband's love – Mary understood so clearly – Alice would despair.

Upstairs in their room, Alice drew aside the curtain. A few light snowflakes blew against the glass. Martin would be coming back to her. To Johanna, to the home he loved. And to the child he hoped would be his son. She could feel it moving: soon, within a month, it would be born, the future of the farm ensured. And Martin must be happier – she was quite certain. He would be fulfilled at last.

Yet Alice was afraid. She longed – for the first time since her marriage – for the safety of the *vardo*, for the sound of Grace's voice and the comfort of her arms. She longed to hear again the sweet clear sound of moorland water, curlews crying as they rose and fell above the shadows of the combe; the steady turning of the wagons' wheels along the dusty road. The freedom she had lost; the world beyond the valley –

'Mother,' Alice murmured in the darkness, 'Mother – why did you bring me here!'

13

It was New Year's Day. As always, hounds were meeting in the morning at Ash Ford, outside the Pennington. A clear blue sky, the air ice-cold; a little snow remaining in the backs of hedges on the highest ground, the ruts and hollows treacherously hard. From the Barton they could hear the tapping, quick and purposeful, of horses' hoofs as riders came along the High Ash road; and across the valley from the kennels close by Nymet Bridge the noise of eager dogs, the crack of whips as Luxton and his lads brought the pack up to the meet. Martin guessed that they would find in Jason's Wood.

The milking and the yard work were done early, all the stock was checked. But when Martin called Johanna to get ready – she must come with him to see the meet – she was nowhere to be found. She could not be far away; she had been with him to feed a calf. He was sharp with Alice, grew impatient, wouldn't wait. He wanted to go on to Forda, he hadn't seen his uncles for a year; Mary meant to walk as far as Town – she would pay her New Year visit early in case the weather changed. Alice was relieved to see them go.

She found Johanna in the barn among the hay. She scolded her and then regretted it: the child had done no harm – she had annoyed her father, that was all. Alice couldn't help resenting Martin's hardness. When Johanna asked if they might take their presents down to Rose, he had been adamant – they were not to go. Alice

227

did not argue with him: as Mary had foreseen, his anger frightened her. The packets with their brightly-coloured ribbons had remained beneath the tree.

Alice rarely had Ash Barton to herself. The house did not oppress her as the Rectory had done at first – but it was Mary's house. Her presence was in every room. Even, Alice felt, in the one she shared with Martin. The religious texts – sentimental yet severe – still hung above the bed; all the linen had been Mary's; the old tin trunk that came with her was the only object Alice called her own. She hadn't minded that – possessions had been few enough when she was still a gipsy. But when Mary went to Rincombe Alice glimpsed a different life: in that perfect month with Martin she had known how their marriage might have been.

Lately the longing to escape had almost overwhelmed her. She remembered how that other winter – it seemed so long ago! – she believed that she would die if she did not go back to Martin: now, each morning when she woke she felt it would be death to stay. The change appalled her. Only the knowledge that Johanna needed her could give her courage, only the coming child gave any hope.

But this afternoon the house was quiet, calm. Alice felt surprisingly – and thankfully – at peace. Downstairs was cheerful with the Christmas evergreens and sunlight warmed the upper rooms: on impulse – as if establishing her own authority at last – she went into each one.

At the far end of the passage, by the second staircase, was a narrow room that Martin said had been a chapel long ago: one wall curved up into the rafters, with a high slit window through which eastern light came like a shaft above Johanna's bed. Alice liked to think that she was sleeping safely there. The room that had been Eleanor's, then Martin's, led out from the chapel. In the passage by the other door stood a heavy wooden chest. Tentatively

Alice opened it: a pile of neatly folded clothes, a wooden horse, a small rag doll. A straw hat with a faded ribbon, a pair of buttoned boots. All Eleanor's. Mary never mentioned her, Martin only rarely – and then in a way that had made Alice realize how much her death had hurt him. Only Robert ever told her just what she had meant; would Martin have as much affection for his daughter? Now, Alice wasn't certain that he would. She hated doubting him . . .

Francis' room. Unused and dusty. Only the riding-whip above the fireplace to remind her of the man who had confronted her at Jason's Wood. At the funeral she'd hardly recognized him – neat, well-dressed, black hair smoothed down. So different from the careless-looking youth whose arrogance had roused her anger, who had made her feel – at first – alone, without defence. She could not imagine him as husband to that cool fair woman, Margaret Trenaman – the one who had been close to Martin once . . . And what had happened, Alice wondered, to the gun that Francis had been searching for: what had her brother Charlie had to do with it? And where was Charlie now? She missed his wildness, even all that boasting – he'd cared about her, tried to take their father's place. Sometimes when she was alone or with Johanna she would sing the songs, remember all the tunes he played – but lately even thinking of them made her sad . . .

And Mary's room. At the doorway Alice hesitated. She had never, in nearly five years at Ash Barton, gone in there . . . It was colder, the failing winter sun was almost down behind the hill. And there was something chilling, too, about the way the room appeared so ordered, scrupulously neat, impersonal: every sign of Robert had been cleared away. Nothing frivolous and no concession to its owner's femininity. Except, perhaps, for the silver brushes and the photograph beside them on the dressing-chest. A picture, Alice realized, of Mary's mother: even late in middle age she had been beautiful. And Francis standing by her, Mary on his other side, her hand in his . . . No. Not Francis but an older man, so like . . . Alice recognized Tom Cheldon: Martin's Uncle Tom whom she had seen with Francis after Robert's funeral. Even then she'd wondered why he never came here to the farm. She had sensed that he was watching her, it made her feel uneasy. In the way that Francis Ford had watched her in the lane; he too had made her feel unsafe . . . Somehow, Tom Cheldon was a threat . . .

It came as an overpowering certainty. The answer to the questions she had asked so often since the day John Reed had taken her to find Euphemia's grave. Before that, even –

'Who was the man?' she had asked Grace before she left. 'I can guess it,' Grace had said, 'from what your father told me – and from what he would not say. But it could be dangerous for you: don't think or speak of it again.' And Isaac's words – 'Because of it Will died. It was Ash Ford folks that got him in the end.'

In Ash Ford churchyard, whenever Alice saw the carved inscription on the stone, she wondered. Euphemia's baby had been named for Will, the brother she had loved. But the second name – had Thomas been the father of her son? Was he the man who caused Will Penfold's death?

Alice knew the answer.

She had left Johanna in the parlour. As Alice went downstairs her apprehension grew: how long had she been there in Mary's room? She hurried, almost stumbling down the last few steps. The parlour fire was out, the door into the kitchen passage open wide. An icy draught was blowing from the yard. 'Johanna?'

But the child had gone. And the packages for Rose were no longer by the tree.

*

The village had turned out to see the meet. A group of laughing girls as usual on the churchyard steps, boys running up and down the lane between the chapel and the bridge, the smallest children sitting on the low stone wall beside the school. Old men with sticks leaned against the iron railing by the pump or made their slow sure way towards a favourite corner by the fire inside the Pennington. Some younger regulars were there already – they had spent the New Year's night in forays from the belfry to the pub, then back again to church to ring yet another peal.

As the hour drew closer, cottage women left their aprons and responsibilities behind and gathered in the chilly sunshine – they always liked to see the huntsmen and the gentry on their well-groomed horses. Roger Braund and his apprentices, of course, were working: a meet was good for trade. Some riders would be strangers – Christmas visitors, perhaps – but most were faces that the village people knew. There were a few young men from Nymet on their bicycles, with several of the more emancipated girls – come home on holiday from distant city work. Apart from these, the Ash Ford crowd that morning differed little from the folk who watched the stag-hounds meet in old Sir Jocelyn's day.

All the Trenamans had come. Even Harry was on horseback: he was changing, Martin thought, becoming more conventional since Ralph had died. There were Margaret and Laura, looking so alike; their features had a clear-cut regularity and hardness that Martin could no longer find attractive – though evidently Francis did. His brother never missed this meet: Martin had come with him many times when they were young – and he'd envied Francis all his horsemanship, his confidence. Secretly, of course, he had been proud; glad to feel that Francis had relied on him. They were strangers to each other now.

'There's George Webber,' Mary said. She watched the

agent as he spoke to Harry. Webber looked across the crowd, acknowledged Mary, turned his mount away. 'I suppose he thinks he'd better cultivate the Squire,' said Mary scornfully. She could be right, thought Martin. He had not seen Webber for a year or two – but he knew the Portsmouth properties had been dispersed. The other Cheldons, as expected, bought their farms: had Webber played his usual dirty game? Martin guessed he had.

'It's getting cold. And they'll be expecting me at Town.' Mary didn't want to wait. It was obvious to Martin that she wouldn't speak to Laura Trenaman – yet they had been so close. His mother, in the last twelve months, had aged: her face was thinner, lined. It had happened since she went to Rincombe, he was sure. Since she went to Tom . . .

'Francis should be home in autumn,' Harry said. He had left his place beside the younger Trenamans, self-conscious on their ponies, and had ridden over to where Martin stood. 'He wrote not long ago. He's had a few excitements over there but he's ready to come back. Harry laughed. 'I suppose we'll have a wedding then –' He saw his friend's expression. 'What's the matter, I'd have thought you would approve to have him settle down?'

'It isn't that –' Martin couldn't tell the truth of it to Harry, even after all these years. 'But he's not secure, he's very young –'

'You were younger when you married Alice. He'll be nearly twenty-five. And Margaret's older . . . They should marry while they can, before things get much worse.'

'What can you mean – get worse?'

'Before things change. If the politicians have their way there'll be a war before this year is out. My father saw it coming long ago – and he was right. No marriage for young Francis then, he'll have to fight the same as everybody else.

'And all of this' – Harry gestured with his whip – 'all we have known, in our cosy little valley, will be gone. We used to talk of it at Oxford, how we'd live to see the old life swept away. And it looks as if we shall!'

The hounds moved off towards the bridge. As Martin had expected they would cross the river, draw the wood.

As he walked rapidly to Forda he thought of Harry's words. He'd said such things before – but never with such certainty. Could he be right? What would happen to them – to Johanna, Alice and himself – their son? Or to Francis and his dreams; to Rose and the dark-eyed little boy, he'd seen them both this morning in the lane . . . If war came, all their lives – the quarrels and the joy, ambitions, fears – would be irrelevant and meaningless. As if they'd never been. All that they had fought for would be gone.

His uncles up at Forda Mill, which had stood for centuries beside the Aish, had led such simple lives. They had never left the valley, never known the world beyond. Their work had not been easy: but it had given every day its purpose, every night its well-earned rest. Martin had believed their way of life to be unchangeable – reaching far back into the past and forward to the generations that would follow. But none of that would matter if there were a war.

He reached the disused quarries where, with Francis, he had come so often as a boy. Always Francis climbed them, never looking back. Always Martin waited, watched in trepidation, feared the climb – and feared to see his brother fall. That difference of character had shaped their lives, determined everything so far. But none of that would matter . . .

Martin saw, across the river, the bracken-covered hill where he found Alice on an autumn day. Now she was safely at Ash Barton with their child. In spite of all the dangers – Mary's hatred and the troubles of the past –

they were together. Nothing altered that. Even if war with all its changes came – as long as he had Alice, Martin could go on. But if he lost her there would only be that darkness, the emptiness he dreaded. Nothing else would matter any more.

The trapper's cottage was deserted. No light from any window, not even a faint blue thread of wood-smoke rising through the stillness of the valley air. No sound of children's voices or a woman's singing: only the steady lapping of the river at the wall. It was bitter cold in the shadow of the trees, in the dim half-darkness of the early afternoon – the calm mid-winter twilight when a mist begins to rise above the water, blue sky fades, and frost-rime stiffens every stem of grass, each fallen leaf.

Alice noticed nothing. She was conscious only of exhaustion and despair. Her breath came heavily and she could feel the baby's weight, oppressive, as she leaned against the cottage door. At her feet the little coloured packages lay scattered. Johanna must have left them there. But she had gone again. Alice hadn't seen her on the Barton path. Wildly, as she ran and slipped along the icy track, she'd called her; having found the cottage empty Alice searched along the river bank, calling for Johanna as she went. No answer – only the rush of water over stones. Once with sudden hope she heard a movement in the trailing willow at the river's edge – and saw a startled hind, eyes staring as it leapt the stony bank and vanished in the darkness of the wood.

When she came back to the bridge that second time she had remembered Ellis. How he would stand there by his gate or disappear – as if not wanting to be seen – into the shed where he had put his rabbit carcasses and traps ... Her terror had returned – supposing Ellis had come back already and had found Johanna ... Alice forced herself to look inside the shed – in case – but there was nothing. Only a strange dry smell that caught her breath, and a mass of webs that clung about her fingers as she closed the latch.

Now, as she rested at the cottage step, Alice thought of Martin. He would surely have come home – she should fetch him, he and Joe would search . . . But how could she face his anger, his distress? The accusation – however justifiable – that she had failed. How could she bear that yet again? She must stay here. Johanna might come back – it would soon be dark, the child would be afraid –

Above the constant noise of water Alice heard a different sound. Faint, high-pitched, yet echoing across the river from beyond the bridge. She heard it twice. And then, almost as if the cry had triggered a response, another cry. It was louder but more distant. More cries mingled with it and above them all a sudden long-drawn note that was repeated, taken up by others – hunting-horns that rang across the valley, called insistently above the baying of the hounds.

But she had heard Johanna first . . . As Alice ran across the bridge she could hear her yet again – crying from the thickets of the wood. But the hounds were closer too, where the gipsy camp had been – they would be coming down the lane – Having found there in the morning the hunt had run their quarry home. Alice knew it, she had seen the hind. They would kill at Jason's Wood.

Thorns and brambles tore her face, her hands, her clothes. Her hair had come unpinned, her boots undone – Alice threw them off. She could scarcely breathe and dared not shout for fear the dogs might reach Johanna first – they were above her, baying and running through the shadows, there were horses in the lane – She found her in a little clearing, curled beside a silver birch; in the half-light, as she held her close, Alice saw the hind slip past . . . But by the time she reached the bridge, Johanna in her arms, Alice knew that it was finished – with a terrible crescendo from the hounds, the shouts of men. A shot. Then silence in the darkness of the wood.

. . . As Alice stood there by the river she remembered. How she'd come to fear the valley's hardness: Ellis and Tom Cheldon, Francis, Mary Ford. The hardness she had found in Martin, that had made her so reluctant to go back; the cruelty that caused Euphemia's death. She could hear the rushing of the water as it swirled against the bridge; and through the rising mist the last high note, so resonant and clear, of a distant hunting-horn. Yet she was not afraid.

In that moment, suddenly, she saw it all as Grace had seen it. There was no question, no confusion: the past, the present and the future coalesced. In that moment they were one – Euphemia, herself, Johanna. At last the suffering no longer weakened her, but gave her strength. She had not failed Martin this time – she would never fail him now. They had almost lost Johanna. Somehow, Alice realized, through Mary's hate. But she had not destroyed their love.

. . . 'Why did you bring me here?'

'And if we had not come? You would have loved him just the same whenever you had met. You must not judge a man by those around him, but love him on his merits – those alone. Nor must you hate his weaknesses, for he cannot change them any more than he can change his virtues. If you love a man, as I loved Will, you may sometimes let him see you know his faults – but never let them make you love him less. His goodness shines more brightly if he has some faults – which may not make him evil, only less than perfect. As we all must be.'

'Why did you not tell me this before?'

'And if I had? What difference would my telling you have made? We do not choose the path that is laid out for us – perhaps we choose how soon or late to follow it, but follow it we must.'

236

. . . There were lights in the lane below the farm. Alice knew it must be Martin. Soon he would reach the far side of the bridge, where she would wait for him.

Martin saw her. Saw her with such gladness and relief that all his anger was forgotten. She was barefoot – with her long bright hair, her gipsy laughter as he had re-membered it at Forda. And she held Johanna in her arms.

She was there as he came down to the river. Alice crossed the bridge. But Martin saw her fall.

14

They found the trapper by the railway line, at a place where deer and foxes often crossed. His body had been torn, his legs were broken where he must have caught them in the line. At his side was a canvas bag of rotting carcasses.

'He must've meant to put his catch on the early London train – they allus calls that there the rabbit train, it gets the morning markets, see. And he'd made a proper fortune at it, no mistake. Two or three hundred pounds in his jacket pocket – good money in they rabbits, see. Jessie Pike's old uncle up to Molland, that works on the estate, he heard it all from the station-master down to Bottrix Mill.'

'Coming home, he was, to find that girl of his. Her'll get his cottage, sure now – 'twas a blessing in disguise. Mind, Rose was fair cut up about it, funny thing after all he did to her.'

'They say she do be helping to the Barton: they've had some upset there and no mistake. Martin's fair out of his mind since his wife and baby went. First one then t'other. Now old Ellis. They do say trouble comes in threes.'

'But things weren't never right up to the Barton, not since Martin Ford took up with that there gipsy maid. Don't never get across they gippoes, see – they'll put the evil eye on you . . .'

'Joe Pike knows all about it, don't'n? Come on Joe!' There was no reply. 'Come on then, Joe!'

From his corner in the Pennington Joe stared. He had – as usual these days – been drinking very hard. Alone.

'You fools!' he said. 'You bliddy stupid fools!'

Martin did not know there was a war. The week that it became official there were thunderstorms throughout the county. When a bolt of lightning struck the church spire at King's Nymet folk agreed it was symbolic: had Martin been aware of it he would have said it was a judgment on the Fords. He was conscious only of the intervention – divine or diabolical – that had brought destruction to Ash Barton, death to Alice and his son. If there was any conflict, any field of battle, it was here – upon the land he cherished. Here, within himself.

Later, when peremptory powers beyond the valley ordered requisition of his heavy horses, removal of his wagons – anything with wheels – he noticed. When young men – the lads that he had often seen in hay-field or in public house, at shooting matches, harvest suppers, village fairs – went off to be more cannon-fodder, boys of Kitchener, he mourned. When Harry – now another Captain Trenaman – went missing, was reported shell-shocked, invalided home, it tore at Martin's heart. Was he to lose yet more? How soon would Harry, just like all the others Martin loved, fall victim to the nameless, faceless gods? In time he shared the general grief, the national pain – yet within himself each loss was another wound to add to those already suffered. Often, as the war went on, he thought that he would rather fight and be destroyed for an illusion – military glory – than remain at home and battle with his demons, with the enemy that had laid waste his farm.

That year he had not seen the spring. When Johanna – with a sweetness that was but another grief – brought early daffodils that she had found with Rose and John in Barton Wood, he held them for a moment – gave them back. He could not bear emotion, had no resources left.

He worked mechanically: the routine kept him alive. The lambing came and went, the shearing and the hay. For months he would not – even for a market day – leave home. He did not neglect the farm: that would happen later, when – one autumn morning – he would realize that there could never be a purpose to his harvest. That nothing – as he had known long before the loss of Alice – would matter any more.

At first he blamed Johanna. Yet he clung to her as the only vestige of his love, and she quickly came to dread his moods. The alternate terrifying swings of temper, one minute violent, the next in tears. Then she turned to Rose. If Martin hated that – the knowledge that Johanna was so often with his brother's child – he suppressed it for the sake of Alice. Mary was glad to see Johanna drawn away: the less she saw of Martin and her home the better. It suited Mary to get the Barton back. Martin didn't care what happened to the farm. He ignored his mother, except when she was openly antagonistic to his child. 'If you ever harm Johanna,' he said to her one day, 'as you harmed Alice, I shall kill you. Do you understand?' Mary did. She would not willingly provoke him – he was too like Robert now.

Only Harry – in the months before he went away to France – could manage to get through to him. He understood, as no one else would ever do, just what Aiice meant. In the poems he wrote in war-time Harry would see Alice – in the purest sense – as Martin's soul: the inspiration he had needed to achieve perfection in himself, perfection of his land. And he recognized the harsher, more ironic truth – that Martin, having given up so much and fought so hard for Alice, could not bear the loss. Harry never spoke of it, he could see it was no use. But he was there whenever Martin wanted him: he hoped that time would ease the pain. Deep down, he believed it never could.

*

Francis had come back. The wedding had been cancelled. He would fight for King and Country – just as Harry had predicted, just like all the rest. The rest, that is, of the rural middle class. Among the valley people lay a fierce reluctance to be forced away from roots and ties: the recruitments and the pressures from above did little to affect the attitude of farming men. The womenfolk were more susceptible to dreams of glory – and coercion from their betters. By degrees their husbands and their sons would yield: but among the patriotic murmurs and the righteous indignation against anything that smacked of 'foreigner' or 'from away', there was a genuine and vocal anger. 'Us bain't going,' they protested, 'until us be fetched!'

Margaret was proud of both her men. Like others of her kind she saw no further than the need and the reward: no question that the war was right. She became absorbed, as Laura did, in her private contribution to the cause – her sacrifice of happiness in the interest of the public good. When Harry went back home, his mind and heart destroyed, his body wrecked, she wept for him – but it was unthinkable that he should not, as soon as he recovered any strength, return to battle. And when Francis, home at last on leave, made it clear that he would fight no more, Margaret was at first bewildered – then incensed. It was just as when Ralph Trenaman had died: how could fate do a thing like this to her – how could anyone desert his loved ones in this way!

Francis knew that she would never understand. No one would see it as he did. He had had five years of revolution out in South America – had witnessed, he thought, all the horror and the degradation of the world. Now he knew that he had not. Nothing had prepared him for the horrors of the war in France: no human being with any dignity could wish that on another, let alone himself. He remembered what Ralph Trenaman had shown him out in Mexico: the truth about established governments who used their helpless citizens like heaps of twigs for firing – to fuel a conflagration they could not control.

He handed Margaret all the trophies of their long relationship. She gave him back his ring. For her it was the end of all that she had cherished, waited for, since childhood – she would survive, like other single women of her class, alone among the wreckage of the war. She would grow old and bitter in the emptiness of Nymet House.

But Francis felt, for the first time since he had abandoned Rose, a cleaner, purer man. In prison he would count that as a bonus for a conscience that was clear. This time when his mother read his letter she did not weep or comment. She went upstairs to Francis' room, took every dusty relic of his old Ash Barton life and burnt them in the yard. It did not occur to her to change her will. Even now, she would never let a gipsy child inherit, whatever Martin hoped.

When Martin heard of it – his brother's latest aberration – he could only laugh. He laughed out loud to think that Francis – in spite of everything he'd done – should discover that he had a conscience after all. He saw it as another gesture – yet another crazy bid to gain attention: Francis as a pacifist. His brother, who had always played with guns, had always hunted, killed? The notion just amused him, roused no old affection, left him cold. Nothing Francis did could matter any more . . .

Martin saw Johanna running wild. In his curiously hermetic way of life – his lack of interest in the outside world – his daughter was his link with all that he had known before. Dimly Martin felt that he was keeping faith with Alice; he still heard her voice, still looked for her. Johanna would grow up a gipsy, as her mother wished.

Yet he had his moments of unease. She was always

242

wary, always self-contained. And she had never lost her tendency to wander – even Mary was concerned by that. Perhaps it was the influence of Rose: yet she was watchful with her boy. It seemed to be Johanna who would rather roam the woods than go to school; Johanna who was found at night by Martin swimming naked in the river, and who one day walked right up to Forda on her own. Most of all, it troubled Martin that his child – by force of circumstance – should find her only friend in Francis' son. Whenever Martin met the boy the memories of all that bitterness, of the division that would never now be healed, came flooding back. And the more he saw John Ellis with Johanna, the more deeply Martin felt his other loss: Francis – who had cared so little for his child – might, if he chose, leave his share of Ash Barton to a son.

One morning Martin heard the children down in Barton Wood. They were somewhere near the cottage where Rose Ellis had met Francis – where Tom Cheldon, long ago, had left Euphemia. The past held no importance now for Martin. But the children did. He knew the cottage roof was falling in, and getting dangerous ... When he reached it he found the broken door had rotted, fallen off; Johanna and the boy were playing there among the bracken that had grown up through the floor.

In a recess in the corner near the fireplace was a woodstack – logs and faggot bundles that entirely filled the space where once a ladder had been put to reach the sleeping-loft above. The ladder, like the door, had rotted – it leaned precariously on the stack. When Martin reached to pull it safely to one side he saw behind the faggots something of a different colour, a more distinctive shape. A ray of sunlight gleamed on metal as he pulled it free. He knew, as he ran his hand along the barrel, that his fingers would find something to establish – without any doubt – to whom the gun belonged. And it was there, he rubbed it clean to make quite certain – but he knew.

Martin had seen it many times. The silver mark of old Sir Jocelyn Pennington.

When he got back home he went straight up to Francis' empty room. He locked the door and took away the key. He said nothing to his mother. Weeks went by during which he took the gun apart and cleaned it carefully, obsessively. One morning very early he went down into the marsh and tried it. As he heard the shot ring out he thought of Francis – and the morning that he climbed the hill to Middle Aish. The morning Martin met Grace Penfold first. His fear of her, and all his anger at his brother . . .

Suddenly it seemed to Martin that the years had vanished, as if nothing – only emptiness – had ever been. He could think of nothing but the gun. He was quite certain Francis must have stolen it – and hidden it down in the cottage where he had made love to Rose. His brother hadn't just betrayed the girl and left her with his child; he had not only thrown away his loyalty to go with Trenaman. He was a thief – a liar. Martin had the proof. And he had thought that Francis didn't matter any more . . .

Beneath it all, he had loved Francis. Long before his love for Alice, that feeling for his brother had kept Martin whole. Now even that was gone. The darkness he had kept at bay since Alice died was closing in. He had tried to see Johanna as a light that would illumine what remained of life. But Martin saw it was no use: he could find no future, now he had lost that one small remnant of his past.

When Alice came into his life he recognized her as his hope. But Francis – the brother he had known from the beginning – had been Martin's faith.

The tallet door was swinging wide. They found Martin in the hay. Beside him – with its newly polished metal gleaming – lay Sir Jocelyn's gun.

*

Francis saw the child. She was a gipsy child, that was for sure; no one could have doubted it. The quick bright glance, half shy, half bold. Eyes dark grey as water in the winter light, a darker blue with fear – or, much more rarely, laughter. He came to know her smile, as sudden as a shaft of sun – yet a shaft of pain to Francis. She was like his brother then . . . He saw her pure uncomplicated joy in something small or simple – a fallen feather or a strange smooth coloured stone beside the dusty road. Her brows were straight and black, themselves like small neat feathers; and again – her eyes, confiding yet equivocal. Her mother's eyes. Perhaps her chin was bolder than Alice's had been – a hint of Mary's blood. But Francis had no wish to think of that. He wanted to find Alice in the child – his brother's child, whatever Mary Ford might claim with the malevolence of age and disappointment. Even now, when she could have no cause, she would bid to separate her son from the woman he had loved. Even after death, Martin roused that anger in her.

Francis knew it. And at last, hated Mary for it. Once, he hadn't cared. But seeing Alice in Johanna made him wish that he had cared for Martin more – that their brotherhood had been a deeper thing. Mary had divided them. And later, Alice – though Francis' jealousy had been, like all his feelings, far more to do with pride than need or love. He had never until now felt any need to love. So he believed, so he'd always told himself when drawn to any girl he might have cared about: he had only wished to take whatever she might give.

But Johanna, still a child, compelled him. Quickened in him feelings he had thought long dead. Maybe, Francis thought, he had loved Alice after all . . .

'I am sorry for it, *chal*. But it served the *gorgio* right. If my sister hadn't married him she might have lived.'

He had heard the sound of Charlie's fiddle, from the

245

gateway to the camp. The girl was dancing. There was an air of rapt remoteness in her gaze – her head thrown back and hair about her shoulders like a straight smooth curtain, blacker than her mother's hair had been. Her skin, a clear dark gold against the brightness of a coloured sleeve; her fingers stretched and taut, in a gesture both accomplished and abandoned – like the movements of the women he had seen in Mexico. Their dancing to the music he had heard across the empty spaces of another valley – greater, far more lost than this to which he had returned.

'I would have killed him, *chal* – you needn't doubt it.' Charlie put more wood into the fire. Then he laughed. 'But maybe that was why I put the gun in there – I saved one *gorgio*, but I caught another one instead!'

Charlie looked across the fire towards Johanna. 'We will keep her safely, since you ask it. But only till you come. If she had been her mother we should never have her back. But you took trouble for the old one when you might have left him – as any other *gorgio* would. I knew it then –'

The gipsy leaned across and touched Francis on the sleeve in a gesture he remembered from so long ago. 'I knew it, *chal*. You are one of us – and so is she.'

The hillside grass was scented, sweet. Long ungrazed, it had overgrown the track, which had dwindled to a narrow hardened line, untrodden save by fox or deer. When the traveller came to where the path divided he turned towards the river, following its course; at last he reached the ruins of a cottage, deep among the oak and ash – a place where he had come as child and lover, long ago. Between its walls of crumbled cob, its mossy fallen stones, the pink and white of bramble flowers, the summer fern, he found the gipsies' tent. A lurcher lay asleep, while half a dozen yellow chickens pecked at last year's leaves. The river's music, ever present, held no threat; it mingled with the hidden song of birds, the sigh of wind above the wood.

Two women waited there. One, old and blind, expected him. Already in imagination she had seen him leave the mines, the city, far behind – had known that he would cease his wandering in search of profit, his heartless exploitation of the land. She could feel, as he approached, the weariness of spirit and the need that brought him home. And she foresaw that at this summer's close, when harvest gave men strength to face the winter cold, she would return to a church among the apple trees – to Will.

The other – still a girl, black-haired – ran to him as he came. Her look, her voice and laughter, were all that he had hoped – had scarcely dared to hope – as he neared his journey's end. In her he saw the past, its loss and pain: his brother's child – now, by the ancient tie of blood, his own. He was dispossessed, yet in this inheritance – this promise – rich at last.

*

A wagon leaves the lane. Slowly it climbs from mist and shadow to the higher road. In early light, in purer air, the rough land shines, already touched by autumn gold. The wagon turns and moves towards the Moor.

There are no gipsies in the valley now.